Rowena gasp
caught

Her heart hammered her ribs as she stared up into his smoldering black eyes. She knew better than to show fear, but her racing pulse would not obey the command to be still. Swallowing her terror, she took refuge once more in words.

"I'm not afraid of you," she declared, meeting his stony gaze. "You didn't hurt me when you had the chance. You won't hurt me now. You need me too much for that."

Boldly spoken, but her fluttering heart belied her bravado. She could feel the rise and fall of his chest through her bodice. Her own breath came in shallow gasps, as if she'd been running uphill. Every nerve in her body was taut and tingling, but a strange fascination had taken the place of fear. He was so large and wild and so…beautiful, like an unbroken stallion…!

My
Lord Savage

Elizabeth Lane

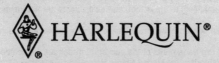

HARLEQUIN®

TORONTO • NEW YORK • LONDON
AMSTERDAM • PARIS • SYDNEY • HAMBURG
STOCKHOLM • ATHENS • TOKYO • MILAN • MADRID
PRAGUE • WARSAW • BUDAPEST • AUCKLAND

ISBN 0-373-29169-8

MY LORD SAVAGE

Available from Harlequin Historicals and
ELIZABETH LANE

Wind River #28
Birds of Passage #92
Moonfire #150
MacKenna's Promise #216
Lydia #302
Apache Fire #436
Shawnee Bride #492
Bride on the Run #546
My Lord Savage #569

Other works include:

Silhouette Romance

Hometown Wedding #1194
The Tycoon and the Townie #1250

Silhouette Special Edition

Wild Wings, Wild Heart #936

Please address questions and book requests to:
Harlequin Reader Service
U.S.: 3010 Walden Ave., P.O. Box 1325, Buffalo, NY 14269
Canadian: P.O. Box 609, Fort Erie, Ont. L2A 5X3

For PowderPuff

Prologue

Virginia
February 19, 1573

Black Otter lay in the stinking darkness of the hold where the white men had flung him. Slimed with blood, his wrists and ankles twisted against the iron manacles that held him prisoner. Although he had been viciously beaten, his ribs cracked and purpled, his eyes swollen shut, he felt no pain. He was beyond pain, beyond fear, even beyond grief. The only emotion left to him now was white-hot rage.

A whisper of reason told him that he'd been taken prisoner in the attack on the village, that he'd been knocked unconscious by a blow to the head and carried onto the great, winged canoe where the white men lived.

Reason, darkened by despair, reminded him also that Morning Cloud, the wife of his heart, was dead. His arms had caught her as she fell, her chest shattered by a blast from the mouth of a white man's firestick. In the space of a single breath her life had

slipped away. Too stunned to react, he had been cradling her limp body when the sharp blow had struck
his head from behind. He had awakened in shackles.

Morning Cloud, at least, was beyond danger. But
what of his children? Black Otter writhed in his
bonds, yanking at his chains in impotent fury as he
thought of his son Swift Arrow, a stalwart lad of nine
winters, and his shy young daughter, Singing Bird,
budding with the promise of womanhood. They had
been in the village that morning, but he had not seen
either of them since the beginning of the attack. Had
they escaped into the forest or were they lying dead
somewhere, the boy's skull shattered, the beautiful
girl-child spread-eagled and bloodstained where the
white men had slaked their lust?

Black Otter clenched his teeth to keep from
screaming out loud. He could not let the white men
hear his torment. He could not let them know how
close they had come to driving him mad.

Willing himself to be calm, he filled his lungs with
the foul, dark air and forced his rage-numbed mind
to think. There was nothing he could do for his wife.
But if his children were alive, he had to get free and
find them. He had to get them to a safe place before
it was too late.

A rat scurried across his outstretched leg, triggering
a jerk of revulsion. The great boat's belly was overrun
with the filthy creatures. The smell of their droppings
mingled with the rank odors of seawater, rotting fish,
urine and mold.

Black Otter could hear the rats squealing and rustling in the darkness around him. He could hear the
creak of the massive timbers, the steady lap of waves

against the hull, and, faintly, through the closed wooden door overhead, the strange, metallic babble of white men's voices.

Sooner or later, he calculated, they would come down for him. This time he would be ready.

Black Otter moved more cautiously now, testing the limits of his manacled arms and legs. He could not maneuver far, but yes, it would be possible to fight. The men who had captured him did not look like seasoned warriors. If there were not too many, he would have a fair chance against them. The chains themselves could be used as weapons, to club, to slash, to strangle. He would strike to kill, leaving only one of them alive to unfasten the iron bands. Then he would be gone with the speed of a panther in the night.

The great boat was anchored in an inlet, not far from shore. If he could gain the open air it would be an easy matter to leap over the rail and—

Black Otter's thoughts fled as a new sound penetrated his awareness—the slow, labored groan of wood and the even tread of moving feet. He heard a thud and felt a shudder pass through the body of the great hull as if something heavy had been lifted into place. Voices were bawling out orders—or signals, perhaps, in their alien tongue. Black Otter raged against his shackles, bewildered, fighting a fear so terrible that it had no shape or name.

Motion rocked the hull as the lap of waves became a murmur like the current of a fast-flowing river. Only then did he understand what was happening. Only then did desolation crush him with a weight so over-powering that he screamed.

The great boat had pulled up its anchor and spread its huge wings to catch the wind.

It was moving out to sea.

Chapter One

Cornwall
June 10, 1573

Mistress Rowena Thornhill pressed anxiously against the tower window, her skirt of plain russet billowing behind her to fill the confined space of the landing. For a moment her tawny eyes strained to see the world beyond the leaded diamond panes. Then, impatient with the narrow view, she unlatched the sash from its dark wooden frame and flung it open to the sea wind.

The salty air stung her face and loosened tendrils of her tightly bound chestnut hair as she leaned over the stone sill. Beyond the courtyard, the hilly moor, abloom with clumps of gorse and flowering sedge, swept off in every visible direction, ending to the south with rocky cliffs where seabirds cried and circled above the surging waves.

Threading across the land between the cliffs and the rambling old manor house was a narrow road, rutted almost hub-deep by generations of passing carts and wagons. It was on this road that Rowena fixed her worried gaze, stretching beyond the sill to see the place where it disappeared over the eastern horizon.

No horse. No rider. Nothing. And the sun would be setting in less than an hour's time.

Her father often made the journey to Falmouth. As a scientist, he liked to wander the docks, buying "curiosities," as he called them, from the sailors—a monkey or parrot, perhaps; maybe an unusual shell or some odd sea creature plucked from the depths and pickled in salt brine. Any and all of these things he would bring home to his laboratory where he would spend days, even weeks, prodding and observing his new prize and taking copious notes in his leather-bound journals.

In more vigorous years these writings had earned Sir Christopher Thornhill a reputation as one of England's foremost scholars. But he was getting old now, too old to be riding the long, dangerous road alone. Next time, Rowena resolved, she would insist on his taking one of the stable grooms with him or go along herself, despite his protests that the teeming waterfront was no place for a lady.

She lingered at the window, her fingers toying with the heavy ring of keys that hung from a cord at her narrow waist. How would she face life when her father passed on? she found herself wondering. In the seventeen years since her mother's death she had filled her days with managing the house and servants and assisting him in his laboratory. This crumbling old manor house and her father's work had consumed her whole life. But he was nearing seventy, and she could sense the looming frailty in the stoop of his shoulders, the slight unsteadiness of his hands. What would she do when the halls no longer echoed with his ponderous footsteps? What would she do when the laboratory lay still and empty?

Marriage? An ironic little smile tugged at a corner of her too wide mouth. Who but an old sot would want her? A spinster two years past thirty, shy and mannishly tall, with a long, narrow face that had always reminded her of a horse? Even with the enticements of house and land, the prospect of finding a worthy husband was hardly worth considering.

She would, of course, carry on her father's scientific work. But who would take her research seriously? Who would read the scribblings of a mere woman, let alone give them weight and value?

Rowena's gaze drifted toward the sea where petrels and kittiwakes wheeled above the cliffs. High above them a single soaring albatross rode the wind, its outstretched wings as still as if they had been carved from white marble.

As she watched the bird's flight, Rowena was seized by a yearning so powerful that her lips parted in silent response. The walls of the ancient house seemed to close around her, shutting her in like the gates of a prison. The heavy folds of her skirts and the rigid constriction of her corset seemed to drag her down like the weight of iron shackles. Even her own rational mind, hardened by a lifetime of common sense, held her back from following the cry of her heart—to shed the chains of house and clothes and reason, to spread her wings and soar with the albatross over the oceans to places she would never see

in her sober lifetime; places whose very names reso-
nated with music—Cathay, Zanzibar, Constantinople,
America…

Pulling back into herself she dropped her gaze from
the sky to the spot where her long, pale fingers rested
on the limestone sill. When she glanced up again
there was a dark speck moving along the distant road
toward the house.

Little by little the speck materialized into a
wagon—a ramshackle one-horse dray with two men
hunched on the seat and a long, dark form lying
across the open bed. Rowena's hand crept to her
throat as she recognized her father's gelding, Blackamoor, dancing alongside the wagon on a tether. The
gelding's saddle was empty.

Her long legs took the steps two at a time as she
raced downstairs to what, in grander days, had been
the great hall. Her slippered feet flew across the rush-
strewn floor, their swift passage releasing the scent of
crushed rosemary behind her.

By the time she reached the front door, Rowena's
heart was hammering with dread. What had possessed
her to let her father go off alone this morning? She
should have ridden along on the pretext of some errand or devised an excuse to keep him at home. Whatever disaster had befallen him now, the fault was at
least partly her own.

The front doors opened straightaway onto the
moor. Rowena burst outside to see that the dray was
still a considerable distance off. Too agitated to wait,
she caught up her skirts and broke into a headlong
run that bruised her feet through the thin leather house
slippers. The sea wind tore the pins from her hair as

she plunged toward the road. Would she find her father hurt? Ill? Even dead?

At the crest of a long hedgerow she paused for a moment to rest. Her ribs heaved beneath the constricting stays of her corset, and her breath came in agonized gasps, but she had halved the distance between herself and the dray. Only now did she have a clear view of the two men on the seat. One of them was the driver, an unkempt hireling she had often seen in town. The other—

Rowena's knees buckled with relief as she recognized her father's stoop-shouldered frame and low-crowned woolen hat. He was all right. She had worried herself to a frenzy for nothing.

But why had he taken the trouble to hire a dray? What was the nature of the dark, mysterious shape that lay across the planks behind him, wrapped in what appeared to be a canvas sail? Had Sir Christopher purchased some exotic new specimen? A large fish, perhaps? A dolphin? A dead seal? She thought of the long marble dissecting table in the laboratory and the exhausting days and nights to come as they labored to learn and catalog their discoveries before putrefaction made the work impossible.

"Rowena!" Her father's sharp-edged voice rang out across the distance. His arm beckoned her to come, but she was already running toward the roadway, her skirts gathering green burrs where they trailed behind her.

By the time she reached the edge of the road she was too winded to speak. She stood warm and panting, her hair streaming in the breeze as the dray, drawn by a spavined cart horse, lumbered toward her.

"Rowena. Good." Her father nodded in his terse way. "I'll be needing some help with this specimen. Ride Blackamoor back to the stable. Tell Thomas and Dickon to be in the courtyard when we arrive. Have Ned clear out the barred room in the cellar and spread the floor with clean straw. Quickly."

"The cellar?" Rowena stared up at him, dumbfounded. "But how can you mean that? The place is little more than a rat warren! No one goes down there, 'tis so dark and damp and moldy! Father, I truly do not understand—"

"Soon enough you will. Hurry, now." Sir Christopher reached in front of the driver, seized the slack reins and pulled the plodding nag to a halt. Blackamoor, impatient for stall and feed, snorted and tugged at the tether that held him to the side of the dray.

"Steady, there." Rowena eased closer to the high-strung gelding, caught the bridle and, with her free hand began unloosing the tether. While her fingers worked the knot, her gaze was compellingly drawn to the canvas-swathed bundle that was lashed with thick ropes to the bed of the dray. From what she could see of the thing inside, she could judge nothing except that it was long—the length of a tall man. Her lips parted in astonishment as she saw a slight movement and realized that beneath its heavy wrappings the creature was breathing.

"Father!" She spun around to face him, her heart pounding. "The beast is alive! You must tell me what it is!"

"Later, Rowena." He dismissed her demand with a scowl. "The less said here, the better. We can talk at the house. Now, ride."

The knot parted, freeing the gelding's bridle. Rowena swung expertly into the saddle, legs astride, skirts bunched over her thighs. As she paused to gather the reins, her eyes fell once more on the dray's tightly bound cargo.

Mounted, she could see what she had not been able to see from the ground. The edges of the canvas sail had parted at the near end of the bundle to reveal a face.

A human face.

The face of a man.

Rowena's heart lurched as she leaned closer, oblivious to her father's impatient glare, oblivious to everything except the sight of those riveting male features.

The eyes, set beneath straight ink-black brows, were closed. Deep-set, they lay in the hollows of a fiercely noble face that seemed all bruises and jutting bones, fleshless beneath taut bronze skin. A lock of black hair—all she could see—trailed across one purpled cheek. For all his evident strength the man looked ill and starved. He smelled of vomit and seawater, evidence of a long, rough ocean voyage. But why in heaven's name was he lashed to the bed of the dray? Surely, in his condition, there was no danger of escape.

Compelled by a strange urge, Rowena leaned outward from the saddle and extended her right hand toward the stranger's battered, motionless face. Ignoring her father's sharp-spoken warning, she brushed an exploring fingertip along one concave cheek. The cool skin was as smooth as the finest tanned leather, the long, rugged jaw bearing not a trace of beard stubble. It was almost as if—

Rowena gasped and snatched her hand away as the man's eyelids jerked open. The eyes that glared up at her were as black as polished jet—their hue so deep that she could see no distinction between iris and pupil.

But it was not the startling color of those eyes that froze her as if she had been turned to stone. It was the blaze of hatred she had glimpsed in their depths— a hatred so pure, so intense, that it seemed to rise from the depths of hell itself.

She wrenched her gaze away. "Father—"

"Not now, Rowena," Sir Christopher snapped. "Later, once the brute's safely locked away, I'll tell you everything. Go, now, there's no time to lose!"

Rowena shot her father a look of horrified dismay. Then, knowing there was nothing to be done here, she wheeled the horse and galloped off toward the house.

Black Otter willed himself to not struggle as the two burly white men seized his arms and began dragging him off the bed of the cart. Over the course of the terrible sea voyage, he had taken on the desperate strategy of a trapped animal. Watch and learn. Wait for the best chance. Then strike to kill.

Early in the voyage he had come close to killing one of the men on the ship. The young brute had been tormenting him, jabbing him with the end of a smoldering stick. For one careless instant the fellow had come too close, and Black Otter, driven by pain and anguish, had lashed out at him. Flinging the iron links of his wrist manacles around the sailor's neck, he had squeezed and twisted, taking a perverse satisfaction in the man's thrashing, his labored gasps.

Then a shout had rung out from above, and the man's cohorts had come pounding down the hatchway to fall on Black Otter like a pack of dogs. They had beaten him so savagely that he had drifted in and out of consciousness for more days than he could count on the fingers of both hands.

That beating had taught Black Otter a lesson he would not forget. Never again would he strike out at his captors without weighing the odds. If there was little to be gained he would contain his fury, caging it like a wild beast. But if the chance came to break for his freedom, he would kill any white person who stood in his way.

Including the woman.

He felt her eyes on him now as he struggled to stand on the reeling ground. Golden eyes, darkly set in a long, pale face. He remembered the touch of her fingertip on his face, her low gasp as he opened his eyes. Had he frightened her? Good, he had wanted to frighten her. He wanted to frighten them all.

Straining against the weight of his shackles, Black Otter straightened to his full height and glowered defiantly at them—the woman, the old man and the lesser people who had come out of the enormous lodge. The two burly men, who seemed to be taking orders from the old one, gripped his arms, half supporting, half restraining. In his full strength Black Otter could have broken their bones with his bare hands. Chained, starved and ill, he had little power to resist.

The woman turned to the old man and spoke.

Maybe they were going to kill him now, Black Otter
thought. If that was so, he would not submit meekly.
Among his own people, the Lenape who lived on the
banks of the great sea river, he was a powerful *sakima,* a chief, as well as an invincible warrior. Even
here, in this alien place, he would die a warrior's
death. And he would not die alone.

For all her proper upbringing, Rowena could not
help staring at the stranger. Filthy, bruised and unsteady on his feet, he stood between the two stable
hands with the majesty of a captive lion. He was taller
than almost any man she knew. His pitch-black hair
formed a matted mane that streamed past his massive
shoulders. His face was striking—but then, as Rowena discovered, she could not look long at his hawk-
like features with any kind of ease. The hatred in
those infernal eyes blazed back at her with such fury
that she was forced to lower her gaze.

Beneath a patina of welts, cuts and bruises, his
body reminded her of—yes—the drawing of a Greek
statue she had seen in her father's library. Rowena's
eyes traced the flow of muscles beneath his bruised
mahogany skin, their names clicking senselessly
through her mind—the deltoids, the pectorals, the flat,
hard rectus abdominus that rippled downward to disappear beneath the twisted, dirty bit of leather that
covered his loins.

Apart from the loincloth he wore nothing below
except a pair of rotting soft-soled leather slippers, the
like of which she had never seen before.

As the dray lumbered back toward the road, Rowena drew closer to her father. "Who is he?" she asked softly.

"No need to whisper," he snapped a bit impatiently. "The primitive wretch has no understanding of the queen's English."

"Father, who *is* he?" Rowena demanded, more forcefully this time.

"An Indian. From America. I bought him today in Falmouth."

"You *bought* him? As a slave?"

Sir Christopher looked askance. "Certainly not!" he huffed. "Look at the fellow—far too much a savage for any kind of decent service."

"Then why would you do such a thing? Out of Christian pity?"

Sir Christopher shook his head, then fixed her with a level gaze. "No, Rowena," he said, "I bought him as a curiosity."

"As a *curiosity?*"

"Yes, my dear. As a rare specimen. For the purpose of study."

Chapter Two

"By my faith, have you lost your mind?" Rowena spun to confront her father, horror overcoming her usual deference. "A specimen, indeed! Father, you can hardly collect and catalog a human being as you would a bird or a fish!"

"And what makes you so sure the creature is human?" Sir Christopher challenged his daughter. "I have it on good authority that his speech—if you can call it such—is nothing but monkey gibberish, and that he attacked and nearly killed a seaman aboard the *Surrey Lass*. All told, the brute seems considerably more beast than man. Whichever he may be, I mean to study him and find out."

Rowena's gaze darted from her father to the tall, dark American savage who, even now, looked ready to spring on her and devour her flesh. Over the years, she had put up with innumerable monkeys, fish, reptiles, tropical birds and even one aged performing bear, all of which her father had kept penned in his laboratory until they sickened in the cold English climate and died—after which they'd gone straight to the dissecting table. Much as it saddened her, she had come to accept the fate of these creatures as part of her father's work. But a man—even the raw, untutored heathen who stood before them now? No, she would not stand for it! This time Sir Christopher had gone too far!

"Father!" Rowena seized his arm, gripping it so hard that the old man winced. "I beseech you in the name of humanity, don't do this!"

"And what would you have me do instead?" Sir Christopher thrust her away from him, scowling at her over the top of his thick spectacles. "Should I let him go? Should I turn the poor devil loose to roam the countryside like a mad dog and probably end up being shot or hanged?"

Rowena exhaled slowly, knowing she had no counter to his question. "Very well, then, get me the keys to his manacles. If the man is going to live here, the least we can do is give him a good washing and some proper clothes." She wheeled away from her father and took two strides toward the defiant prisoner.

He did not move, but the blistering rage in his black eyes stopped her like a wall. Rowena hesitated. Her hand crept to her throat as she glimpsed something else beneath that rage—a sorrow so deep and so desperate that it tore at her heart.

"No closer," her father cautioned her from behind. "The creature is dangerous. Given his freedom, there's no imagining what he might do, especially to a woman. You're to keep a safe distance from him, Rowena, at all times."

Rowena studied the prisoner across the span of a

few paces. Dangerous? Yes, certainly. He was a wounded animal, maddened by pain and fear. But what if she were to reach out and touch him in gentleness, in compassion?

Her hand stirred, but even that slight motion ignited a fresh blaze of hatred in the man's eyes. Rowena felt as if she had stepped too close to a fire and been singed from head to foot by a sudden flare.

Before she could gather her wits, her father spoke gruffly to the two servants. "Take him to the cellar and lock him into the barred room. You'll find the key hanging on the wall behind the door. Leave him a little water and a slop bucket—pray that after two months at sea the wretch will know what to do with it."

"How can you just shut him down there in the dark?" Rowena had found her tongue and was determined to speak. "Look at the poor creature! He needs food and warm clothing! He needs some measure of kindness in this strange place!"

"All that he will get soon enough!" Sir Christopher retorted. "But first, as with any wild beast, we must break that proud spirit of his. Only after he has learned dependence on his masters will he be docile enough to study."

"Father, there are rats down there, and heaven only knows what else—"

"Hush, Rowena! My mind is made up! We can talk at supper." Sir Christopher turned away from his daughter and unleashed his irritation on the servants. "What are you staring at? Get him downstairs—and watch him, mind you. I was told that the creature is uncommonly treacherous!"

The two husky Cornishmen tightened their grip on the prisoner's arms and began dragging him toward the back door of the house. Until that moment the man had not made a sound, but as the three of them reached the stoop, he suddenly threw back his head and uttered a shattering cry—a sound so savage and primitive that it raised the fine hairs on the back of Rowena's neck and startled a flock of jackdaws perched on the edge of the roof. The cry was not born of fear or pain—that much Rowena knew at once. No, her instincts told her, it was a warrior's battle scream, an outburst of sheer, defiant rage.

Startled, the two servants drew back for an instant, and suddenly the dark stranger was free. He lunged across the courtyard, dragging the weight of his shackles as if they'd been made of twine. In full health, he might have made his escape, but as it was he tired swiftly. Halfway between the house and the stable, Thomas and Dickon caught up with him. A swift kick from Thomas's boot sent the prisoner sprawling facedown in the muck. From there it was an easy matter for the two men to seize his arms and jerk him to his feet once more.

Dripping mud and manure, the savage faced his captors. Then, to everyone's astonishment, he burst into a sudden stream of the vilest profanity known to any English sailor.

"...*Son of a whoring bitch...filthy, murdering redskinned bastard...*" The phrases he spat purpled the air around him. He had learned them on the voyage from America, Rowena realized, sick with dismay. In all likelihood, they were the only English expressions he knew.

A bitter smile tugged at the corners of Sir Christopher's mouth. "Well, well," he said, nodding in satisfaction. "At least we know the creature is capable of learning human speech. Take him to the cellar."

Rowena half expected the savage to strike out again, but he had exhausted his strength for the moment. He offered no more resistance as Dickon and Thomas gripped his arms and dragged him into the house.

Black Otter felt as if the great lodge had swallowed him whole, as a giant frog might swallow a fly.

His gaze darted furtively over whitewashed walls and ceilings higher than a man's reach, over huge, ornate pictures made entirely of thread, over tables and chairs that looked as solid as the trunks of great trees. At first he had planned to memorize the way inside so he might know it when the time came for his escape. But he had long since given up. The place was a maze of corridors and chambers as complex as the inside of a termite nest. Surely, with such a lodge, the old man who had taken him from the ship must be the chief of all the white tribe.

One of the rooms he had passed through appeared to be used for nothing but cooking. The fire pit was built into one wall like a cave, and over the crackling flames, the carcass of a large animal hung roasting on a metal spit. Loaves of fresh brown bread lay on long tables. Black Otter had never seen so much food in one place. The mouthwatering aromas had made his stomach contract with hunger, but no one had offered him food or even a sip of water. He had been dragged through one immense room after another and, at last, down a long, narrow passageway that ended in a pool of darkness.

A third man, plump and pale, joined them now. He was carrying a torch made of twisted reeds dipped in pitch. The foul smoke stung Black Otter's eyes and nostrils as they forced him downward into the black space that opened up before them. His moccasin-clad feet stumbled on the rough stone steps.

Fear closed around his heart as the clammy air, redolent with mold, filled his lungs. It was cold and damp down here, below the earth. And without the torch it would be darker than the belly of the great boat. Even if they did not kill him at once, he would die slowly in this place. He would die like a caged animal, from want of sun, air, warmth and freedom. And he would never know what had happened to his precious children.

Torchlight flickered over mildewed stone walls, then over moldering crates and barrels that looked as if they had not seen daylight in years. Black Otter heard the faint drip of water and the scurrying sound of rats.

One of the men spoke as the torchlight came to rest on a framework of rusty iron bars. A door creaked open on corroded hinges, revealing a tiny, cavelike room that looked as if it had been hacked from the living flesh of the earth. Realizing he was about to be shoved inside the terrible place, Black Otter began to struggle—a waste of strength. With a quickness that belied his size, the largest of the white men struck out with one meaty fist. Black Otter saw the blow coming, but he was powerless to dodge or counter.

He felt a flash of pain as the massive knuckles crunched against his cheekbone. Then the torchlight exploded into swirling stars, and he pitched forward into darkness.

Rowena toyed with her supper, too agitated to eat. "I understand none of this!" she declared, pushing her plate to one side. "You say you paid a hundred fifty pounds for the man! A small fortune, Father, and far more than we can spare! What under heaven possessed you to do such a thing?"

Sir Christopher lifted his tankard and took a draught of ale to wash his mouth free of bread and meat. "My dear Rowena," he answered, scowling, "I grant you, a hundred fifty pounds is a considerable sum, but you must look on it as an investment."

"An investment?" Rowena glared at him.

"An investment in the future. Mine and your own." He leaned forward across the long, bare table where the two of them sat. A single candle sputtered between them, etching his face with stark ridges of light and shadow. He looked old and tired.

"Listen to me, child." His earnestness all but made her weep. "We both know my reputation as a scholar has faded over the years. I am no longer consulted by the queen or invited to lecture at Oxford. But with the new discoveries I hope to make, all that will change."

"You talk in riddles! What new discoveries?" Rowena asked, her concern deepening. Had the great Sir Christopher slipped over the edge of reason?

"Think of it, Rowena!" The candle flame, reflecting in his spectacles, transformed his pale eyes into blazing lights. "Spain has already gained a solid foot-hold in the Indies. While there is time, England must seize her own piece of this bright new world. The vast country to the northwest, rich in furs and land and treasure, is ours for the taking, save one obsta-cle—the savages who live there!"

Rowena gazed at her father, excitement clashing with dismay. The Spanish conquistadores had long since subdued the more civilized tribes of tropical America—the Aztecs, the Mayans and, far to the south, the Incas. But the northern forest dwellers were savage brutes, rumored to be more beast than human. Their ferocity had long kept white invaders from their shores.

And now one of them was here in England, locked in the cellar of this very house.

"Think, Rowena!" Sir Christopher's voice rasped with emotion. "Think what we might learn if we can communicate with the creature—if we can subdue him, teach him to speak, perhaps even press him to serve as a guide and interpreter!"

"He'll serve as nothing if he dies of the cold and damp in the cellar," Rowena snapped. "A hundred fifty pounds, indeed! You might as well have—"

Her words died in a little choking sound. She stared at her father, thunderstruck. "By my faith, you didn't just happen across that poor wretch in Falmouth, did you? You planned this, all of it!"

"Hear me out, Rowena." Sir Christopher could be as strong-willed as his daughter. "What I did, I did for my own good reasons."

"How long did it take you to arrange it?" she de-manded, trembling as she rose to her feet. "Six months? A year? What did you have to do to get him?''

"I put up printed notices in the taverns around the docks," he answered with the cold stubbornness of a rock in the Narrow Seas. "The notices declared that I would pay one hundred fifty pounds for a healthy savage from North America. A messenger brought me word yesterday that a captain, newly arrived, had such a specimen—"

"A captain, indeed! A privateer, you mean! No better than a pirate!"

"In truth, I did not think to ask." Sir Christopher had marshaled his defenses now. The set of his shoulders and the jut of his jaw declared that he had taken his position and would not be moved.

"And not a word to your own daughter!" Rowena fumed. "Indeed, why did you neglect to make me privy to your plans?"

Sir Christopher speared a morsel of beef with the point of his knife and used it to jab the air emphatically as he spoke. "Because you would have behaved exactly as you're behaving now. And you would not have succeeded in changing my mind, Rowena. Not by a whit. The discoveries I make about this creature and his world will restore my favor with the queen. Yours, too. Perhaps you might even be offered a position at court—"

"I have no wish to wait upon the queen, Father. My life is here in this house with you."

Sir Christopher sagged in his chair, an expression of profound sadness stealing over his once-vigorous features. "And what kind of life have I given you, child? When I pass on, you'll be alone here. No husband, no children—''

"Let the savage go," Rowena demanded gently. "Take him back to Falmouth and put him on a ship for the New World. I'll pay his passage myself out of the dowry of jewels my mother left me."

Rowena's father shook his head. "You know as well as I do he would never survive the journey. Likely as not, the captain would take your money and throw your savage overboard at the first sign of trouble."

"My savage?" A bitter smile tugged at the corners of Rowena's mouth. "So now he's *my* savage, is he?"

"Why not, since you seem to have taken up his cause?" Sir Christopher scowled at the tidbit of meat on the end of his knife, then brought it to his mouth and began the tedious chewing that his meager teeth allowed.

"Well, then, as long as I have claim to him, I want him out of the cellar," Rowena said. "There are empty chambers aplenty in this house. The least we can do is lock him in a warm, dry place with ample food and bedding."

Sir Christopher downed the remains of the meat with a swig of ale. "What? And have him leap out of a window or attack the first poor soul who comes in to feed him? No, Rowena, as long as the creature is a danger to himself and to others he will remain behind bars. As for you, you are not to go near him, nor is any other woman in this house. Leave the tending of him to Thomas and Dickon." He pushed back from the table, his chair scraping on the stones. "And leave the breaking of him to me. I mean it."

"Breaking?" Rowena paused in clearing away the platters, something she often did if the evening meal lingered past the time for the servants to retire. "You talk about him as if he were a wild animal!"

"That is precisely what he is." Sir Christopher rose wearily to his feet. "I wasn't always the doddering old fool you see before you, my dear. Just give me a little time. Believe me, I know how to break a beast— and a man."

Black Otter gripped the iron bars, his eyes straining to see into the murky darkness that lay beyond his cell. The effort was useless. For all he could make out, he might as well have been blind.

How long would they keep him here? Time lost all meaning when the sun was gone. At least, in the belly of the great boat, he had caught occasional glimpses of light from above. He had been able to hear men moving and shouting on the decks overhead and, in time, had learned to tell day from night by the sounds they made.

Here there was nothing but darkness and bone-chilling cold. Nothing but the scurry of rats and the faint, distant drip of water. Nothing but his own burning rage to keep him from giving in to madness.

He thought of the two husky men who had dragged him through the great lodge and down the dark stairs. He pictured the pale, plump man with the torch and the old one, the chief of all the white men. He remembered the woman, tall, like a man, but with a disturbing grace about her, the skirt of her odd cos-

tume flaring around her legs like the inverted cup of
a huge, dark flower. One by one he focused his anger
on them, letting it burn hot in the cold darkness. Even
her. Even the woman. He hated them all.

But anger would not get him out of this place,
Black Otter reminded himself. For that he would need
a cool head and the cunning of a fox.

He had explored his small prison from top to bottom, fingers probing the straw, the walls, the fasten-
ings that anchored the heavy barred door. The enclo-
sure was solid stone, with not so much as a niche that
could be widened into an opening. The bars, as well,
were too strong to bend and too closely spaced for
even a child to squeeze through. His only chance of
escape lay in seizing the instant when one of his captors opened the door. For that he would need to be
on constant watch.

The iron manacles ground into his scab-encrusted
wrists and ankles, raising an ooze of fresh blood as
he moved into a shadowed corner and eased himself
into a low crouch against the wall. He had found the
water jar earlier and taken a cautious sip. It was fresh
and cool, and after the foul stuff he'd been given on
the boat, it had taken all his willpower to keep from
gulping it to the last drop. Even now, his parched
throat cried out for more. But he could not surrender
to thirst. There was no way of knowing how long the
water might have to last.

With a broken exhalation, he leaned back against
the wall, closed his eyes and tried to rest. To take his
mind off the pain of his battered body, he thought
about Lenapehoken, his homeland, with its deep forests and clear-running streams; and he thought about

his children. He pictured Swift Arrow bounding toward him along a mossy forest trail, his small brown face split by a reckless grin. He imagined Singing Bird kneeling beside the fire, her gaze lowered, her young features—awkwardly balanced but holding the promise of beauty—soft in the golden light. He would return to them, he vowed. Whatever the cost, if they lived he would find them. He would gather them into his arms and the three of them would be a family once more.

Whatever the cost....

Rowena lay on her bed, her hair spread in a wild tangle on the pillow. Above her the midnight moon glimmered through the leaded windowpanes. She had been tossing for hours, it seemed, turning this way and that, willing herself to sleep. But it was no use. Her body was tired but her churning mind would not grant her release.

Frustrated, she sat up, swung her legs over the edge of the bed and brushed her sweat-dampened hair back from her face. Her chamber, closed as always against the night vapors, was warm and stuffy. Rowena hesitated, then rose and strode to the window. Vapors be damned! She needed fresh air!

Flinging open the sash, she stretched on tiptoe and let the sea wind wash her face and body. She was naked beneath her shift, and the coolness through the soft, damp linen was as poignant as a caress. The curve of the crescent moon gleamed like a Saracen's blade in the dark sky. Waves crashed and murmured against the rocks at the foot of the cliff.

Rowena's thoughts returned once more to the savage, *her* savage, locked away from light and warmth and air. She remembered his eyes, the anguish she had glimpsed beneath the glaze of hatred.

What torments was he suffering down there alone in the darkness? Was he hungry? Injured? Even dying? Could she make the prudent choice and harden her heart against his need?

Or was it already too late?

Trembling, she closed the window and fastened the latch. Almost without willing it, she found herself moving to the wardrobe, slipping her light woolen dressing gown off its hook on the door. A voice in the back of her mind shrilled that she was setting out on a madwoman's errand, risking her father's anger and her own safety. Rowena paid it no heed. How could she rest in her soft, warm bed when a fellow being was suffering under her very roof?

Resolutely now, she gathered a wool-stuffed quilt from the foot of her bed. Then she glided across the room and opened the door into the hallway. Sir Christopher would scold her, to be sure. But she would face that unpleasantness tomorrow.

The house was dark but Rowena's bare feet knew every knot in the cool wooden floor, every step of the long staircase that curved down into the great hall. The rushes whispered beneath her soles as she skirted the table and hurried to the kitchen. The upper floors of the house she knew by heart, but not the cellar, whose darkness was like the wet black pit of a mine. She would need a light to find her way.

Groping amid the clutter, she found a candle and lit it with a coal from the fireplace. The light glowed eerily in the cavernous kitchen, flickering over soot-

blackened iron pots, shelves, cupboards and long tables. Rowena found a loaf of bread in the pantry and
tucked it under her arm with the quilt. Much as she
loved her father, she could not condone his plan to
starve the savage into submission. Not after glimpsing
the pain in those proud, black eyes.

As she made her way down the rough stone stairway, a mouse scurried across her bare foot. Rowena's
lips parted in an involuntary gasp. If only she'd
thought to wear her slippers—

But there could be no going back now. If she returned to her room for the shoes, her courage would
surely fail. She would shut herself in, draw the bed
curtains and spend the rest of the night hidden beneath the coverlet, quaking like the coward she was.

For as long as she could remember, Rowena had
harbored an unspoken terror of the cellar. Perchance
something about the place had frightened her when
she was too young to remember; or one of the maids
had told her horrible stories to keep her from toddling
down the dark stairs. Whatever the reason, her skin
crawled as she descended the long passageway. She
cupped a protecting hand around the candle flame,
fearful that some stray draught might blow it out.

At the center of her fear lay the barred room. In
Rowena's lifetime it had been used only for storage.
But it was well known that the long-ago Thornhill
who'd built the great house had used it for a very
different purpose. People had died in that room.

Past generations of the Thornhill family had shown
a penchant for barbarism, Rowena reflected. But not
Sir Christopher. Not, at least, until today. Had the
dark trait surfaced at last in her own gentle father?

The damp cellar air rose around her like a miasma, smelling of mold and rot. She thought of the savage huddled alone in the darkness. Was he frightened? Angry? Would he understand that she had come to him in the spirit of kindness?

Rowena tried to imagine how he had been captured, chained and taken from his home. A man such as he would have fought like the very devil. Why hadn't the ship's crewmen captured someone more docile? A woman, or even a child?

The answer to her question came at once. The privateers had wanted their captive to reach England alive. They had chosen a strong man—a warrior—because he would have the best chance of surviving the miserable voyage.

Darkness, as cold and heavy as the body of a snake, pressed around her as she reached the bottom of the stairway. The candle seemed little more than a sputtering pinpoint. She inched forward, protecting the tiny flame. By its dim light she could make out a jumble of stacked boxes and barrels and, beyond them, the stark outline of iron bars.

Rowena paused, holding her breath and listening. She could hear the faint drip of water from an underground spring and a low rustling noise that could have been a rat. But even in the stillness, she heard no sound at all from the barred room.

She crept closer, the candle thrust ahead of her. Now she could see the bars clearly. She could see into the cell beyond them, all the way to the far wall.

No one was there.

Forgetting caution, she hurried forward. Had the savage escaped? Had he died on the way to his dark prison? Or had her father simply decided to put him somewhere else?

Rowena reached the bars and pressed against them, raising the candle to see into the far corners of the small room. Only then did she notice the straw piled in the shadows—a long, bumpy mound of it, the size and shape of a man's body.

Relief swept over her as she lowered the light. Cold and weary, the savage had taken the only sensible course of action. He had burrowed into the straw like a wild animal and gone to sleep.

Rowena's breath hissed out in a jerky release. Her errand of mercy would be easier now. She had only to push the bread and the quilt between the bars and go. When he awakened the savage would discover her gift, and if he was as intelligent as he appeared to be, he would understand that even among the English there was compassion.

Dropping to a crouch, she set the candlestick on the stone floor to free her hands. She was about to push the bread between the bars when a rustle in the shadows reminded her of the rats. An unguarded loaf would only serve as bait for the horrid creatures, drawing them by the score into the cell. The bread would be gone before the captive could wake up and drive them off.

Rowena hesitated, torn. She could call out and rouse him. But that in itself would be a heartless act. Sleep was the only blessing left to the wretched man. If, perchance, he was dreaming of his homeland and loved ones, why awaken him to misery?

She would push the quilt and the bread through the bars, she resolved. Then she would reach through with both hands and wrap them into a single bundle. Nothing would hold the rats off forever, but at least the quilt might delay them.

The quilt was so thickly padded with wool that it had to be unfolded and stuffed inch by inch between the bars. As she worked, Rowena kept a wary eye on the mound of straw, ready to draw back at the slightest stir. But there was no movement or sound from the sleeping captive. Clearly he was too exhausted to be of any danger.

All the same, her fingers trembled as she guided the crusty loaf through the narrow space. Nothing remained now except to wrap the bread securely in the quilt.

It would only take a moment, Rowena assured herself as she leaned forward and slid her arms into the darkness beyond the bars. Just a moment of fumbling, and then—

Her thoughts exploded in a paroxysm of fear as a rough, brown hand shot out of the shadows, seized her wrists and yanked her hard against the bars.

Chapter Three

Rowena fought for balance as the savage wrenched her forward. Her head struck one of the bars, setting off an explosion of pain. She sagged for an instant, the candle flame spinning in her vision. Then, as her senses cleared, she began to twist and claw in earnest.

"Let me go!" She spat out the words, forgetting that he would not likely understand her. "I'm not your enemy, you fool! I'm here to help you!"

His grip tightened around her wrists. She felt the crushing of bones and tendons. Rowena whimpered as he wrenched her flat against the bars. She might have screamed, but she knew no one else in the house would be able to hear her. Not from this deep, dark place.

She could see the savage's face now by the light of the guttering candle. His cheekbones were gaunt bronze slabs. His jet eyes were as cold as a panther's. She could smell him, too. His scent was a trapped animal's, thick with the musk of rage and terror.

"Let me go," she gasped, weak with pain. "They'll come for me…they'll punish you—"

He growled something under his breath—a guttural, menacing phrase whose meaning Rowena could only guess. The grip of his manacled hands shifted, and for the space of a heartbeat she thought she might have reached him. But no—he was only crossing her wrists so that he could wrap a length of his chain around them, leaving his right hand free. By the time Rowena realized his intent, it was too late to jerk away.

She was on her knees now, her body molded to the bars. The savage's face was a handbreadth from her own. Rowena shuddered as his black eyes impaled her. "Tell me what you want," she whispered, choking back panic. "If it is within my power—"

Her words ended in a gasp as his huge hand knifed through the bars and caught her at the waist. She would have wrenched herself away, but the iron grip on her wrists kept her pinned against the bars. She froze, her heart pounding, as his fingers groped the span of her waist, fumbling awkwardly with the knotted sash of her robe.

Rowena's eyes closed as the knot came loose and the robe fell open. The bars were strong, she reminded herself. Aside from hurting her hands, the savage could not truly harm her. All the same, her heart seemed to stop as his fingers seared through the thin fabric of her shift, moving urgently along the curve of her waist, then lower, skimming her hipbones. His dangerous touch triggered subtle tuggings and tightenings in the moist core of Rowena's body. A tiny moan quivered in her throat.

She thought of the candlestick, the candle still flickering on the floor where she had left it. One well-placed kick could tip it into the straw that lined the cell. The straw would begin to smolder, then burst into leaping flames...

She could not move.

His touch became more demanding, more frantic. Rowena could feel the anger in him, the rising tide of frustration that grew until it exploded out of him in a single word.

"Key!"

She stiffened against him in sudden awareness. The savage had evidently learned on the ship that a key was needed for opening locks. He had even managed to learn the word. And last evening in the courtyard, the ring of keys hanging at her waist had caught his sharp gaze. He was looking for those keys now.

Finding nothing, he drew back from the bars. His eyes seethed with anger. "Key!" he demanded again, jerking her arms so hard that she whimpered. "Key! Give me!"

"No!" Rowena began speaking volubly, with no idea of how much he could understand. "I don't have any keys with me. And even if I did, even if I were to let you out of this place, it would do you no good. You'd be lost in this land. You wouldn't know where to go, where to hide, how to find food and clothing. You wouldn't have the first idea how to get on a ship and return to your own country. You must stay here for now. *Stay here!*" She emphasized the words, praying he would understand their meaning. But he only glowered at her, his eyes so hot with pain and hatred that their gaze all but withered her spirit.

"I don't have the key," Rowena said again, resisting the painful pull on her hands. *"No key."*

The savage stared at her, then snorted with disgust and let her go so abruptly that Rowena tumbled backward into a pile of moldering firkins. The small barrels came bumping and rolling down around her, making such a commotion that she feared someone in the house would hear. She sat up, rubbing her bruised temple, as the racket subsided.

The candle had burned down to a glowing stub. By its faint light she could see the savage, standing now, behind the bars of his prison. The fierce majesty of his presence filled the wretched space. Who had he been in that other faraway world? Rowena found herself wondering. What would he tell her if she could understand his alien tongue?

But this was no time for idle questions. She would need to get the candle at once, before it sputtered out and left her in darkness. She felt the savage's eyes on her as she crept forward and snatched the candlestick from its place on the floor. The sudden motion fanned the flame, causing the light to dance crazily over the walls of the cellar. As Rowena scrambled to her feet she glimpsed his face—the grim mouth twisted wryly at one corner, disdainful, amused, as if he were silently laughing at her. She felt a sudden surge of irritation. Her temper flared like tinder as she swung back to face him.

"I'm not afraid of you!" she snapped, not caring whether he understood or not. "And I have better things to do than put up with your bullying! If you're too blind to see that I'm your only friend in this place, there's nothing more to say! You can stay down here by yourself and rot!"

She wheeled abruptly and stalked toward the stairs.

Her exit would have done a queen proud if her candle had not, at that very moment, burned to the end of its wick. The fragile light flickered and died, plunging the cellar into pitch blackness.

Only Rowena's anger kept her from giving way to panic. She could not, *would* not let the savage know how terrified she was, she vowed as she groped her way across the cluttered floor. She had suffered enough humiliation without giving him cause to laugh at her again.

The memory of his searching fingers, hard and rough through the fabric of her shift, brought a surge of heat to her cheeks. She'd had no choice except to let him touch her, Rowena reminded herself. But that did not in any way excuse her from responding like a cat in heat. What could she have been thinking? That he wanted her? That any man could want her? What rubbish! He had wanted nothing except the key to his prison. Failing to find it, he had flung her away like a piece of tainted meat.

What had she expected? In the name of heaven, what had she wanted? Rowena inched forward, her face burning with shame in the darkness. Behind her, where the savage stood, there was nothing but silence.

Her shoulder scraped against a wall, and in the next instant her groping feet found the bottom of the long stairway. Sick with relief, she toiled her way upward, one hand clutching at the cold stones for support.

Eternities seemed to pass before she emerged into the corridor on the ground floor of the house. The shadows were more familiar now but they gave her no comfort. The very walls mocked her folly as she fled across the great hall and stumbled up the stairs.

Reaching her own chamber, she bolted the door, flung herself into her bed and hastily drew the curtains. Even then the laughing demons would not be shut out. Rowena lay hot-faced and quivering beneath the covers, waiting for the mercy of dawn.

Black Otter fingered a corner of the quilt the woman had pushed through the bars of his cell. It was a wondrously fine thing—thick and soft, its covering smoother than doeskin. The fabric still smelled of her body—a pungent, flowery aroma that was nothing like the scent of his own people. Raising it to his nose, he inhaled deeply. The odor flooded his senses, awakening a spark of heat in his groin. He frowned at the sensation. Was he so woman-hungry that the very scent of this tall, pale creature could rouse him to desire? If that was so, he was even worse off than he'd thought.

Flinging the quilt down with a snort of self-disgust, he turned his attention to the bread. The loaf was fresh and soft beneath its crisp outer crust. Black Otter was starving, but he kept a tight rein on his appetite as he broke off one small piece and tasted it. Like the water, it might have to last him a long time.

The bread was light and chewy in texture, a far cry from the dense, flat maize cakes he had eaten all his life. But the flavor—yes, it was good. More than good. It was all he could do, in fact, to keep from bolting the entire loaf. But Black Otter was a disciplined man, his will tempered by experience. He ate only enough to dull the edge of his hunger. Then he wrapped his body in the quilt and settled himself against the wall, still clutching the bread to guard it from the rats.

The woman had brought him this gift of food and warmth, he reminded himself. She had come alone, at great risk, to do him the first kindness he had known in this strange land.

He remembered her moon-white face in the flickering candlelight, her large, cat-colored eyes wide with fear. It had not been easy for her to come to him—he had not made it easy. But even when he'd done his best to frighten her, she had not lost her courage. For that she had earned his grudging respect.

And he was not ungrateful for her gifts, Black Otter mused as he sank deeper into the softness of the quilt. Gratitude, however, was not the same as friendship. All whites were his enemies, this tall, strong-minded female among them. But if ever the chance came for vengeance he would remember this night and, perhaps, let her live.

He had resolved to not sleep, but as the warmth crept into his aching body he felt his eyelids grow heavy. The woman-musk scent of the quilt stole around him, awakening subtle urges in the depths of his body. He remembered touching her through the thin cloth, his fingertips tracing the long curve of her waist in search of the keys. If his hand had moved higher—or lower—would he have discovered her to be like the women of his people? Would his fingers have found the quivering softness of her breasts, the moist, secret cleft of her womanhood? Would her breath have caught and quickened at his touch?

Black Otter exhaled, pushing her image from his mind. Such careless thoughts would only do him harm.

They would lull his spirit, causing him to lower his guard and miss the chance that would surely come. For such a lapse, he would never forgive himself.

He stared into the darkness, striving to fill it with the faces of those he had loved and remembered— pretty Morning Cloud who had died in his arms; their children, their friends, all of the people who made up the big, warm extended family of the village. He would return, Black Otter vowed. No matter what he had to do, no matter who he had to hurt, he would return.

His eyelids were growing heavy again, and the quilt was as soft and enfolding as a woman's arms. Black Otter was drifting deeper, and he knew he could not battle sleep any longer. The white woman's aura seeped like perfumed smoke through his senses. He smelled her, tasted her, and saw her dark-rimmed eyes in the candlelight. He heard her breathy gasp as his fingers touched her flesh.

As he sank into slumber, hers was the last image he saw.

"By my faith, have you lost your mind?" Sir Christopher confronted his daughter across the breakfast table. "What in heaven's name were you thinking last night?"

"That our prisoner was in need of some common kindness." Rowena willed herself to meet her father's angry eyes. She knew better than to deny what she had done last night. Her quilt had already been discovered in the savage's cell.

"The creature is dangerous, Rowena. He could have hurt you, even killed you!"

"As you can see for yourself, he did neither. I

came away from the encounter quite unscathed.'' Rowena avoided glancing at her wrists, which bore small, dark welts where the savage had jerked his chain around them. She had chosen a gown with long, lace-edged sleeves that covered all but her fingers. Her father did not need to know everything that had happened.

"This time you were fortunate," Sir Christopher snapped. "But the savage is not to be trusted. You're to have nothing more to do with him, and that's that!"

"I suppose I should respect your wishes," Rowena answered quietly. "But I am the only person in this place who has treated him kindly. You may discover that he trusts no one else."

Sir Christopher cursed under his breath, swallowed his ale too quickly and broke into a fit of coughing. Rowena was on her feet at once, sprinting around the table to pound the old man between the shoulder blades until his raised hand signaled that he was all right. As the coughing subsided she bent closer, pressing the tankard toward his chapped lips. He waved her away.

"Don't fuss over me!" he grunted. "I'm a man, not some ancient dotard who needs to be fed and wiped."

"That I know." Rowena sighed as she reined back the impulse to dab a bead of spittle from the end of his jutting chin. Only then did she notice the folded letter, its wax seal already broken, lying next to her father's plate. A groan escaped her lips as she recognized the oddly back-slanted handwriting.

"Not Edward Bosley again! What does he want this time?"

"Need you ask?" Sir Christopher crumpled the letter between his arthritic hands. "The wretch is out of money again and asking for a handout! Just because he married your mother's younger sister and worried her into an early grave, he thinks he's entitled to bleed me dry!"

"Tell him no," Rowena said. "If it were up to me, that's what I would do."

"Even if he were to inform you that he could find no more work in the theater and as a consequence his landlord was about to throw him into the street—in which case he would be forced to come and take shelter with us?"

Rowena sagged against the side of the table, remembering Edward Bosley's last visit. "How much does he want?" she asked.

"Twenty pounds. For now."

"And twenty pounds again next month, I'll wager. Very well, I'll see that the money is sent." Rowena returned to her chair and forced herself to take a spoonful of porridge. "Now, about the savage, Father—"

He scowled up at her, eyes narrowing sharply behind his spectacles. "No, Rowena," he said. "I know where this discussion is leading, and there's no use—"

He broke off as Thomas burst into the hall. The husky Cornishman was out of breath. His fleshy face was as pale as a slab of lard.

"'Tis the savage, sir!" Thomas gasped. "He looked to be asleep, so I told Dickon to open up the door and get the slop bucket. The bastard jumped poor Dickon and got him by the throat! I managed t' gèt the door shut, but Dickon is locked in the cell with the savage—that is, if 'e's not kilt by now!''

"Bloody fool!" Sir Christopher was on his feet. "See what you've done!" he said, turning angrily to Rowena. "Your so-called kindness did little more than lessen the creature's fear of us! Now there'll be the devil to pay!"

"Oh, hurry, sir!" Thomas's eyes bulged wildly. "The red 'eathen keeps screamin' something about a key! If we don't get down there…" The rest of his words were lost as he wheeled and raced back toward the corridor. Sir Christopher, feeling his arthritis, labored after him.

Rowena bumped her hip as she plunged around the corner of the table. The heavy key ring at her waist jangled as it struck wood.

Pausing, her father shot her a stern backward glance. "And where do you think you're going?" he demanded.

"I'm coming with you," Rowena said. "If there's anything I can do—"

"Haven't you done enough harm already? Stay up here where you belong!"

"With all due respect, Father—" she began, but this was no time for an argument, and they both knew it. With an indignant huff, Sir Christopher turned on his heel and hobbled furiously toward the corridor. Rowena caught up her skirts and rushed after him. Dickon, for all his size and strength, was the gentlest of souls, an innocent creature with the mind of a child. He had grown up on the manor and, as a youth, taught her to ride her first pony. She could not bear the thought of his being hurt. As for the savage—

Rowena forced all concern for the dark-skinned prisoner from her mind as she pressed past her father in the narrow corridor. This was no time for sentiment. If it came to a choice, Dickon would be the one saved. The savage, for all his worth, would be destroyed like a rabid dog.

From the top of the stairs she could see the yellow flare of torchlight on the walls. She paused while her father, his breathing alarmingly labored, came up behind her. He was too old for this ordeal, Rowena realized, her own heart pounding. His reflexes were too slow, his judgment too impaired by his years. She could not allow Sir Christopher to pit himself against the primeval strength and lightning instincts of the man in the cell.

She alone stood a chance against the savage.

Murmuring a plea for forgiveness, Rowena turned, pressed a hand against her father's chest and shoved him backward into the corridor. Before the stunned old man could react, she wheeled and flung herself into the dark stairwell, pausing only long enough to slam the door and bolt it fast behind her.

"Rowena!" Sir Christopher pounded impotently on the massive oaken planks. "Open this door at once! Open it, I say!"

Closing her ears to his cries, Rowena hurried down the stairs, down and down, into the very maw of danger.

Fear hung in the dank cellar air, its presence so acrid that she could almost taste it. In the hellish glare of the torchlight, Thomas stood outside the cell jabbing a long wooden pike through the bars. The savage had backed into a shadowed corner, just out of his reach. One muscular brown arm was wrapped around Dickon's throat. The other gripped the hapless servant's waist.

"Keep back, mistress," Thomas warned as she moved closer. But Rowena scarcely heard him. Her attention was riveted on the drama in the cell. She could see the glint of firelight on Dickon's bulging blue eyes. She could see terror in every line of his plump, gentle face. Behind him the savage was no more than a black shadow, but she knew he was watching her.

"Key!" His voice rasped out of the darkness, pleading, demanding. Rowena felt the weight of the brass ring at her waist. One of the keys, old and rusted, was a twin to the key Thomas had used to open and lock the door of the cell. But she had no key that would free the prisoner's manacled wrists and ankles. Her heart sank as she realized there might be no such key, except, perhaps, aboard the ship that had carried him to Falmouth.

"Rowena!" Sir Christopher's muffled voice rumbled through the locked door as she glided like a sleepwalker toward the bars. "Have you gone mad? Let me in!"

Rowena pretended to not hear. Her father would be frantic, she knew, but a tragedy lay in wait here. If she did not act swiftly and courageously someone would die in this wretched place.

As she drew closer she could hear the whimpering sounds that came from Dickon's throat. His face was an ashen lump above the dark band of the savage's arm. Thomas was still jabbing uselessly with the pike. Rowena laid a hand on his arm. "Stop," she said in a low voice. "You're only threatening him. It won't help."

He hesitated, and for the space of a heartbeat Rowena feared he would argue. But Thomas was a servant and she was mistress of the great house. In the end he withdrew the pike and backed reluctantly away. From the top of the dark staircase, Sir Christopher continued to pound and rage. "Mind the door, Thomas," Rowena said. "Keep my father safely out of this. Don't let him interfere or you'll answer sorely for it."

"Aye, mistress," Thomas muttered, his voice weighted with reluctance. He would answer sorely in any case.

Rowena could feel the savage's black eyes on her as she fumbled with the cord at her waist, freeing the ring of keys. Her unsteady fingers found the oldest and rustiest among them and thrust it into the lock.

The corroded mechanism balked for a moment, then the tumblers clanked into place and the door opened.

Rowena could see the savage clearly now. His height and bulk filled the far corner of the cell. Black hair streamed in his battered, feral face. Black eyes glowed amber in the dancing torchlight. He looked like the devil incarnate, she thought. Only the sight of Dickon's blanched face and bulging eyes kept her from bolting to safety and locking the door behind her.

"Hold on, Dickon," she muttered, clutching the ring of keys. "I've come to get you out of here."

Brave words. But Rowena felt her spirit quail as her eyes met the savage's desperate gaze. There was a fair chance she could fool him long enough to free

the terrified servant. But what would the savage do
once he discovered that none of her keys would unlock his manacles?

She stepped into the cell and felt the stench of fear
close around her, thick and dark and fetid. Beyond
the barred door, even her father had fallen silent. She
could hear nothing but the crackle of burning pitch,
the labored sound of Dickon's breathing, and the
drumming of her own heart.

Dickon's pale eyes bulged in the torchlight. Behind
him, the savage seemed no more than a tall, black
shadow. Only his arm and his massive fist had sub-
stance where they caught the light. She could see the
chain now, passing in front of the groom's plump,
white throat. A single jerk would be enough to break
his windpipe.

Swallowing her terror, Rowena forced herself to
speak. "Don't be afraid, Dickon," she said gently. "I
won't let him hurt you. See, I've brought the keys.
That's what he wants."

Dickon's eyes flickered in response. His breath gurgled in and out, blocked by the pressure of the chain
against his neck. "Let him go." Rowena spoke
slowly and clearly to the savage, holding the key ring
just out of easy reach. The Indian made no response.

"I said, let him go!" Rowena's hand dropped onto
the bruised knuckles of the powerful hand that
gripped the chain. The light contact sent a shock up
her arm, a sensual chill that jolted through her veins.
She felt the responding jerk of his hand. It took all
her self-control to keep from leaping backward.

"Key! You open!" He rasped the words, shaking
a manacled wrist in her face. The motion tightened

the chain around Dickon's neck. The groom gurgled in terror.

"Let him go!" Rowena ordered, punctuating the words with emphatic gestures. "You let him go, or no key. Understand? No key."

"I...kill." The chain tightened across Dickon's throat. "Kill him...kill you."

Rowena's knees threatened to buckle beneath her petticoats. She willed herself to stand tall and speak fiercely. "You kill, you die!" she said. "Right here. Right now."

Thomas moved the torch closer to the cell, shining the light directly in the savage's eyes. The black pupils contracted sharply. Then slowly the chain slackened against the groom's throat. The links slithered in the torchlight, and suddenly Dickon was free. He stumbled forward, half paralyzed by fear.

"Go on, Dickon," Rowena said softly. "You're all right now. Thomas will let you out."

Dickon lurched toward the door of the cell. Rowena heard the ancient hinges creak behind her as Thomas opened the door. Then the iron bars closed. She was alone in the cell with the savage.

Her savage, she reminded herself. She had come to save him as well as the hapless groom. Now he stood before her in wretched majesty, his shackled arms extended, his eyes squinting in the torchlight.

How long could she play this game of pretense? And where would it end?

Rowena was about to find out.

Chapter Four

Black Otter stood watching as the woman lifted the heavy ring of keys into the light. Strange, his own people had lived from the dawn of time without benefit of locks and keys. But here, in this alien world, keys seemed to control everything.

His heart dropped as he realized there were more keys on the ring than there were fingers on his two hands—large and small keys, in a bewildering mix of shapes and metals. He had thought one key would open any lock. Only now did it strike him how wrong he had been. Keys appeared to be as diverse as people, each fitting inside its own lock as a man would fit inside the woman he loved; and the chance that one of these keys would fit the shackles from the great boat were small indeed.

Fumbling with her key ring, the tall woman selected a large key and extended it toward the lock that held the iron around his wrist. Black Otter's eyes flickered from the lock to the key, which was far too large for the tiny opening. Couldn't she see that it wouldn't fit? What was she trying to do?

Feigning perplexity, she tried to force the end of the key into the lock. Questions swirled in Black Otter's mind. What sort of game was she playing? Did she really think he was foolish enough to be taken in?

From the top of the stairs, Black Otter could hear the muffled shouts of the old chief and the pounding of his fists against the door. Why had the ancient one been shut out of this dark place, and why had a mere woman risked her life to enter his prison? So many questions—and no answers.

The musky fragrance of her hair crept into Black Otter's nostrils as she leaned close. He had come to loath the odor of white men. It was sharper and more pungent than the familiar smell of his own people. But the scent of this woman was lighter, richer in a way that made his loins stir. He steeled himself against her nearness as she selected yet another key, this one also far too large. She was only playing for time, he realized, his spirits darkening. None of her keys would unlock his terrible bonds.

Her hand brushed his skin, its touch cool and soft. Black Otter checked the impulse to tear his arm away and rebuke her. Let her finish this silly game. He had nowhere to go. And she had given him a much better hostage than the blubbering coward he had set free. Her menfolk would do a great deal to rescue such a woman as this.

"What is your name?" Her feline eyes glittered up at him as she spoke. Black Otter understood the phrase but chose not to answer. To tell her his name would be to give her a part of himself—a power she could use against him if she chose.

"My name is Rowena," she said, touching the hollow of her throat with her free hand. "Ro-we-na." She paused as if expecting him to mimic the three syllables. Black Otter gazed impassively over her head toward the door of his cell, willing himself to ignore her. But his mind was not so easily conquered, nor was his body.

He remembered touching her in the night, the exotic scent of her flesh, the smoothness of her skin and the slender curve of waist and hip beneath his seeking hand. He remembered the sharp intake of breath, the quickening of her heartbeat. Yes, for all her pallid face and golden eyes, she was a woman like any other.

"Rowena." She repeated the name again as if he were a backward child. "I am your friend."

The last phrase was one Black Otter did not understand. He had heard nothing like it from the men on the great boat. The words intrigued him. But this was no time to learn more of a language he had come to despise.

"Open!" He growled the word, shaking his manacled hand in her startled face. "Open it!"

Fear flashed in her tawny eyes, but she stood her ground. Outside the cell Black Otter could see the two men, one pressed against the bars, the other still collapsed on a heap of barrels—cowards, both of them. Only the woman faced him with a warrior's courage. For that she had earned his grudging respect.

But he was growing tired of her game. Key or no key, there had to be a way to end the torment of the chafing iron bands and dragging chains. The men would have to find it if they wanted their woman to live.

With the speed of a striking puma he caught her waist. His manacled hand whipped her around and jerked her hard against him so that he was holding her from behind with the chain at her throat, exactly as he had held the trembling fool before her.

"Open it!" he thundered, shaking his free fist at the two men who stared, dumbfounded, through the bars. "Open it...I kill...*kill!*"

Rowena kept perfectly still, willing herself to not show fear. The savage's sudden move had caught her off guard, but it came as no great surprise. She had hoped to calm him with kind words and a gentle touch. But she should have known better—and she should have realized she could not deceive him by stalling with her keys.

Would he really kill her? Reason argued against it. She was of no worth to him dead. But her own fear whispered otherwise. How could she expect civilized—or even reasonable—behavior from a man with the reflexes of a wild animal?

"Mistress, what shall we do?" Thomas's terror-filled eyes pled with her through the bars.

Rowena's eyes flickered obliquely to the manacled wrist that lay along her shoulder. In the hellish glow of the torchlight the flesh lay swollen and suppurating beneath the crusted iron rim. Infection had already set in. Gangrene would be next, and the savage would die in agony. Yes, the shackles had to come off at once.

"We have an anvil and some blacksmith tools in

the stable," she said, thinking fast. "Fetch them at once!"

Thomas hesitated, then shook his shaggy head. "Nay, mistress, I'll not leave you alone with the creature. Your father would have me drawn and quartered."

"Then send poor Dickon if his legs will carry him!" She strained to speak against the chain that pressed her throat. "Hurry!"

She held her breath as Dickon staggered toward the stairs. "You've naught to fear," she whispered to the savage as if he could understand. "We mean you no harm in this place, but if you want to live, you must stop fighting—"

The chain tightened against her throat as the savage muttered something harsh and guttural in her ear. Rowena could feel the hard length of his torso against her back and the rib-crushing grip of his arm beneath her breast. Each taut, shallow breath stirred tendrils of hair at her temple. She had never been this close to any man—least of all a bare-skinned primitive who could kill her with a mere jerk of his wrist. By all rights she should have been swooning in terror. Instead, the fear that gushed through her veins was as heady as a dive into a churning ocean wave. Her senses were exquisitely heightened. Every nerve in her body seemed to be tingling, alive....

"You think you can frighten me." She forced herself to speak in a calm tone, as if she were conversing over a leg of veal at the dinner table. "Well, you're quite mistaken, My Lord Savage. A wild man you may be, but you're no simpleton. You would hardly be fool enough to harm your only friend in this place. Perhaps we might—''

Her words were interrupted by a sudden commotion from the top of the stairs as Sir Christopher burst through the door that Dickon had opened, knocking the unsteady groom aside. ''Rowena!'' Her father's voice, hoarse from shouting, rumbled down the dark stairwell. ''By my faith, if the brute has harmed so much as a hair on your head—''

''Go to him, Thomas.'' Rowena gasped the words against the icy pressure of the chain. ''Help him down the stairs. And see that you don't alarm him. I'm really quite...safe.''

Thomas muttered his assent and turned to go, but before he could reach the foot of the stairs, Sir Christopher staggered into the torchlight. The old man's face turned ashen as he caught sight of Rowena in the cell, imprisoned by powerful bronze arms. His mouth worked in horror as he stumbled through the clutter of boxes and barrels.

''Rowena, child—'' He gripped the bars, looking small and drawn and old.

''The savage has not harmed me, Father, and *shall* not, God willing,'' Rowena said quickly. ''But if you think to leave him in these festering irons another day, you may as well kill him now and be done with it!''

Sir Christopher had recovered his wits, and now he thundered at her through the bars. ''Be still and listen! You should have done as you were told and left this matter to me. You could have spared us both!''

''Father?'' Rowena stared, dumbfounded, as he drew a small tarnished object from a pocket in the folds of his robe. Her knees crumpled beneath her as she realized what it was.

"The key," he snapped. "Given to me by the captain who sold me the wretched creature." He shot Thomas a sharp glance. "Open the cell."

The chain had gone slack against Rowena's neck as the savage stared at the key. "Give it to me," she insisted. "He trusts me—as much as he trusts anyone in this place."

"So I see." Sir Christopher glared at her. "Hold your tongue, mistress. You've done quite enough damage already." He strode into the cell and halted just out of the savage's reach. "Let...her...go," he said, as if speaking slowly could make him understood. "Then...we...use...this." He held up the key, letting the well-thumbed bronze catch the flaring torchlight.

The Indian's hand flashed outward like the swipe of a cat's paw. But Sir Christopher had anticipated this move. He stepped backward, well out of reach. "No," he said. "You let her go. Let her go now."

Black Otter studied the old chief cautiously—the aging body, stooped and frail beneath the somber black robe, the pale eyes squinting behind what appeared to be two transparent shells. Only a coward would harm such an ancient being. But could the old man be trusted? Black Otter had known nothing but cruelty from white men. How could he expect anything else from their chief?

But why wonder? All he really needed was a hostage, and the chief would be more valuable, even, than the woman. With the old man as his prisoner he could demand anything he wanted, even passage back to his homeland.

Slowly and cautiously Black Otter loosed his grip on Rowena's slender body. She stumbled to one side, leaving traces of her musky warmth on his skin. The old chief's eyes flickered toward her. He uttered a gruff command, most likely ordering her to leave. Instead she edged backward to the bars, crouching there, her skirts pooling around her. The two of them were father and daughter, he realized, glancing from one proud face to the other—a good thing to know when the time came to bargain.

The old chief approached him cautiously. Black Otter stood motionless, waiting. He had never set eyes on the key to his shackles, having been unconscious when the iron bands were clamped around his limbs. But every instinct told him this key would fit perfectly into the locks.

In the silence of the underground room he could hear the faint drip of water and feel the ripping cadence of his own pulse. He willed himself to keep rigidly still as the gnarled fingers inserted the key into the tiny opening. His breath stopped as the hidden mechanism ground, clicked, separated.

The woman gasped as the iron band parted and fell away, exposing the raw flesh of Black Otter's wrist. With more haste now the old man thrust the key into the second lock. A quick turn, and both hands were free. Tongues of fire blazed up Black Otter's arms as the blood gushed into long-constricted vessels. He clenched his hands into fists, biting back the urge to scream with pain. Soon he would be free. Soon...

The ancient chief glanced down at Black Otter's

legs. To unfasten the ankle bands, he would have to drop to his arthritic knees, exposing himself to treachery from above. As the old man hesitated, Black Otter's eyes caught a flicker of movement from the corner of the cell and heard the woman's voice.

"I'll do it, Father." Without waiting for a reply she snatched the key from the old man's hand and dropped to a kneeling position on the floor. Black Otter's ankles had suffered even more from the chafing irons than had his wrists. They were swollen with fluid and raw with infection. He waited, in silence, teeth clenched against the pain he knew would come.

Her pale hands were cool and as soft as flower petals against his tormented flesh. *Rowena.* Her name echoed in his mind as she worked the key into position. A liquid name, as smooth as flowing water on the tongue. No he would not kill this harmless creature. Nor would he kill the old chief who was her father. They had shown him kindness and he, as a Lenape warrior, was bound by honor. But the toad-faced cowards who had dragged him down into this black hole—yes, on them he would take a warrior's vengeance. He would strike without—

Black Otter's body jerked in sudden agony as the iron band fell away from his ankle and dropped with a clatter to the stone floor. The pain of flowing blood lanced up his leg into his groin, so hot and intense that only his warrior's discipline kept his mouth clamped shut, his throat silent.

The last iron band, he knew, would be the worst. Over the three long moons of his imprisonment, the rusting iron had worked into his swollen flesh, spawning odorous poisons that seeped like snake venom into his blood—poisons he knew would kill him if the irons were not removed and the wounds treated with healing herbs—if he could but find any. But where, in this accursed land—?

In the midst of his thoughts the rusty lock parted. The rush of sensation was so searing, so unspeakably painful, that Black Otter disgraced himself with a low groan. Sweat broke out on his face, streaming in small rivulets down his temples, his cheeks, as the realization struck him.

He was free.

The urge exploded in him to *run*—to shove these foolish people aside, to flee up the stairs and out of this great smelly warren of a house, to find fresh air and blue sky, to find the sea...

The door to his cell was ajar. Reason fled as he ripped it open, knocked the burly man out of the way and lunged toward the stairs. Behind him, the old chief was shouting, but his voice was drowned by the roaring sound that filled Black Otter's head, a sound like the crash of ocean waves in a mighty storm.

Above, at the side of the stairs, the reed torch flickered in its bracket on the wall. If he could reach it, he would have a weapon—a weapon he could swing like a war club or fling into the straw, setting the hateful lodge aflame.

He struggled upward, head throbbing, limbs screaming in agony. The flame of the torch filled his vision, the light haloed by unearthly rings of green and violet. He strained upward to seize it, but his arms were as heavy as tree trunks and his legs suddenly refused to support him. The roar in his head grew, and now he was sinking into it like a swimmer in a dark ocean. Deeper, deeper, he struggled until it closed over his senses, leaving nothing but blackness and silence.

Clutching her skirts, Rowena pushed past her father and raced up the stairs to where the savage lay slumped beneath the torch.

"Keep away from him, Rowena!" Her father's voice echoed off the dank stone walls. "Leave the brute to me and to Thomas."

"So you can throw him back in that cell to die of his wounds?" She crouched beside the dark head, gazing down at the crumpled length of the man—the bruised torso, the ropy muscles, devoid of fat, the bloodless cheeks beneath the bronze patina of his skin. Where the torchlight fell on his face she noticed, for the first time, the blue tracery of birds in flight across his forehead and the small spear-shaped figure at the corner of his mouth. There were tattooed lines on his arms, as well, faint, like the river lines on an old map. This man's mind would be a treasure trove of stories and adventures, Rowena knew. Suddenly she wanted to hear them all.

Crouching above her savage like a protective hawk, she glared at her father. "We'll be taking him upstairs, and putting him in a clean bed," she said. "Thomas, fetch Dickon to help us. Quickly, before he awakens."

Thomas glanced from master to mistress, then, as if sensing the stronger will, worked his way around the sprawled Indian and sprinted up the stairs.

"Are you mad?" Sir Christopher rasped. "After

what the creature nearly did to you? I say throw him back in the cell like the wild animal he is!''

''It was you who paid a hundred fifty pounds for him!'' Rowan retorted hotly. ''For that grand sum, Father, do you want a living being or a corpse?''

Sir Christopher's shoulders sagged in surrender to his daughter's logic. ''Very well,'' he growled. ''But he must be locked up like the wild beast that he is. We can hardly have him prowling the halls or leaping out of the windows.''

''No, certainly not.'' Rowena eased the battered head into her lap, her mind groping for a solution that would mollify her father. ''The small chamber at the end of the upstairs hall—we set up a cot there when Viscount Foxley visited last November, for his manservant, as I recall.''

''The window—''

''Higher than a man's head, and securely barred. 'Twill do for our savage, I think. But we must have the means to watch him, Father, and to pass food and slops.''

''A simple matter!'' Sir Christopher was becoming caught up in the plan he had opposed so vehemently. ''We'll have Thomas saw two openings in the door, one at eye level and one above the floorboards. That way, we can observe the savage and even communicate with him without risk to our safety.''

''A splendid idea, Father.'' Rowena glanced down in sudden alarm as the dark head stirred in her lap. The savage's eyelids fluttered. He moaned a word—a name, perhaps—in his own tongue. His body jerked in agitation, as if he were dreaming.

''Hush now.'' Rowena brushed a fingertip across

his forehead, tracing the line of winging birds. "You're safe with us, My Lord Savage. We've no reason to harm you."

Slowly the twitching limbs relaxed. The powerful chest rose and fell as the Indian slipped back into unconsciousness. Rowena supported the fierce head between her knees, her senses taut and wary, as if she cradled a sleeping leopard in her lap.

"My Lord Savage, indeed!" Sir Christopher hissed. "You're making a pet of him, Rowena, a folly to be sure! The creature's as dangerous as a wild boar, and if you allow him so much as a modicum of liberty, there'll be the very devil to pay!"

Rowena brushed an exploring hand along the line of one jutting cheekbone. Her heart contracted with dread as she felt the searing heat of his skin.

"I fear our savage may be too ill to be dangerous," she said. "If the festering's gotten into his bloodstream, 'twill be all we can do to save his life!" She twisted toward the light at the top of the stairs, straining upward in sudden agitation. "By heaven, where are Thomas and Dickon? If they've fallen into some kind of mischief—"

As if her words had conjured them, the two Cornishmen appeared that very moment at the top of the stairs, Dickon carrying the camphorwood chest that held Rowena's collection of salves and ointments. "Hurry!" she whispered, the sound echoing up the stairwell. "Put that chest down, Dickon! I need you to help carry him upstairs!"

Dickon did as she'd ordered but his face was gray with terror as he stumbled down the stone steps. "Don't be afraid," Rowena coaxed him, frantic beneath her own calm demeanor. "Just hurry—for the love of heaven, hurry!"

Rowena slumped on a low stool beside the cot, her legs too weary to hold her. Afternoon sunlight slanted through the high, barred window of the tiny room, falling on the savage's bloodless face. All day she had watched as he drifted on his red tide of fever, sleeping like an exhausted child one moment, muttering incoherently the next. Now and again his eyes would shoot open, but there was nothing but confusion in their black depths. He seemed unaware of her presence, lost in the nightmare visions of his own heat-seared mind.

From the hallway Rowena could hear the rhythmic, nasal wheeze of Thomas's snoring. Sir Christopher had posted him as guard outside the sickroom. A needless precaution, as were the linen lashings that bound the captive's body to the bed. The savage was too ill to get up and walk—and if he were otherwise, Rowena knew, all the bonds and guards under heaven would not suffice to hold him.

Pouring cool water into a pewter basin, she wrung out a cloth and sponged his burning face. What compelling features he had, she mused. They were as fierce as the mask of an eagle, the bones jutting sharply beneath smooth olive skin, the eyes set so deeply as to be lost in pits of shadow, the mouth, thin-lipped but oddly sensual in the long, squared frame of his jaw. Her hand lingered as she passed the cloth over the flying birds on his forehead. What sort of man had he been in that faraway world from which he had been so cruelly torn? A warrior? A leader of his tribe? Aye, a lord in his own right. She could scarcely imagine less.

"No change in the creature?" Her father had entered the room so quietly that Rowena was startled by the sound of his voice. She glanced up to meet the worry in his eyes, then shook her head.

"Strange how swiftly the fever came upon him," she said. "It was almost as if the shackles were holding it in check—but that's hardly possible, is it? If it were, he'd have likely lost his hands and feet."

"No success with your salves and potions, I take it?" Sir Christopher was skeptical, Rowena knew, of the herbs she gathered on the moor, ground with a pestle and blended with tallow or bitters. The concoctions had proven their merit on sick and wounded animals, but she had never tried any of them on a human being before.

"I made poultices of boiled comfrey for his wrists and ankles and bound them with linen—oh, and I managed to get a half cup of mint tea down him before he began fighting me."

"As would any man with a tongue in his mouth," Sir Christopher scoffed. "Mint tea, indeed! A cup of stout ale would do him more good!"

Rowena glanced sharply up at her father. "Well, at least you're calling him a man now! That's a bit of progress! Mayhap we should have a doctor in to look at his wounds."

"A doctor?" Sir Christopher made a small choking sound. "And have the whole county and beyond learn what we're harboring here? My dear, the witch hunt ensuing from such a discovery would be the ruin of us all!"

"You should have thought of that before you paid those brigands to kidnap a man from his own home!" Rowena snapped.

"You don't understand!" The urgency in her father's voice chilled Rowan's blood. "Once the savage is able to speak for himself, perhaps even accept Christian baptism for the sake of appearances, 'twill be a different matter entirely. But for now, his presence must be kept secret!"

"And if one of the servants, say, Thomas or Dickon, can't keep still? You know as well as I do what too much drink can do to a man's tongue!"

"They'll keep their silence or lose their positions. I've already made that quite clear. And after all, how much can they reveal? Only you and I know where the savage came from. As far as the servants are concerned, we're sheltering some poor raving Gypsy lunatic I brought home from Falmouth."

"Father, this whole venture will come to no earthly good!" Rowena picked up the cloth from the basin and wrung it out with a vehement twist. "Look at the poor wretch! You had no idea what you were planning, did you? No notion of how you were going to care for him, how you were going to communicate with him, how—"

"That's quite enough lecturing!" Sir Christopher snapped. "I am your father, after all, and entitled to some degree of respect."

"Of course you are!" Rowena bit back a sob of frustration. "But, by heaven, this creature's not one of your apes or foreign birds! You can't just stuff him into a cage and—"

A sharp moan from the savage cut into her words.

Glancing swiftly down, she saw that his eyes were closed, but his head was rolling back and forth on the pillow. His body jerked, straining at the linen strips that bound him to the cot.

"There…" She sponged his burning face with the damp cloth. "There, now, it's all right. Rest…"

Little by little the savage's body relaxed beneath her touch. His breath eased out in a long, powerful exhalation as he slipped back into his dark void.

Silence hung heavy in the small chamber, broken only by the cry of a storm petrel and the sound of the sea beyond the high window. At last Sir Christopher sighed, a tired and broken sound. "I've been a selfish old man," he said. "And I've done you no good service, child, keeping you here in this lonely old house with no friends your own age."

Rowena glanced up at him, caught off balance by this sudden turn of conversation.

"You've given your poor, tender heart to every wounded bird and fox and hare that's found its way onto the grounds," he continued gravely. "But as you pointed out yourself, this creature who lies before us is no mere beast of the field. He is capable of doing you more harm, my dear, than a veritable menagerie of wild animals."

"Father—"

"No, let me finish. You've defied me at every turn in this matter, Rowena. But for your own safety and my own peace of mind, I insist on your obedience this time. You're to keep away from this chamber and leave the tending of the savage strictly to me."

Rowena sprang to her feet, a flood of impassioned protests surging in her mind. The savage trusted her—

more so, at least, than anyone else in this place. He *needed* her.

But wisdom and experience constrained her to hold her tongue. She recognized the finality in her father's tone. There were times when Sir Christopher could not be defied, and this was one of them.

"Your concern is for naught, Father," she argued, still hoping to persuade him. "The savage is too weak to do me harm, and with Thomas here to guard me—"

"My dear child." Sir Christopher laid a gentle hand on her arm—a rare gesture of affection on his part. "'Tis not so much the safety of your body that troubles me as the safety of your heart."

"With all due respect, Father, you presume too much!"

"Do I?" The sadness in his voice struck her harder than any blow. "Even the appearance of evil is dangerous. A mere whisper of scandal could mark you for life, ruin any future prospects—"

"You mean the chance of my marrying respectably, let alone well?" Rowena managed a bitter chuckle. "At my age, Father, that's hardly a consideration!"

"You think so poorly of yourself?" Sir Christopher glowered at her over his thick spectacles, then waved an impatient hand in dismissal. "Never mind! You could stall me with arguments until the fires of hell burn out, but I'm not going to change my mind! Off with you now, before I order Thomas to drag you to your chamber and lock you in!"

"Father—"

"No, Rowena. There are other things around the house that need your tending as much as this poor Indian. Go now and leave him to me. You are not, under any circumstances, to enter this room again!"

Chapter Five

*L*azy golden flames, tipped with azure, flickered in the warm darkness of the lodge. Shadows danced on the inner walls, playing on the willow framework and its overlay of woven reed mats. The rich fragrance of the salmon that lay roasting over the coals on its bed of green willows perfumed the evening air.

Cushioned by soft beaver pelts, Black Otter sat cross-legged on the floor of the lodge, his children nestled on either side of him. "Tell us the story you heard in the Wampanoag village, Father," Singing Bird begged him, "the story of the great whales."

Black Otter pinched a bit of tobacco from the squirrel skin bag that hung around his neck, worked it into the bowl of his clay pipe and lit it with a coal from the fire. The mellow smoke curled upward as he puffed in silence for a moment, then spoke.

"Long ago, it is said, the Wampanoag people traveled to the island where many of them dwell to this day, led by a wise and good giant named Maushop. For many years they lived in peace there, and then one night Maushop had a fearful dream."

"What was the dream about?" Swift Arrow asked,
even though he had heard the story countless times.

*"The dream was about white men who would one
day come to this land and cause grievous harm to fall
upon the people here. Maushop was so troubled by
the dream that he decided to escape to the sea. He
invited the people to follow him."*

"Did they follow him, Father?"

*"Some of them did. And as the water covered their
bodies they turned into great whales and swam away,
leaving the others behind."*

"And did the white men come?" Swift Arrow
asked.

*"Not yet. But they will come. We have seen their
great canoes on the water."*

"Will they come here?" Singing Bird pressed close
against her father's side.

Black Otter closed his eyes, willing away his own
fears for these, the children of his body, and for all
the Lenape, the people, who were children of his
heart. *"They may come,"* he said. *"But our braves
will be ready. They will protect you—I will protect
you, my little ones, with my very life."*

With my very life...

The dream vanished as Black Otter's body jerked
in a sudden spasm of consciousness. His eyes shot
open, the pupils shrinking abruptly against the sunlight that fell across his face. The air was fresh and
cool, rich with the familiar salt tang of the ocean.
Sucking it deeply into his lungs, he forced his twitching muscles to lie at rest.

Was he home? Had the eternity aboard the great

boat, the bone-rattling ordeal on the cart and the horror of the rat-infested hole been nothing more than a
terrible dream? Had his exhausted mind created everything—even the phantom oval of the white
woman's face in the darkness and the gentle touch of
her hands?

Whatever the truth, he could not lie here with his
mind swimming in circles. He had to get up. He had
to discover what had happened and face his enemies
as a *sakima* and a warrior.

Struggling from the depths of exhaustion, he willed
his limbs to stretch, to stir. Only then did he realize,
to his horror, that he could not move. The entire
length of his body was bound by a veritable net of
cloth strips to the frame of the bed where he lay.
Singly, he calculated, the strips would be flimsy
things, easy for a man to break. But their combined
strength held him as firmly as the iron shackles. They
bound his arms straight against his sides, his legs flat
against the surface of the bed. He was as much a
prisoner as ever.

Black Otter sank back onto the pillow, resolving to
not waste his strength until he could think things
through and devise some kind of plan. As the fog
lifted from his mind, he became aware of a prickling
sensation along the calf of one leg—an odd tingle,
merely irritating at first, then puzzling, almost frightening, as if some small animal were gnawing at his
flesh beneath the light cloth covering. Black Otter's
heart contracted as he thought of the rats.

Summoning his self-control, he raised his head off
the pillow, seized a fold on the cloth in his teeth and
began tugging it upward. Little by little he pulled it,

the strain knotting the muscles of his neck. He could
see his own bare feet now, see his ankles, wrapped
in dark-stained bands of cloth. A harder pull and he
could see his bruise-mottled lower legs. That was
when he saw the dark, liver-colored lumps of flesh
that clung to his skin. His stomach lurched as he realized what they were.

Leeches! Not the small, harmless wormlike creatures that lived in the streams and ponds of his homeland, these were monsters, each one longer and
thicker than his thumb. And they were swollen with
blood—his blood!

Black Otter's chest heaved with revulsion. Rats,
leeches… What sort of people were these whites, who
used animals to torture and torment their captives? As
a warrior he was prepared to endure pain. But to lie
here like this, while these hideous creatures sucked
the very life from his body—

Overcome by the urge to tear away the clinging
horrors, he began to thrash and jerk wildly. But his
lashings were skillfully done. He could scarcely
move, let alone peel off the leeches. A tide of disgust
washed over him, churned by rage, by grief and by a
despair so deep that, at last, it erupted from the depths
of his body in a wrenching primal scream.

Rowena was on the moor above the cliffs gathering
wild fennel when the cry reached her ears. She stiffened, pierced by agony in the distant sound. An animal, she thought. Some poor creature had toppled
over a ledge and screamed its way down to a watery
death.

But the cry had not come from the direction of the

sea, she suddenly realized. It had come from the house.

The basket of herbs dropped unheeded from Rowena's hand as she caught up her skirts and plunged toward the house. For the past two days she had forced herself to respect her father's wishes in the matter of the savage. But she had lived every moment with a sense of impending tragedy. Now, reason shrilled, her fears had come to pass.

Sides throbbing, she raced over the threshold, across the great hall and up the stairs. One cry—that was all she had heard. But such a cry it had been, so wrought with rage and anguish that even the memory of it chilled her blood.

As she gained the upstairs hallway she saw Sir Christopher hurrying from the direction of his own chamber, hastily tugging up his breeches. At the sight of him Rowena's knees buckled with relief. At least her father was safe. But what of the savage? What of the scream?

They reached the doorway of the tiny chamber at the same time. From the other side of the locked door there was nothing but an ominous silence.

"What happened?" Rowena seized his arm. "Do you know?"

Sir Christopher shook his head, looking pale and confused. "I left him for just a few moments to visit my chamber. He was asleep, or so I thought…"

"Here—" She shoved her hand into his pocket for the key, wishing he had carried out his plan to have Thomas cut holes in the door. "Is the savage still bound to the bed?"

"Aye, that he is—or was, in any case. What are

you doing, girl? You can't just open that door and go blundering into Lord knows what. Run and fetch Thomas first!''

But Rowena had the key and was already thrusting it into the lock. Reason argued that she was no match for an enraged Indian warrior and she should heed her father's words. But the anguish in that cry echoed in her heart, and she knew that, whatever lay within the tiny chamber, she could not turn aside from it.

The lock clicked open and Rowena hurled herself against the door. If the savage had gotten free and was waiting to attack or escape, at least her sudden entry might catch him off guard.

The damp wood stuck in its frame for an instant, then came free with a suddenness that sent her stumbling forward. But she met no monster waiting to seize her in his bronze arms. The savage lay securely lashed to the bed, his body rigid, his obsidian eyes gazing fixedly at the open beams of the ceiling. Beads of perspiration glittered on his ashen skin.

Had he really cried out? Heart pounding, Rowena ventured closer. He made no sound as she bent over him, but his eyes held an animal's unreasoning terror—an animal's helpless rage.

The muslin sheet that covered his rangy body lay askew, exposing his bare legs. Rowena reached down to cover him, then gasped as she saw the leeches fastened to his flesh.

''Is this your doing?'' She turned angrily on her father who stood in the doorway, looking pale. ''Leeches, father? Those blood-sucking little horrors?''

''I did what I thought best.'' Sir Christopher's

voice rattled oddly in his throat. "I know you set little store by bloodletting, but as you see the brute is conscious, and the fever appears to have broken."

"As it might have in any case. Look at him! He understands nothing about your precious leeches! No wonder he screamed! Who indeed would not?" Her gaze darted to the savage, then back to her father. "Will you remove your bloody pets or must I do the job myself?"

Sir Christopher stood his ground against her outrage. "The leeches are sucking out the poisoned blood. I'll remove the creatures when they've finished their work. Until then I'll thank you not to interfere!"

"How can I not interfere?" Rowena flung. "I've done my best to respect your wishes, Father, but for all your good intent, you're torturing the man!"

"Enough!" The aging eyes were stony behind the thick lenses. "All that I've undertaken here is for your own good! Why do you refuse to see that?"

Rowena's mind scrambled for a retort, but it was the savage who broke the brief silence, speaking not in his crude English but in a birdlike tongue she had never heard before, its flowing syllables angry, passionate, demanding—and strangely beautiful.

He was pleading his own cause with an eloquence that transcended the barrier of language; and the rise and fall of his powerful voice was as compelling as music.

Sir Christopher's eyes had taken on a glazed look. "See," he muttered thickly, "nothing but monkey gibberish!"

"No more monkey gibberish than French or Spanish!" Rowena spun back to face her father, bracing

for more heated debate, but her anger died the instant
she saw him. Sir Christopher was clutching the door
frame, his face the color of unbaked dough. His
mouth was oddly twisted with a thin trail of spittle
glistening long the side of his chin.

"Father!" She sprang toward him with a cry, but
before she could reach his side, he collapsed. His arthritic legs buckled beneath him as, with a little moan,
he slid to the floor.

Rowena flung herself down beside him where he
lay, so small and frail that his body seemed to have
disappeared beneath the ample robe. Her desperately
seeking finger slid along his jawline, probing downward to find his jugular pulse. Yes, praise heaven, he
was alive—but in what condition? His eyes were
closed, the ever-present spectacles crushed and bent
beneath his weight. His jaw was slack, his skin
clammy. Was it apoplexy? She could not be certain.
She only knew that she had to get him into his bed.
But she could not carry his dead weight alone.

Raising her glance, she saw the savage's sharp,
black eyes watching her intently. Could she trust him
to help her? No, she dismissed the thought as swiftly
as it had come. The savage was a danger to all who
came near him—even to her.

Tearing her eyes away from him, she dragged her
father's inert body into the hallway, slammed the
chamber door shut behind her and turned the key,
which she had left in the lock. Then she wheeled and
raced toward the stairs, shouting for help.

Black Otter lay motionless on the cot, listening to
the clamor of voices and running footsteps outside the

door of the tiny room. He had seen the old chief fall, and he had seen the daughter's fear. The old man was not far from death, a fact that was causing a great uproar in the great lodge. Things would have been different among his own people, where the passing of generations was understood and accepted. This would have been the time for a new chief, already chosen, to step forward so that the life of the people might continue as before. Where was the new chief here? There appeared to be no one in authority except the woman.

Rowena.

He fixed his thoughts on her now to keep his mind off the leeches that clung to his flesh, sucking away vital blood. His cry had been a lapse, an explosion of pent-up rage, grief and fear, unworthy of a trained warrior. But he was in control once more, his heart hardened against pain. He could endure, he *would* endure until the day he reached Lenapehoken and held his children in his arms—or mourned over their graves.

But his children were far away now. It was only the thought of *her* that kept his mind flowing like calm water. He recalled the way she had looked bending over him, her hickory-colored hair tumbled by the ocean breeze, her long, pale face flushed and glowing like the inner surface of a shell. His starving senses had drunk in the scents she had brought from the outdoors—the earthy smell of grass and spring wildflowers, the tangy aroma of the sea.

He remembered the horror that had flashed in her golden eyes when she saw the leeches. She had turned on her father in anger then, pointing, accusing. Was it possible that she had not been part of the plan to torture him? Had she been trying to protect him against the men of her tribe?

Could it be that she was an ally, the only ally he had in this place?

Impatient with his own questions, Black Otter jerked at his bonds—and felt, for the first time, a slight yielding, a barely perceptible stretching of the cloth strip that bound his shoulders to the bed frame. His heart jumped. Cautiously he shifted his shoulders and tested the fabric again. It gave—perhaps a finger breadth more.

Pulse racing, he glanced toward the locked door. With the old chief's sudden attack of illness, the great lodge would be in an uproar. No one would think to look in on him. If he could break free of the bed and find a way outside…

Fevered with excitement now, he began working his shoulders hard against the bonds. At first the movement was slight, but as time crawled by, the woven fabric began to stretch. Black Otter's muscles flexed and rippled, causing the cloth bands to cut into his skin, but gaining, with each effort, an additional finger breadth of slack. He strained and twisted upward, like a snake shedding its skin. Suddenly his upper body was free. His hands tore at the wrappings. At last he could sit up. At last he could reach the bloodsuckers on his leg.

There were five of the loathsome creatures, black and swollen with his blood. He peeled them away with exquisite care, remembering his experience with smaller leeches and how their buried heads tended to remain and fester in the flesh. When the first one came

free he flung it across the room, shuddering with revulsion. By the time the remaining four were gone
his ribs were heaving, his skin rank with sweat. Fighting nausea, he pulled the last of the linen strips from
his legs. Relief swept over him as he noticed that the
flesh on his wrists and ankles was beginning to heal.
Perhaps for the first time in three moons, he would
be able to walk.

For the first few steps his unsteady legs would
barely support his weight, but as Black Otter forced
himself to walk about the room his strength and balance began to return. The urge to run reawakened. It
stirred, grew until it became an inner scream, driving
him to the brink of desperation.

As the freedom hunger burst in him, he leaped for
the high window. His hands caught the bars and he
hung there for a moment, swinging his weight in an
attempt to loosen them. But the bars were solid, set
in stone, the spaces between them far too narrow for
him to pass through. Only his eyes could reach beyond them into the sky where seabirds wheeled and
soared. Their cries reached his ears, filling his heart
with such longing that, if he could have done so,
Black Otter would have pushed through the small
opening and hurled himself into the sky.

Churning with frustration, he dropped from the
window and turned his rage on the door. It was made
of solid hardwood, the planks as thick as his wrist
and bolted with strips of iron. A full grown he-bear
could not have broken through it, let alone a man. As
for the lock—yes, he remembered hearing the key
turn after Rowena closed the door. Even with her father lying on the floor she had not forgotten.

Seizing the latch, he gave it a furious twist. The small click he heard was no louder than the whisper of a beetle in the summer grass, but it was enough to stop his heart for an instant.

Scarcely daring to breathe, he twisted the latch again. This time he felt it give and heard the subtle movement of the metal parts inside the door. Black Otter swallowed his amazement. He had heard the sound of the key in the lock and known what it meant, but now the door appeared to be unlocked. Had Rowena, in her haste, failed to turn the key far enough? Or could it be that the device was so old its inner parts had worn away? No matter. He would not get another chance like this one.

Still numb with disbelief, he tested the latch and felt it yield to the pressure of his hand. The door itself stuck slightly in frame. Black Otter's nerves screamed as he nudged it open to the barest crack.

Through the sliver of space he could see into a dim passageway lined with massive wooden doors. There was no one in sight, but he could hear the loud murmur of voices from a room at the far end. Straining his ears, he could make out the throaty timbre of Rowena's voice and the gruff response of the burly man who had guarded her. The plump, slow man with cornsilk hair—the one Black Otter had seized as a hostage in the dark hole—was there, too. The poor, frightened creature seemed to be weeping. There were other voices in the room, as well, that Black Otter did not recognize. All of them seemed to be talking at once, some frightened, others hostile. These white barbarians were very different from his own people.

Clearly, they had never been taught to work together for the good of their tribe.

Black Otter was about to open the door further when a boy of about thirteen winters burst out of the room and came racing down the passageway. Black Otter drew back, holding his breath, but the youth hurried on past him, to disappear down what appeared to be a stairway. Was he going for help, or to summon the man who would be the new chief? It made no difference. All that really mattered was getting out of this place, and the youth might have just shown him the way.

Heart pounding, Black Otter stepped out into the passageway and closed the door softly behind him. From the far room, the voices still clamored in their unpleasant language. He forced them out of his mind as he slipped like a shadow along the wall in the direction of the stairs. The urge to run was like a cry in him, but right now his freedom, and perhaps his life, depended on stealth. He had no war club, no spear, no bow or arrows, and his body was weak from the ravages of his illness. He was as vulnerable as a wounded fox.

He could see the top of the stairs now and hear, from somewhere below, the opening and closing of a heavy door. Was it the sound of the boy leaving or, perhaps, someone else coming in—someone who might be coming directly upstairs?

Black Otter stepped backward into the shadowed recess of the last doorway. Holding his breath, he listened for the sound of approaching footsteps. If someone were to come up the stairs, he would have no place to go except—

His reflexes jumped as the door creaked behind him and gave way to the pressure of his body. Instinctively he whirled, ready to fight for his life. But no one was there. The door had simply been left ajar, and his own weight had pushed it open. He hesitated for the space of a heartbeat. Then, still uncertain of the danger from below, he slipped through, into the room.

The morning sun, streaming through the high glass windows, blinded him for an instant. He squinted furiously, unable to see anything but brightness. Then, slowly, his eyes began to adjust to the light. Shapes and colors swam into focus. Objects took on clarity and detail. Black Otter stared, dumbfounded by what he saw.

The walls of the room were lined with tall wooden boxes, all of them open in front and separated into compartments. Every niche of space was filled, some with odd-shaped jars, some with bowls and trays that were heaped with what appeared to be dried animal parts—hooves, paws, ears and bones—more bones than Black Otter had ever seen in his life.

His senses prickled with premonitions of danger as he examined one jar, then another. They contained more animal parts—eyes, hearts, unborn young, floating in a heavy brine that reeked of salt and death. Turning away in revulsion, Black Otter found himself facing a long table, its surface a single slab of polished gray stone.

A chill, like a breath of icy wind, passed over his body. What sort of place was this—and what sort of evil walked this great lodge? Was Rowena part of it?

At that moment he desired nothing more than to

leave this room of death, but as Black Otter turned to go, his eye caught the unmistakable gleam of sunlight on polished metal. The brightness came from a shallow wooden tray that sat on the table's far corner. His heart lurched as he saw what reflected the sun's rays.

Lying on the cloth that lined the tray, arranged like blackbirds on a branch, was an assortment of small, narrow-bladed steel knives.

He stared at them in wonder, measuring, judging each one with his eyes. Choosing the longest one, he picked it up and tested his grip on the handle, which was made from the same metal as the blade itself. The knife's weight surprised him, for it was no bigger than a feather from the wing of a fledgling hawk. So did the exquisite keenness of the blade, which left a threadline of crimson when he touched it with his finger. Yes, he would take this one. As a weapon, its small size left much to be desired. But at close range, it would be useful enough.

Clutching the knife in his fist, he turned and moved toward the closed door. He was about to open it when his ears caught the sound of footsteps coming swiftly and lightly down the long corridor. Holding his breath, he waited for the footsteps to pass. To his consternation, their cadence slowed as they came closer. He heard them hesitate, then pause directly outside the door.

Black Otter slipped into the shadows behind a tall cabinet, knife ready, as the latch clicked. The evil in the room pressed around him, choking his senses as the door began to open.

Poised for attack, he waited.

Chapter Six

Rowena paused outside the laboratory door. Her hand stilled on the knob as she struggled to collect the scattered pieces of what, until this morning, had been her life.

Her father lay resting in his bed, alive but paralyzed on one entire side of his body. He was lucid enough to know her and to speak coherently, but the left side of his face was frozen as if it had been cast in wax. No one, save God, knew how long he could live in this condition, but Rowena knew it was time to prepare for the worst.

She had sent one of the stable boys for the nearest doctor, but there was none closer than Falmouth. How could she stand helplessly by and wait if there was anything she could do to ease her father's suffering? For all she knew, the attack could well have been her own fault. If she had not lashed out at him for his treatment of the savage—

But casting blame was useless. Only action counted now, that, and the hope that she was doing all she could for him. In the laboratory was a cupboard where she kept her herbs and potions for treating animals. At least she could brew something for the pain, a tea, perhaps, that would allow him to rest more comfortably until the doctor arrived. Thomas and Dickon were there, in her father's chamber. They could watch him while she carried out this simple task and fetch her quickly if he took a turn for the worse.

Forcing herself to move, she opened the door into the sunlit room. The brightness dazzled her eyes. Rowena blinked furiously, seeing the table and its surrounding cabinets through a shimmering blur. She could barely see her way—but no matter, she had grown up in this room, amid the clutter of books and jars and exotic specimens. She could have found her way blindfolded.

The cupboard that held her herbal collection stood on the far side of the room. She groped her way toward it, her mind still spinning with the enormity of what had happened. Even if Sir Christopher lived, she knew his work was finished. She would never again walk into the laboratory to see him bent over a specimen, muttering to himself and scribbling furiously in his journal. She would never again share the excitement of a new discovery or sit for hours over the remains of supper, arguing some obscure point of anatomy or philosophy until the candles guttered and died, leaving them in darkness.

Hot tears stung Rowena's eyes as she stumbled forward. Grief was a black weight inside her, swelling, growing, threatening to burst and shatter her into a thousand pieces. She had to control her private emotions, she reminded herself harshly. There was no one else to see to things now that her father was ill. The laboratory, the household accounts, the house and servants, the grounds, the horses and livestock were all her responsibility now.

As was the savage.

Her heart dropped as she remembered how she had left him—lashed to the frame of the cot, the leeches fastened to the flesh of his leg. Dear heaven, how long had it been? The poor wretch could be delirious with fear!

She whirled abruptly—only to collide with a solid figure that loomed out of the brightness. Blinded by light and tears, Rowena could see nothing but a hulking silhouette, but the arms that closed roughly around her were familiar, as was the powerful hand that smothered her cry. She should have known that *he* would not be contained by linen bonds and rusting locks. She should have guessed he would be here.

Only when she felt the cold blade against her throat did she become truly frightened. Sir Christopher had kept his dissecting knives sharp enough to split a human hair along its length. One careless move and the razor edge would slice her throat.

"Out!" the savage's voice rasped in her ear. "You—me—we go!" The words emerged awkwardly, formed with effort. He had learned more English aboard the ship than even she had suspected.

"Out!" He used his free hand to jerk her around so that her spine pressed against the hard-muscled wall of his chest. Rowena stumbled over her skirt as he shoved her forward toward the half-open door. His hand caught her waist, pulling her up and back against his nearly naked body. Dizzy with fear, she swayed against him, feeling the shaft between his thighs as

distinctly as she felt the small, sharp blade at her throat. A startling heat surged through Rowena's body—strangely exhilarating, combined as it was, with her terror.

Would he really kill her? Reason and hope argued against it. She was, after all, of no use to him dead. But the voice of fear shrilled otherwise. She could not risk what the savage might do if she screamed for help or struggled to escape.

"You haven't the slightest notion what you're doing!" she stressed as he propelled her toward the door. "Kill me, and you kill your one true friend in this place! You'll be hunted down and destroyed like a mad dog!"

The savage muttered a gruff command in his own tongue, probably ordering her to be still. He could not understand her, of course. But Rowena was too agitated to keep silent. She chattered on, the words a balm for her own fear.

"Even if you get away, where will you go? You have no clothes...no money...not the barest knowledge of the land or the customs..."

They had reached the open doorway of the laboratory. He paused to glance up and down the corridor, then pushed her toward the stairs. Where his body pressed hers, Rowena could feel the desperate tension in him, the relentless urge to be free.

"I know you want to go home," she gasped as his brute strength swept her down the stone staircase toward the great hall. "But you must stay here for now. Let me help you—let me teach you—"

He jerked her to a halt at the foot of the stairs. His eagle's gaze swept the vast room, from the long,

empty dining table to the small open doorway leading
back to the kitchen, then fixed on the front door—a
massive slab of solid oak fortified with cast iron
hinges and crossbars.

"Out!" He shoved her along the wall, the blade
cold and sharp against her throat. Rowena prayed silently that no one would come in and surprise them,
for such an encounter would surely end in death—the
savage's, her own or that of her would-be rescuer.

"In heaven's name, you must not do this!" she
pleaded, stumbling against the blade and feeling the
sting of its edge, followed by a thin trickle of blood
down the side of her neck. "Out there you'll surely
die! Here, inside this house, is your only hope of
safety!"

Ignoring her agitation, the savage dragged her toward the front door, where he paused. Rowena needed
no prodding to understand what he wanted. His hands
were occupied with keeping her prisoner. He would
expect her to open the door herself.

She pressed the latch at once, knowing she had
little choice. The heavy door was unlocked. It creaked
inward without a touch, pushed by the force of the
wind that blew in over the cliffs. The savage gasped
softly as the breeze struck his face, carrying with it
the fragrance of the blooming moor and the sea beyond. His chest swelled, lean ribs rising as he inhaled
the fresh air.

He might have rushed into the open at once, but
Rowena pushed backward, resisting as she pondered
her dilemma. Once clear of the house, the savage
would surely bolt and disappear, an act that would
lead, inexorably, to his own destruction. Yet it might

be equally risky to stay here where someone could happen on them at any moment.

"Go!" He pushed her out the door ahead of him, still pressing the knife against her throat. Rowena stumbled across the threshold and into the brilliant afternoon sunlight. Behind her, she felt him hesitate. He stood still for the space of a breath, his eyes taking in the broad sweep of the moor, abloom with gorse and yellow hedgerow, dotted here and there with clumps of thrift and wild bluebells. His gaze lifted to the cobalt sky where kittiwakes circled above the cliffs. Once more the savage inhaled, filling his lungs with the scent of freedom...

A freedom he could never truly know.

Black Otter had glimpsed this land on the miserable cart ride from the sea. But only now did he grasp the vastness of it, the sweep of open hills, the waving ocean of grass and wildflowers. His own people were forest dwellers, accustomed to the shelter of alder and hickory above their heads. Here he was shocked by the sudden sense of his own vulnerability. After the long moons of terror and confinement he quivered like a forest creature cast into the open.

Instincts honed over a lifetime shrilled at him to run. There were no iron bars or locked doors to shut him in now, no heavy shackles to weigh him down. There was nothing to hold him back.

Nothing except the clasp of Rowena's pale hand on his arm.

Only then did Black Otter realize that he was no longer holding her. His knife hand had dropped to his side, and the opposite arm had released its threatening grip around her waist. *She* was holding *him* now, her clasp warm and urgent on the bare flesh of his arm as if she feared he would fly away like one of the white birds that flocked above the cliffs. And she was speaking to him, her low, rich voice arguing passionately in that accursed language of hers. Black Otter could catch little of what she said—no more than a word here and there. But the vehemence in her voice and the pressure of her fingers told him as much as he needed to know. She was determined, by any possible means, to keep him from leaving.

How far would she go? Would she scream for help? Betray him at the first opportunity? He fingered the blade in his hand, testing its keen edge. He might be wise to kill her now, to turn and slit her soft white throat before she had a chance to cry out.

His fingers tightened around the knife in response to the thought—but no, he swiftly checked himself. The Lenape did not make war on helpless women. Besides, Rowena might prove useful as a hostage, or even as a guide. He would take her with him. But she must understand that he was no longer a captive and would never be again. She was his prisoner now.

He scanned the open moor, knowing his only chance of escape lay in finding a hiding place as soon as possible. Choosing the most likely route, he seized Rowena's arm and exploded into motion, running full tilt down the long slope toward the sea.

Rowena gave a little cry as the savage's powerful hand caught her wrist and jerked her roughly downhill. He dragged her with him across the moor, moving so swiftly that at times she seemed to fly behind him. Brambles snagged her skirts, tearing the hems to ribbons. Roots and stones bruised her slippered feet.

"Stop—in the name of mercy—" She tripped over a badger mound and went down in a clump of brambles, ripping the sleeve of her gown from shoulder to wrist. The savage's dark glance flashed back at her as he paused just long enough for Rowena to scramble to her feet. She knew where he was going now. A furlong beyond the house, where the land sloped eastward, a wooded hollow had been cut by a stream that sparkled like a diamond shower where it spilled out over the cliffs. Once the savage gained the cover of such a place, he would vanish like the wild creature he was. He would be free. Free to starve. To kill. To die.

"I beg of you—" she gasped, her lungs all but bursting. "We must go back! Please—my father—he needs me—"

Her words, of course, had no effect on the savage. He plunged down the grassy slope like a bounding deer, the sunlight rippling on his coppery skin, the wind streaming through the ebony mane of his hair. Rowena stumbled after him, her mind in turmoil. Her own father had caused this man to be snatched from among his own people. If the savage came to grief in this alien land, the wrong would be on Sir Christopher's head for all time. Could it be that she owed it to her father's immortal soul to protect this wild creature?

"You're still weak!" She lurched after him, biting back pain from the stitch in her side. "You'll catch a chill out here come nightfall! It's springtime yet—

our nights are cold, and you with scarcely any clothing—''

The hollow lay before them, dense with hawthorn
and feathery bracken where the stream surged among
the stones. A change seemed to come over the savage
as he slipped beneath the trees. He was in his own
element now, and he flowed like a shadow through
the undergrowth, moving down to where the stream
flowed like a thread of silver beneath the trailing willows. Rowena stumbled after him, too winded to carry
on her one-sided argument.

At the water's edge he stopped. Bruised, scratched
and exhausted, Rowena sank to the earth beside him.
Her gown was torn to ribbons, her long chestnut hair
tangled by the sea wind. Her ribs heaved beneath the
constricting stays of her corset. The savage's bronze
fingers remained locked around her wrist, but even if
he had let her go, she could not have run away.

The stream gurgled at their feet, splashing over
stones on its path to the sea. The savage dropped to
a crouch and used his free hand to scoop up water.
For the space of a heartbeat he hesitated, then turned
and offered Rowena his brimming palm.

Startled by the gesture, she shrank back from him.
The black eyes darkened. He spoke to her gruffly in
his own tongue; then, when she only stared at him,
he frowned thoughtfully and came up with the word
in English.

"Drink," he ordered, scooping up a fresh handful
of water and thrusting it toward her.

Rowena bent her head and sipped the water, hesi-
tantly at first, then thirstily, her lips brushing the rim
of his large brown hand. The sweet-salt taste of his

skin mingled with the coolness of the water. She drank again and again as he lifted the brimming cup of his palm from the stream.

Water spilled onto the bodice of her high-necked gown. The wet fabric clung to her breasts, outlining her tautly puckered nipples. As his gaze dropped and lingered, Rowena felt a hot tide of color flood her skin. This was madness! Her father lay gravely ill, dying, perhaps, at this very moment. And here she was, drinking from the hand of a nearly naked savage and blushing like a girl.

Grief and guilt tore at her heart. She had to get away, had to get back to her father's bedside at once. But even as urgency pulled her one way, Rowena knew where duty lay. Her father's life was in God's hands. But Sir Christopher, the scholar, would never forgive her if she returned home and left their prisoner at large.

The savage took a brief sip of water, eyes alert, watching the trees. Then he rose to his feet once more and moved warily down the hollow in the direction of the sea. Rowena scrambled along behind him, slowing him down and making far too much noise. She knew he would be able to travel faster without her. But she had no need to question his reason for dragging her along. Her value as a hostage outweighed any hindrance she might cause—an awareness that gave rise to a new and daring plan.

"Oh—" Rowena dropped to the ground in a clump of bracken. "Oh, stop—my ankle—"

He turned, scowling darkly down at her. His hand jerked at her arm in a none-too-gentle effort to get her on her feet.

"No." Rowena shook her head, grimacing in a show of pain. Her free hand tugged up her skirts to reveal her awkwardly twisted foot in its thin leather slipper. She pointed to her ankle. "It *hurts!*" she whimpered. "I can't go another step!"

Had she fooled him, or had she only succeeded in making him angry? Rowena held her breath as he glanced one way, then the other, every sense straining for signs of danger. Patterns of light and shadow played across the broad planes of his chest as he paused to twist the dissecting knife into the tangle of his hair. There was no fat beneath his coppery skin, only the sinewy contours of rib and muscle. Even after the ordeal of his illness, he looked strong enough to kill her with his bare hands.

Still wary, he dropped to one knee, twisted off her shoe and cupped her heel in his hand. His long, sensitive fingers explored her ankle through the thin woolen stocking, checking expertly for any sign of injury. Her breath caught as those fingers moved upward a hand breadth, then shifted back to her foot, massaging the long arch, the narrow base of the toes...

"*Pah!*" He shoved the shoe back onto her foot with a snort of disgust and rose to his feet, towering above her. His muttered comment made it clear that he had seen through her trickery.

"*No!*" Rowena insisted, refusing to be budged. "It *hurts!* You can't expect me to keep up! Not un-less—"

Her words ended in a gasp as he bent, caught her beneath her shoulders and knees and slung her over his shoulder like a sack of barley. Her head and upper body hung down his back, her dangling hair sweeping the taut curves of his buttocks.

"Let...me...go!" she muttered between clenched teeth, knowing full well he would pay her no heed. "My father will have you drawn and quartered! He'll—"

Rowena choked on her words as the truth struck with brutal force. Her father would do no such thing. Sir Christopher would no longer be there to protect her, to guide her, to scold her. *He* was the one who must be protected now, and she had vanished from the house right when he needed her most.

Black Otter strode down the wooded hollow, his footsteps keeping to the edge of the stream. Rowena's tall, womanly body hung over his shoulder. She had stopped struggling, but she continued to plead and argue, her words interspersed with outbursts of furious weeping.

He was sorely tempted to toss her to the ground and watch her run away on the ankle she had so clumsily pretended to injure. A kildeer dragging its wing to lure an enemy away from its nest could make a more convincing show than this willful white woman. She had made every effort to slow him down, and he was growing weary of it. He was growing weary of carrying her, as well. The long days of confinement and illness were beginning to tell on him, and Rowena's weight—she was no small woman—seemed to grow heavier with every step.

Birds scolded and twittered in the trees. Their calls were strange to his ears, but the sound of the sea, echoing from somewhere ahead, was the sound he remembered. The sea was his only path, his only link to home.

The sides of the hollow grew higher and steeper as the stream wound its way downward. Gnarled tree roots and jutting granite boulders made the way more and more difficult, especially with the burden of Rowena's weight on his shoulders. The weakened state of his body was beginning to tell, and he was tempted to stop and put her down. But then she would only resume her delaying tactics, and he had no time to indulge her. He had to get as far as possible from the house before her hulking protectors could miss her and follow their trail.

Black Otter froze as his ears caught a low rumbling sound, like distant thunder at first but moving closer at a speed far too swift for a storm. Instinctively he ducked behind a boulder. Rowena slid off his shoulder and, with a sputter of indignation, collapsed on a bed of ferns. Only then, with her weight gone, did he lift his head to see it just above the trees—a stout wooden bridge crossing the hollow, no more than a stone's throw ahead of them.

For the space of a breath he stood staring at it. Then, as the rumbling sound grew louder, he felt Rowena's hand tugging urgently at his arm.

"Down!" she whispered. Understanding at once, he dropped to the ferns beside her. There, screened by rocks and willows, they watched the bridge and waited.

As the rumbling grew closer, Black Otter's ears began to hear it as not one sound but as a blend of many—the cadence of thundering hooves, the jingle of metal, the breathy snorting of large animals in motion—a cacophony that was joined by the hammering of his own heart. He could feel Rowena beside him. He could feel the tension in the long, tapered fingers that pressed into the flesh of his arm. She was afraid, he realized, and not for herself, but for him. He remembered the gift of food and warmth that had sustained him in the darkness of the underground cell. Could it be that this strange, pale creature was trying to protect him?

His thoughts scattered as the most amazing conveyance he had ever seen burst onto the bridge. Black Otter's breath stopped as he saw it. His bone-jarring ride from the sea to the great lodge had given him a taste of white men's travel. But that day he had been chained and wrapped from head to foot in a torn sail, his mind groggy with the sleep medicine that had been put into his food. Now he crouched transfixed, his eyes staring in awe.

A flat structure the length of a large canoe was rolling across the bridge on four turning wheels. He could see the boxes and bundles piled on the back, and the three people—two men and a woman—who sat on the bench near the front. This was wonder enough—but the four deerlike beasts pulling it took his breath away. They were massive creatures, as brown as polished hickory, with broad, muscular chests and flaring nostrils. Their massive hooves churned mud as they raced over the bridge and out of sight.

"Horses," Rowena whispered close to his ear. "Horses."

Horses. Black Otter's lips formed the word as the apparition vanished. He had heard tales of such beasts, carried by travelers from the south and spread from village to village. He had heard that white men sat upon their backs as they raced like the wind into battle. He had dismissed such reports as wild rumor—until now.

He felt the touch of Rowena's hand on his arm as he gazed, still transfixed, at the empty bridge. The physical awareness that surged through his body like a tide of fire caught him off guard. Her warmth spread over his skin; her pungent woman scent crept into his nostrils, stirring dark little whorls of heat in his loins.

At this perilous moment, when he should be thinking only of escape, Black Otter found himself remembering the feel of her slender foot in his palm, and how he had fought to keep from sliding his fingers upward to the petal-soft flesh of her thighs and the nest of honey that lay at their joining.

His cheeks burned as he became aware that his manhood was fully aroused. He dared not look down. The barest glance would draw her attention to what his skimpy leather loincloth could not hide.

Even his thoughts were racing down forbidden paths. What sort of woman was she, this Rowena? If she were to discover his secret, would she pull him down beside her on their bed of moss and ferns? Would she lift her skirts and open her long, pale legs to him, drawing him to her soft, moist core until they joined like a key fitting into its lock? Would she cry out with pleasure as he thrust into her deep and hard, driven by a hunger that matched her own?

No, she was already pulling away from him, her eyes downcast behind their veil of golden lashes, her cheeks warm with color. Her beauty struck him like a blow. She was aware of his desire, but she was as modest and shy as a maiden of his own people.

Who was this woman? What was her place in this strange world?

His fingertips caught her chin, forcing her to look up at him. She met his gaze unflinchingly. He could see the pulsing of a vein along the curve of her ivory throat and feel her trembling beneath his touch. Tiny flecks of color—greens and blues and browns—shimmered in the golden depths of her eyes. How different she was from the women he had known—and yet, for all her strange appearance, how very like them.

The stillness around them was broken only by the babble of the stream and the distant cry of seabirds. Black Otter burned to shatter that stillness with words, to shout the story of what her people had done to his village and his family. He had not spoken honestly with another human being in nearly four moons, and the urgency to do so was like a scream in him. Frustration roiled in his chest, threatening to burst and to destroy their fragile truce.

Without warning, he seized her wrist and, with a jerk of his head, indicated that she was to come with him. Fear flickered across her face as she hesitated, but he gave her no time to argue. Pulling her behind him, he plunged ahead, moving deeper into the hollow where the stream splashed and murmured on its way to the sea.

Chapter Seven

"We simply must go back!" Rowena's words failed to calm her galloping pulse as the savage dragged her along the rocky bank. "By now they will have missed us! They'll follow our trail! No one will believe you meant me no harm—"

She winced as the toe of her slipper struck a stone. His hand tightened hard around her wrist as she stumbled, then regained her balance. *Did* he mean her harm? Was that why he had lifted her chin and stared into her eyes, his gaze searing her to the roots of her soul?

Rowena had glimpsed the state of his body. Although she had never known a man's intimate touch, she knew enough about animals to recognize a male arousal. Did he mean to ravish her in these deep green shadows? Was that what her heart believed he would do? Then why wasn't she screaming for help or struggling to break away? Why had she suddenly become a stranger to herself, a woman she neither knew nor understood?

A finger of sunlight probed through the overhanging branches to play across his naked shoulder. Beneath his tawny skin, her savage's muscles rippled like a panther's. He moved with the supple grace of a woodland creature, scarcely stirring the bracken where he passed. The ragged leather loincloth, hanging from its knotted thong, barely covered the flesh of his lean buttocks.

An ache, like the tightening of a knot, stirred in the depths of her body. As the daughter of a scientist, she knew what the act of mating entailed, but she could not imagine herself as part of it. She could not imagine being loved by any man, especially by this man who moved as if he were fashioned of light and shadow—this man who, by turns, terrified, fascinated and aroused her.

He came to a sudden halt beside a sharp bend in the stream. His dark eyes gazed down at a narrow sandbar that jutted into the lee of the current.

Dropping to his knees, he jerked her down beside him onto the stream bank. His fingers released their grip around her wrist, leaving a red band of heat. No, she surmised at once, he was not bent on having his way with her. The swiftly glimpsed bulge beneath his loincloth had diminished and, for the moment, he seemed more interested in the smooth expanse of sand than in her dubious charms. Rowena's pulse slowed to a nervous canter.

Still ignoring her, he reached up and slipped the small knife from the tangle of his hair. Taking it in his fingers, he bent over the sandbar and began to draw, using the pointed tip like a quill.

An oval and a line appeared, then more lines were scratched in the fine wet sand. It was a human figure,

a man. The savage glanced up, as if to make certain
she understood as he pointed to the drawing, then to
his own chest.

"Yes!" Rowena leaned forward and brushed the
small figure with her fingertip, then pointed at him.
"I understand. This is you."

He nodded curtly, then began to draw again. Rowena watched as the steel point etched a line of small
dome shapes behind the man. "Tortoises?" Rowena
guessed. "Wait—no, houses!" Pine trees, placed here
and there, confirmed her guess. "A village! Your village!"

He did not look at her, but continued to draw in
the sand. His fingers tightened around the knife as he
sketched another figure beside the man. It was the
simplest of drawings, but even before it was finished,
the care he took with the lines—each one adding
grace and life—told her it was a woman.

Carefully he added the suggestion of long hair, then
the outline of a garment that resembled a shift. "Your
wife?" Rowena asked.

He answered in his own language, and although she
could not understand the words, Rowena caught the
edge of bitter grief in his voice. Yes, his heart was
there on that other shore with a black-eyed Indian
beauty whose passions matched his own.

A dark flush of shame stole over her features. How
could she have imagined he would want her? She was
as plain as mud and well past the bloom of youth. He
was seeking her sympathy, hoping for her aid. In his
own desperate way, he was using her.

Her hands withdrew into her lap, the fingers inter-
weaving, clenching in a tight ball. It was time she

grew up and faced the truth. No man would ever want her, not unless he wanted something else, as well—her house, her lands or her aid. Even the oily Edward Bosley, her late aunt's widower who'd cornered her in a hallway and squeezed her breast on his last visit, had only wished to hurt and humiliate her. Rowena had clawed his face and fled, leaving him to stagger, bleeding, back to his chamber.

The savage had sketched two more figures in the sand. This time—aye, by heaven's mercy, she should have known there would be children. She saw them now, a boy and a girl, drawn by a hand that gripped the knife intently. This time he did not look at her. He seemed to avoid looking at her, in fact, as he shifted farther along the sandbar and, with one incisive stroke, drew the line of the shore, adding here and there a few waves to show the sea.

He was a skilled artist. The sailing vessel he drew was recognizable as a frigate, perfect in its small proportions. Clearly every detail of the vessel had fascinated him. His face darkened, however, as he scratched jagged lines above the village. His mouth tightened. His eyes narrowed to slits. Yes, he was drawing fire. Rowena could almost see the leaping flames, smell the smoke and hear the screams of terror. The monsters aboard the frigate would have shown no mercy.

The savage's breath exploded in a sharp hiss as he jabbed the knife point into the figure of the woman, stabbing, furrowing the sand until the graceful little drawing was obliterated.

Rowena's throat constricted in horror. "She... died?"

His grief-ravaged face answered her question.

"And your children?"

If the savage had understood, he gave no sign of it. He seemed lost now, immersed in the nightmare of memory. Jabbing again with the point of the knife, he gouged a circle around the figure of the man. His fingers whitened on the handle as he cut a deep slash in the sand, gouging a line to the frigate. This time he was telling Rowena something she already knew. But one question remained unanswered.

She pointed to the figures of the two children. "What happened to them?" she asked.

Only then did he look up at her. His eyes held the look she had glimpsed on that first day, the same anguish, the same helpless fury. He had told her all he could, Rowena realized. The children were lost to him. He had no way of knowing whether they were dead or alive. Yes, that would be the worst of it. The urge to know would be a demon in his soul, driving him day and night, giving him no peace.

"I'm sorry." She spoke instinctively, touching his bare arm. The savage recoiled like a wild animal, turning on her a look of such pure rage that she tumbled backward into the bracken, her skirt pinioned by his knee. Quivering with blind fury he loomed above her. She was the enemy now. Her people had burned his village, killed his wife and torn him from his children. Here, for the taking, was a warrior's vengeance.

A shaft of sunlight glinted on the blade in his hand. His eyes were a wounded animal's, liquid with pain. Rowena edged backward as his arm quivered upward, but she was caught fast. There was no escape. His chest jerked as the lethal blade plunged downward…to bury itself in the earth a finger breadth from her neck.

The savage's breath exploded in raw gasps from his lungs as he slumped over her, his face a rictus of shame. He was a warrior, a stranger to so-called civilized ways, but he could not take her life—not even to avenge the woman he had loved.

Rowena worked her arms beneath her and pushed herself up onto her elbows. He twisted away from her, his ribs heaving as he battled spasms of long contained grief.

"There…there, I know…" Rowena murmured the senseless, soothing words she might use to calm a frightened child. Instinctively her hands reached out, touching his skin, sliding up his shoulders. Her fingers trembled as they stroked the knotted muscles—the iron-hard trapezius, the bulging deltoids. He shuddered beneath her touch, resisting, but not pulling away.

"There… Come back with me now. We'll find a way to get you home…I swear it." What in heaven's name was she saying? How could she make such a promise, even to a man who had little notion of what she meant? Her father had been right. She could not just take him to Falmouth and pay his passage to the New World. Even if she could find a ship, what captain would bother to keep such a dangerous passenger on board? The savage—*her* savage—would be thrown over the side as soon as the vessel cleared the harbor.

There was but one reasonable course. She would have to teach him proper English and civilized manners. Only then would it be safe for him to go abroad. But how could she convince him to learn?

Coherent thought fled as her hands slid down along the twin ropes of muscle that flanked his spine. The heel of her hand brushed the leather thong that held his loincloth in place. The jolt of awareness that shot up her arm recalled the time she had touched an electric eel in her father's laboratory—but no, this was nothing like touching the eel. This was a human male—raw, nearly naked and unbridled by social rules. She was playing with a force as dangerous as lightning.

She willed her hand to move upward. By now her heart was thundering, her throat was dry and she sensed a disturbing wetness in the cleft between her thighs. *Run!* the voice of reason shrilled, but her fingers seemed drawn by a magnetic force within his hard bronze flesh. She could not stop touching him.

Black Otter felt himself responding to Rowena's touch. Her hands were warm, her voice as soothing as the lullaby a Lenape mother would croon to her child.

It would have been foolish to kill her when he needed her help. He realized that now. But to hate her? Yes, hate was what he should feel, what he must feel. Hate was the only thing that gave him strength.

Where was his hate now?

She was the enemy, he reminded himself, fixing his thoughts on the memory of the burning village, the screaming people and the life fading from Morning Cloud's sweet face. His wife had looked so hurt, so bewildered as she gazed up at him. No white man had shown her mercy—so why should he spare this white woman with her strange golden eyes? He was a warrior, a *sakima* among his people. His body carried the marks that showed his courage in the face of pain. Where was that courage now? Why had his thirst for vengeance died like a bonfire in the cool spring rain?

He bit back the swell of emotion stirred by Rowena's gentle touch—the urge to lose himself in her ripe, womanly body and let lust blot out the nightmare that had haunted him day and night.

His arousal stirred as she stroked him with her smooth, strong hands. She was far from young, but her touch lacked the boldness of a woman experienced with men. What did she want from him? Was this behavior an invitation to take her here and now, to plunge into her as brutally as he might have driven the blade into her throat?

Frustrated and confused, he turned back to face her. She drew away, her hand suspended in midair. Her parted lips were full and dark, the pupils of her eyes large in their golden pools. Was she afraid of him? There was only one way to find out.

With the speed of a striking puma he lashed out, caught her narrow waist and jerked her hard against him.

Rowena gasped as the savage caught her close. Her heart hammered her ribs as she stared up into his smoldering black eyes. She knew better than to show fear, but her racing pulse would not obey the command to be still. Swallowing her terror, she took refuge once more in words.

"I'm not afraid of you," she declared, meeting his stony gaze. "You didn't hurt me when you had the chance. You won't hurt me now. You need me too much for that.''

Boldly spoken, but her fluttering heart belied her bravado. She could feel the rise and fall of his chest through her bodice. She could feel the rasp of his breathing. Her own breath came in shallow gasps, as if she'd been running uphill. Every nerve in her body was taut and tingling, but a strange fascination had taken the place of her fear. He was so large and wild and so…beautiful, like an unbroken stallion.

''We'd best be getting back to the house,'' she protested in a trembling voice. ''They'll be looking for us. And my father, he'll be needing me—''

The knife dropped soundlessly to the moss as his free hand came up to catch the back of her head. His fingers tangled in her windblown hair, twisting her face upward until his feral eyes were a hand breadth from her own. The sensations that coursed through Rowena's body were as heady as a plunge over a high ledge. She had never been physically close to a man she was capable of loving. Since her youthful years had passed and she had none of the charms that drew men to women, she might never be so close again. Would this be her only time, her only chance in a lifetime of loneliness?

The throbbing crash of the sea echoed in Rowena's ears, blending with her drumming heart as she reached up, hooked his neck with one reckless hand and pulled his head down to hers.

For an instant his body went rigid with shock. Then his startled mouth softened against hers. She felt the flicker of his exploring tongue, its rough tip tracing the rim of her lower lip, tasting her, caressing her.

Need exploded in her as she molded her body to his. Muscular arms, suddenly urgent, clasped her close. One seeking hand found the curve of her hips and pulled her against his pelvis, holding her so tightly that even through her heavy skirts she could feel his arousal. Sweet heaven, the power of that aching, tingling, compelling need! Dizzy with desire she pressed against him where they knelt in the feathery bracken. This sweet madness—yes, she understood now, how it could drive the flesh, drive the spirit until nothing else mattered. Aye, even if she burned in hell, let her know it all, here, now and be ruined! The devil take all her bleak tomorrows!

Black Otter had suspected that Rowena was innocent. Now he would have wagered his life on it. She was so eager, so touchingly awkward as he lowered her to the bed of ferns. But he had no doubt she wanted him. Her hands clung to his shoulders, hesitant, then hungrily demanding as she pulled him down against her. Her eyes were tightly closed, almost as if she were fearful of what came next.

The stiff layers of her clothing frustrated him. If she'd been clad in a doeskin shift, like the women of the Lenape, he could have slipped it upward in a flash; but Rowena's formfitting costume appeared to have been sewn on her body. Her constricted waist felt hard and rigid, far different from the willowy softness his fingers had found the night he'd searched her for the key. Why did white people put their women into such restrictive clothing? It was no wonder they seemed to know so little of loving.

Her enormous skirt, at least, did not deny his seeking hand—but such a tangle of cloth!

She moaned impatiently as he fumbled through a sea of fabric to find, at last, the long, sleek legs hidden beneath. Even these were covered in cloth—soft and fine, to be sure, but not what he was seeking. The worst of it was, the more frustrated he became, the more he wanted her. The urge to be sheathed in the dark, moist honey of her body was a raging fire inside him. To have her—to feel the softness of her breasts and the clasp of her eager legs; to hear her moans of ecstasy as—

Black Otter's thoughts shattered as his urgent hand found, at last, the exquisite smoothness of her bare thigh. The sweet scent of her woman musk tempted him upward. He thought of the crisp mat of hair, the delicate folds, like the opening bud of a flower.

Pausing, he lifted the flap of his loincloth. Yes, he would take her. He would bury himself in the wild, innocent sweetness of her body, lose himself in her exotic aroma. He would drown in sensuality, sinking deeper, deeper until the pain was blotted away, and with it the memory of all he had lost.

The memory of all he had lost.

The leather flap dropped from Black Otter's hand. He drew back from her, willing his passions to cool. He had a quest, a sacred duty to his children and his tribe. If he allowed himself to be distracted by this woman, his resolve would weaken. His soul would drink the waters of forgetting and he would never leave this alien land alive.

She had opened her golden eyes. They stared up at him, bewildered and more than a little hurt.

He rose lithely to his feet, picking up the knife and twisting it into his hair again. Then he bent from the waist and extended his hand to help her up. *"Wendaxa.* Come." It was a command, not an invitation, and when she did not respond, his face darkened into a scowl. He enunciated the foreign words clearly to make sure she understood. "You—come—now."

Rowena glared up at him, her cheeks hot with shame as she battled the urge to crawl into the bushes and hide. What an utter fool she had made of herself, lying spread-eagled in the bracken and offering her body like a common slut! How would she be able to stand looking at him, or at herself? What madness had possessed her to tumble on the moor with a wild man while her father lay gravely ill at home?

Had the savage led her on, or was it only her own imagination that had led her to believe he desired her? No matter. She had never felt more ashamed or humiliated in her entire life!

He stood over her now like a conqueror, demanding her obedience. It would serve the brute right if she stalked off and left him here alone to blunder his way into certain capture or death. But no, she could not abandon him. She had to get him safely back to the manor. She owed her father that much and more.

"You—*wendaxa!* Come!" He growled the order and jerked impatiently on her hand.

Burning with indignation, Rowena let him pull her to her feet. Rage exploded in her as she used her free hand to whip her skirts into place. "I hate you!" She spat the words from the depths of humiliation, not caring whether he understood or not. "If you ever touch me again, I'll have you flogged within an inch of your wretched life!"

He turned away as if he hadn't heard and started

down the hollow, dragging her along with a viselike grip on her hand.

"No!" Rowena dug her heels into the moss. "I've had enough of this nonsense! We're not going any farther! I'm taking you back there!" She thrust her arm in the general direction of the house. "You *wendaxa!* Come with me! *Now!*"

The savage snorted disdainfully and, muttering something that sounded like a curse, continued to drag her down the hollow toward the cliffs. Twisting and struggling Rowena stumbled after him. Ahead, through the lacy spring branches, she could see the stout timbers that supported the bridge.

"Stop!" she gasped, flinging one arm around a half-grown oak and gripping it doggedly. "This is utter foolishness—surely you can see that! You'll only end up with a rope around your neck or a musket ball in your chest!"

Feeling the resistance, he turned. His ink-black brows furrowed into an angry line. His free hand moved upward, and for an instant Rowena thought he was going to strike her, or perhaps threaten her with the knife again. "Go ahead!" she challenged him, biting back her fear. "See how far you get without me! I'm the only hope you have! Harm me and you won't—"

"No more!" he snapped, his patience clearly at an end. His scowl tightened as he groped for more English words. Abandoning the effort, he burst into an impassioned tirade in his own language.

"No!" Rowena glared at him, her face a hand breadth from his own. The last time they had been this close she had kissed the brute. Even the memory brought a flush of shame to her face. "We go back!

There!'' She gestured furiously toward the house.
"Now!''

She should have seen his move coming, but only
as he whipped her back toward him, breaking her hold
on the tree, did Rowena realize he was about to sling
her over his shoulder again. That first time she had
submitted to his manhandling. But no more, she
vowed. Fueled by rage, she fought him, twisting and
clawing like a wildcat.

Seizing her wrists he spun her around to face him.
"Wendaxa!'' he growled, his face as imperious as a
thundercloud. "You come!''

"You don't own me!'' Rowena aimed a kick at his
shin, her foot striking solid bone. "I'm an English-
woman, your better by tenfold! You have no right—''

A faint moan, coming from somewhere below the
bridge, cut off her protest in midsentence. Black Otter
froze beside her, instantly wary.

"Get back!'' She pulled him into the thicket, her
anger forgotten. "You stay here. I'll go and see what
it is.'' She punctuated her words with gestures and was
relieved when he edged deeper into the shadows. At
least he had the good sense to know that if strangers
were about, she was the better suited to deal with them.

Rowena heard the moan again as she parted the
thicket. Her raw nerves prickled as she moved toward
the bridge. The voice had sounded human, more like
a man's than a woman's. Was someone injured and
in need of help? She could only hope the savage
would stay hidden until she had resolved what to do.

Knee-deep in bracken, she did not see the man
sprawled on the slope until she was nearly on top of
him. He was lying faceup with one arm flung over
his eyes—an unkempt, bearded hulk of a fellow clad

in the homespun garb of a tenant farmer and reeking
of too much ale. It appeared that he'd been walking
home from the nearest tavern last night and, too drunk
to find his way in the dark, had stumbled off the near
side of the bridge and passed out where he fell.

The man moaned again as she leaned over him, a
trickle of spit forming at the corner of his mouth. He
did not seem to know she was there. Either he was
still drunk or sleeping off the wages of indulgence.
In any case, he did not appear to have been harmed
by the fall. His limbs lay naturally, with no sign of a
break. Under the circumstances, Rowena concluded,
it would be wise to let the poor fool lie and go swiftly
back the other way. Now if only she could persuade
the savage...

Turning, she glanced back toward the thicket where
he had waited in the shadows. Her heart dropped as
she realized he was nowhere to be seen.

Rowena's dismay grew as she scanned the edges
of the small clearing—every bush, every tree, every
shadow. No, she had not been mistaken the first time.
The savage was truly gone.

Perhaps he had wearied of her constant arguing and
decided he would be better off alone. Or perhaps he'd
been afraid the stranger would wake up and see him.
Whatever the workings of his dark mind, he had vanished. Her savage. Her responsibility. Where was he
now?

With a sigh, Rowena brushed her tangled hair back
from her face. Maybe the unpredictable savage hadn't
really left. Maybe the long days of illness had caught
up with him...maybe he had fainted and was lying
unconscious in the thicket. In any case, the sooner

she started searching for him, the more likely she was to find him.

She took a step, but as she swung her right leg forward she felt a large, hairy hand clamp her left ankle from behind. Jerked off balance she twisted and fell, sprawling across the man's body in a tangle of petticoats.

Fully awake now, he laughed as he seized her waist, flung her onto her back and pinned her with his body. The face that leered down at her was coarse and brutish, with rheumy eyes and several missing teeth.

"Just what I was dreamin' of!" He laughed again, showering her with rancid spit. "No need t' fight, now, me pretty. Ye'll like what I got once it's ridin' 'twixt them long fancy legs o' yours!"

Rowena writhed and kicked with all her strength, but the stranger's smelly bulk held her flat against the moss. When she opened her mouth to scream, his fist crashed into the side of her face. Pain ricocheted through her skull, setting off colored starbursts in her vision. As she blinked them away she felt a warm trickle of blood at the corner of her mouth.

"Not a peep out of ye! Not unless it be the groans of a woman's pleasure!" He grinned down at her, his breath reeking like a boar's. "Be nice t' me, now, an' I'll leave ye' pretty. Fight me, an' ye'll remember it every time ye look in the glass!" Propping himself on one arm, he reached down and fumbled with his breeches. "Open those legs, now," he panted. "I be—"

The words ended in a gurgle as a powerful bronze arm seized him around the throat and jerked him upward. The savage was weakened by illness, but he had the advantage of surprise. A swift blow to the head rendered the man unconscious. He teetered on his sagging legs, then reeled sideways and collapsed facedown on the ground.

As Rowena scrambled to her feet she saw the savage's hand move upward, reaching for the knife he had twisted into his hair.

"No!" She sprang toward him, catching his arm. "You're in enough trouble without a blessed murder on your hands! Leave him be and pray he won't remember any of this when he wakes up!"

The savage scowled down at her with puzzled black eyes. His arm paused, then dropped as if in a shrug.

"Aye, you do understand." She swayed dizzily as the horror of her narrow escape swept over her. The savage could have bolted and left her to her fate. Instead he had risked his own life to save her. A chill passed through her body as she realized he would have killed for her, as well, had she not stopped him.

The pupils of his eyes held her reflection. Rowena stared at the trembling, disheveled man imprisoned within those twin black orbs. Mere moments ago this man had shamed her to the depths of her soul. She could not be so foolish as to expose herself again. She would protect the savage out of duty to her father, she resolved, but her heart would be forever closed to him.

Forever closed to any man.

Forcing her mind to other concerns, she glanced down at the drunkard who lay in a stupor, soughing like a winded ox. He was nearly as tall as the savage, though not so broad through the shoulders or lean through the belly. Still, his clothes…

Rowena gasped aloud as the idea struck her. Bending, she tugged at the man's rough fustian tunic. Then she pointed a finger toward the savage. "You—you take—you wear!'' She gesticulated urgently, praying he would understand. Clothed, he would not be noticed and branded as the wild man he was. As long as he did nothing untoward, he might be reasonably safe.

The savage edged closer to the inert man, his stormy eyes taking in the grease-stained tunic, the rough homespun breeches and canvas leggings, buskined with thin strips of leather. His proud nose wrinkled in obvious distaste.

"You *must* put them on!" Her eyes swept over the savage's splendid body, which could have done justice to the robes of a king. Her instincts told her he understood, but it was equally clear that he saw nothing wrong with his own natural state and did not relish donning the man's filthy garments.

For a long moment he stared downward, deliberating. Then, without warning, he dropped to a crouch, seized the lout's breeches and, with a single lightning tug, jerked them down, exposing a pair of flabby white buttocks.

Rowena spun away, flushing crimson. Crossing her arms across her chest, she stood rigid as a post, staring at the trees while the savage divested the man of his clothing and heavy hobnailed brogans. Neither she nor the savage spoke, but once, from behind her back, she thought she heard a sound from him—a low snort tinged with hidden irony.

She could have sworn it was laughter.

Chapter Eight

Black Otter despised the white man's clothes. The fabric was coarse and scratchy, the neck-to-toe fit too warm and confining for one who had grown up running free with the wind gliding over his skin. The rough cloth made him long for the supple feel of a deerskin robe, tanned with ashes and smoked to baby softness over a fire of hickory logs. No wonder white people had such miserable natures!

Discomfort aside, the worst thing about the strange garments was their smell! Every time he breathed, the odors of sweat and urine, mingled with a sickly sweet aroma like the stench of rotting maize, assaulted his senses. White men possessed so much knowledge and so many wonders. Why did they persist in being so filthy?

Rowena walked beside him, casting him furtive, sidelong glances from beneath her golden lashes. She almost seemed to be admiring him! Was she pleased that he looked more like her own people now? Black Otter dismissed the question irritably. She had been wise in urging him to dress like a white man. He knew he would be safer this way. But the change in his appearance struck him as a betrayal of his own people and his own purpose. He fought the desire to tear the hated coverings from his body.

They had come out of the hollow onto the open moor. Rowena's mahogany hair streamed in the wind, catching the light of the morning sun. She had not argued with him this time when he turned toward the sound of the crashing waves. It was as if, in putting on the white man's clothes, he had earned her consent to go where he wished. Perhaps, in her eyes, he was now "tame" like the wolfish dogs that hung around his own village snarling over food scraps. The notion did not please him.

She had scarcely spoken since they'd left the naked white man snoring in the thicket. Strangely, he missed the sound of her voice. He had understood little of what she said, but her urgency, her passion, had touched him in a way he had not expected. Now the silence between them was large and heavy, unfilled by the calls of seabirds and the crashing of the waves below the cliffs.

Their fleeting encounter in the hollow passed through his mind once more. His loins tightened as he remembered her long, pale legs, the skin as soft as the wing of a butterfly beneath his fingers. Her body had been ready for him, he knew. But, sadly, his heart had not been ready for her.

Regret gnawed at him now. Was he sorry because he had gone too far, or because he had stopped too soon? Black Otter could not say. But why should it matter? Why should anything matter except getting back to the sea and finding a way home?

How would he cross the great water? Perhaps he could steal aboard a great winged canoe like the one that had carried him here. Or, if time allowed, he could fell a tall, straight tree, burn out its heart and fashion a canoe of his own. The crossing would be long and perilous in such a small craft, but the forces of his heart and spirit would drive him onward. Nothing would stand in his way—not even the tall, determined white woman who strode at his side.

Just ahead, the grassy moor jutted upward before it dropped off to the sea. Black Otter's pulse leaped as he plunged toward the sound of the breakers. Rowena struggled to keep pace, clutching her skirts and gasping with effort, as if she feared he would arrive ahead of her, fling himself off the cliff and drown.

The land ended abruptly in a sheer drop. Black Otter's strides halted on the edge of the precipice. His heart seemed to stop as the panorama of sea and sky swept over him. Until three moons ago he had lived on a river that emptied into a long inlet. The great canoe had sailed up that inlet to capture him, and he had spent the entire voyage locked away in irons. Only now, as he stood with Rowena on what appeared to be the very edge of the earth, did he begin to understand the vastness of the ocean that lay between him and his homeland.

The cliff where they stood towered above the water, perhaps twenty times the height of a man's reach. At its foot, the huge waves hurtled violently against the rocks. Eddies hissed and foamed, swirling beneath the onrush of incoming breakers.

Beyond the shore the glistening water stretched across the horizon as far as Black Otter's eyes could see. The glittering waves swam in his vision, dazzling him to near blindness. Seabirds wheeled, dived and squabbled above the spray, their cries like mocking laughter in his ears.

Black Otter felt his legs buckle beneath him as his weakened body overtook his falling spirit. He dropped to his knees, heartsick. How could he have been so foolish as to think that returning home was a simple matter of getting to the sea and climbing aboard a boat that would carry him to the mouth of his own beloved river? The earth was more vast and terrible than he had ever imagined. Here, cut off from all he knew, he was as innocent as a child.

With the scant knowledge he possessed he had no chance of finding his way home. He would become lost or die in the attempt, and he would never see his homeland again—never run free in the forest, never sit before a council fire, never hold his precious children in his arms...

Unshed tears stung Black Otter's eyes as he swallowed the bitter truth. His only hope of returning home lay in learning the way of the white men—their language, their tools, their knowledge of the earth and sea.

It was a simple matter of choice. He could end his life wretched and alone in this alien place...or he could become a white man.

When the savage turned and looked at her, the naked torment in his eyes struck Rowena like a blow. It had been easy enough to surmise that he was longing for his home and children. But she had not anticipated what she saw in his face—the crushed pride, the leashed fury of a captured beast.

Her hand stirred, then dropped to her side as she sensed he would not welcome her touch. For a long moment his fathomless eyes gazed at the sea. Then, shifting his shoulders as if shrugging off a heavy cloak, he turned around and began walking back across the moor in the direction of the house.

They did not speak as they crossed the wide expanse of open land. But Rowena sensed the bitter surrender that had taken place. The sea had done what she could not. Perhaps now he would allow her to help him.

As they neared the house she was startled to see a cart with a team of drooping horses—the very one they'd seen crossing the bridge—tied to the post at the foot of the front steps. Strange, she'd been expecting no visitor today except the doctor, and it was far too soon for him to have gotten word of Sir Christopher's illness. In any case, the doctor always rode a mule. This cart was piled with trunks and boxes. Some travelers, she surmised. Perhaps they'd suffered some mishap and stopped at the manor for aid.

Beside her, the savage had stiffened apprehensively. Then, as his eyes fell on the horses, he stared in rapt fascination and began moving toward them.

"No!" Rowena caught his arm, pulling him back. "Someone's here—it could be dangerous for you. Come! *Wendaxa!*" She badly mispronounced the word, but his eyes flashed in understanding. Running on a diagonal course, they cleared the front corner of the house and made their way more cautiously toward the rear.

"There." She pointed toward the stable, praying that no stranger's eyes were watching from the house.

Even in the clothes of a common laborer, the savage did not look like an ordinary man. His hawkish features, streaming hair and chiefly bearing would mark him in anyone's memory. And once word of his presence got out, he would lose the chance of ever returning home. He would be caged, prodded, examined and paraded like a freak—and in the end, like Sir Christopher's other exotic specimens, the harsh English climate would exact its toll and he would die.

The stable door was ajar. They slipped through, into warm darkness redolent with the smells of sweet hay and the bodies of horses. The fingers of light that probed through the thatched roof revealed a dusty wagon in one corner piled with rakes, scythes, shovels and buckets. A collection of saddles and bridles, polished and well used, hung on a rack along one side. Fresh straw was heaped in the middle of the earthen floor, and along the far wall were six stalls.

Rowena heard the savage's breath catch as he realized what was here. Two of the stalls held the big draft horses, used for plowing and hauling on the manor and its surrounding tenant farms. The third contained Mayfair, Rowena's own blooded palfrey. In the fourth stall, Blackamoor, Sir Christopher's spirited gelding, snorted and tossed his ebony mane.

The remaining stalls were empty, but in any case the savage would have paid them little heed. His eyes were on Blackmoor's splendid head. Like a man sleepwalking, he hesitated, then edged forward as if fearful of startling the beast into flight or attack.

''There's nothing to fear,'' Rowena whispered, nudging him closer. ''Blackamoor is like a spoiled child—he loves petting and attention. Go ahead, touch him.''

The savage understood her tone if not her words. Murmuring softly in his own language he extended a cautious hand. Blackamoor, expecting a treat, reached out and nuzzled the open palm, nipping lightly with his teeth and pushing with his velvety nose. The savage's lips parted in silent wonder.

''Here.'' Rowena seized a wad of hay and thrust it into his hand. The big, satiny mouth closed around the hay, munching amicably in the warm darkness. Rowena saw the savage's throat move, as if he were trying to speak, but no words would come. For him, in this quiet moment, a tenuous bond had formed. For the first time in this alien land, her savage had discovered something to love.

''Mistress?''

The piping voice, coming from somewhere behind her skirts, shot Rowena's heart into her throat. She spun around to find herself staring down at the earnest face of young Will, Dickon's nine-year-old nephew.

''Are you all right, mistress? Were you wanting to ride?'' Will was as bright and precocious as his uncle was dull and childlike. Rowena's knees threatened to buckle as the boy's sharp blue eyes flickered toward the savage, then back to her. ''Mistress?''

She scrambled for her wits and her tongue. ''No, Will, I've no wish to ride,'' she said. ''But—perhaps you can keep an eye on this gentleman while I see to my father, and to the visitors who've just come.''

''Gentleman?'' Will eyed the savage's tangled hair and shabby clothes.

''He's...a foreigner, newly arrived here. He speaks

scarcely a word of English and..." Her eyes darted swiftly to the savage, who had turned away from Blackamoor and was looking at the boy's flaxen head with gentle curiosity. The savage had a son of his own, Rowena reminded herself. Surely Will would be safe with him.

"He will be staying here, in the stable," she said, weaving desperate plans even as she spoke. "Fetch him some food from the kitchen, and then you can show him where to make a bed in the loft. Do your best to make him understand that he should stay there. If he needs anything, come and get me—only me— at once. Do you think you could do that?"

"Aye..." Will frowned thoughtfully. "That I could, mistress. And if he's willing, I could even teach him some proper English words."

"That would be fine, Will. In fact, I'll pay you a penny for every word you teach him! You'll get your money at the end of the week!"

"A penny for every word!" The boy's eyes lit up at the thought of the wealth he would amass. "You needn't worry, mistress. If the gentleman wants to learn I'll have him speaking right proper in no time!"

"I'm certain you will." Rowena glanced at the savage, who was watching her intently. Did he understand what she had just arranged for him? Would he stay here when she went back to the house? "I must go now," she said. "I have to see to my father. But I'll come back soon—you understand? Soon." A sense of urgency overtook her as she spoke the words. She had been gone far too long. Sir Christopher would be needing her.

The savage glanced at her calmly, then shifted his

attention to examining Blackamoor. Aye, he would be all right here, Rowena assured herself as she turned to go. And her father would be relieved to know his investment was in good hands.

She had almost reached the door of the stable when the boy called to her again.

"Mistress!"

"What is it?" She glanced back over her shoulder.

"You forgot to tell me. What might the gentleman's name be?"

She groped for a believable answer. "His name is—John," she said. "John...Savage."

Rowena broke into a run as she left the stable and made for the house. In the past hour with the savage, she had thrust her father's condition behind other concerns, telling herself Sir Christopher was in devoted hands. Now, as worry and guilt overcame her, she felt a scathing flush of shame. While her beloved father lay helpless, perhaps dying, she had been out on the moor behaving like a common strumpet. She had betrayed a lifetime of careful upbringing and common sense by flinging herself at a man she scarcely knew.

Never mind that he had kidnapped her at knifepoint and forced her outside. She had initiated the shameful encounter, and if anything had happened to her father in her absence, she would never forgive herself.

She paused at the back stoop to scrape the mud and straw from her ruined slippers. Then she hurried into the kitchen. The servants were preparing the midday meal as usual, but the everyday bustle and chatter was strangely subdued, as if Sir Christopher's illness had cast a pall over the entire household. The strain in the air was almost palpable. Heart pounding, Rowena steeled herself for the worst possible news.

Bessie, the cook, glanced up from tending the stew. When she saw Rowena her good-natured face puckered in a disapproving frown.

"Faith, mistress, did ye tumble into a bog? Look at ye! Where've ye been so long a time?"

"How fares it with my father?" Rowena asked, dismissing the good woman's concern. "Surely that cart outside isn't the doctor's."

"Nay, 'tisn't the doctor." Bessie's scowl deepened. "But the master be no worse. 'E's even taken a bit of broth. Ye'd best get on up to him now."

"Thank you, Bessie." Dizzy with relief, Rowena rushed out of the kitchen, skimmed across the great hall, and, lifting her mud-coated skirts, hurried up the stairs.

The corridor was cool and dim. Rounding the top of the landing, she heard muffled voices coming from her father's closed chamber. A spirited argument seemed to be in progress. Listening carefully, she could make out the voices of a man and woman, intermingled with her father's stentorian tones. The sound of his voice lifted Rowena's spirits. If Sir Christopher was well enough to speak so strongly, his chances for recovery might be better than she'd hoped.

She was passing the door to her own chamber when she remembered her appearance. The sight of her torn, muddy gown, scratched arm and disheveled hair could upset her father and draw some embarrassing questions from the visitors, whoever they might be. She would take a moment to change her clothes and pin up her hair. Then no untoward suspicions would be raised.

Rowena slipped quietly into her chamber and eased the door shut behind her. Turning toward the wardrobe, she caught a glimpse of herself in the tall, mirrored door. Transfixed by what she saw, she moved closer.

The woman in the glass was tousled and windblown. The bodice of her gown was ripped below the collar, exposing the curve of one ivory breast. Tendrils of damp hair framed a flushed, sensual face with swollen lips and wide, stormy eyes.

She looked like a stranger—coarse, wanton, almost...beautiful.

She lifted a finger to the glass, as if uncertain that the reflection there was truly her own. One hand groped for the button that fastened her collar...

"So you're here at last!" The unctuous, all-too-familiar male voice from the doorway made Rowena's heart drop. "But what's this, my dear?" the voice continued. "By my faith have you been tumbling about on the moor? I must say, mud stains become you!"

Rowena forced herself to turn around slowly, hiding the sick, sinking feeling in her stomach. *Why now?* her nerves screamed. And why here, of all places?

Why did Edward Bosley, her late aunt's widower, have to make his appearance at Thornhill Manor today?

As his indolent gaze slid downward, Rowena's hands crossed over her bodice, covering the rip in her gown. "What are you doing here?" she demanded coldly. "And how dare you walk into my chamber without knocking?"

"Tut, tut, my dear," Bosley clucked in a mockery of concern. He was a large man, who'd been handsome in his youth, but too much drink and rich food had added layers of flab to his face and body, and too much time indoors had faded his complexion to a yellowish pallor. Since her aunt's death he had returned to his former vocation in the theater. His only successful role, however, had been that of King Henry VIII, to whom he bore a striking resemblance.

"Not even an embrace for your poor uncle?" he asked, sidling into the room. "Rowena, dear, where *are* your manners?"

"Not a step closer!" Rowena snapped. "Aunt Margaret is in her grave, where you drove her, and as far as I'm concerned, you're no longer entitled to be treated as one of the family! As for your presence here, my father is far too ill to receive visitors, so you can climb back onto that wretched cart you left outside and—"

"Visitors, you say?" Bosley raised one russet eyebrow as if enjoying some secret joke. "But I'm hardly a visitor, Rowena. If you saw the cart, then you must have seen the baggage piled in the back. I've come *home*, my dear, with all the worldly goods I possess. Your father has agreed to let me live here, at Thornhill Manor, with you!"

The rage that boiled up in Rowena's breast was fueled by two decades of bitter memories. This man had gone through her aunt's money like a rat through cheese curd and broken the poor woman's heart with his flagrant infidelities. In the years since her death, he had sponged off Sir Christopher at every opportunity. And then, on his last visit, when he had cornered her in the hallway...

"Get out!" Rowena seized a hairbrush and brandished it like a battle-ax. "You wretched, conniving leech! No matter what you forced my father to say, I'll not have you living under this—"

"Well, well, Edward!" a throaty feminine voice declared. "What sort of trouble have you gotten yourself into now?"

Startled, Rowena looked beyond him to the doorway. The woman framed there looked to be near Rowena's age, but there all resemblance ended. She was a stunning creature, doll-like in her proportions, her honey-colored hair tightly curled in the fashion of the day. Her artfully outlined blue eyes, for all their beauty, reminded Rowena of two wintry ponds, frozen to ice. There was no trace of softness or warmth in her gaze.

"So, Edward, I take it *this* is the charming niece you've described so often." Her laughter was brittle, without humor. "But is her attire the fashion in Cornwall these days? If so, I fear I'm very much overdressed. Perhaps I should consider going outside and washing down the stable!"

Rowena had been staring, dumbfounded, at the woman, but the word *stable* jolted her back to her senses. "We have servants for that sort of thing," she muttered, feeling as awkward as a cow. What was wrong with her? At least she might have thought of a witty reply.

Bosley stepped forward, sweeping his hand in a gesture of mock gallantry. "Rowena, may I present my half sister, Sibyl? In time, I'm sure you'll come to love her as I do.''

"I took the liberty of finding my own chamber," Sibyl said. "A rather dreary room, if you ask me, but then I only plan to be here for the season. Summers are dreadful in London. The heat! The odors!''

"Sibyl is a woman of the most delicate sensibilities," Bosley said. "Rather than leave her to the miseries of London, I took the liberty of inviting her here."

Sybil pursed her small, heart-shaped mouth. "I'll be needing clean linens for my bed," she said, "and clean towels, as well. I'd have ordered them myself, but there seem to be so few servants about the place…" Her querulous voice trailed off expectantly.

Rowena sighed. "I'll have Hattie see to the linens sometime before nightfall. I can hardly deny you a night's lodging, but your staying here for the season, or even so much as a week, is out of the question. My father is in no condition to receive guests and, frankly, neither am I. Tomorrow morning after breakfast you're to be on your way! Both of you!''

"But Rowena, dear!" Bosley's voice oozed pathos. "We've no place to go, and practically no money! What's to become of us if you turn us out?''

Rowena's gaze took in Sibyl's wine-colored sarcenet gown with its inset of lace above the bodice, the sapphire ring on her hand and the string of pearls that hung nearly to her tiny waist. Were these gifts from some wealthy lover—a lover who had since abandoned her? Was that why the beauteous Sibyl had thrown in her lot with a man such as Edward Bosley?

Rowena glanced at Bosley, then back at Sibyl.

"You appear to have a few things you could sell—enough to tide you over, at least, until one of you could find work."

At the mention of work, Bosley's pasty face paled visibly. "But I could work here, Rowena! With your father so ill, you'll be needing a man to manage the estate—to make decisions, see to the land, the servants, the accounts—"

"I manage those things quite well by myself," Rowena said.

"So I see." Bosley's gaze slithered over Rowena's disheveled hair and gown, making her flesh crawl. "From the look of you, you need someone to take you in hand and see that you're made a proper lady. And since your father's taken to his bed, it falls to me, as your only living male relative to—"

"No!" Rowena flung the hairbrush with the strength of desperation. It glanced off Bosley's cheek, leaving a fleck of crimson. He dabbed at the spot with a forefinger, wincing as he saw the blood.

"Take your so-called sister and get out!" Rowena said coldly. "I was willing to offer you a roof for the night, but you have pushed me too far, Edward Bosley! I'm going to see my father now. By the time I come out of his chamber, I want both of you gone!"

"But, Rowena, dearest, your father gave his word—"

"My father is in no condition to give his word! If you leave at once you'll make Falmouth by dusk. There are inns aplenty along the waterfront. Now, get out of my way!"

Without giving Bosley or Sibyl time to recover their wits, Rowena pushed past them and stumbled into the hallway, fighting back tears of rage and grief. How could she have allowed these terrible people to manipulate her father? If only she had gone to his chamber at once, instead of stopping to make herself presentable, she might have intervened in time. If she found that they had bullied or upset Sir Christopher, she would never forgive herself!

As she raced down the hallway, spurred by an urgency she could not even name, she saw that the door to her father's chamber, which had been standing ajar when she'd first come upstairs, was now closed. The sight of that closed door unsettled her, but she swiftly reassured herself that it was no cause for alarm. Perhaps Sir Christopher had wanted to rest. Perhaps he'd asked Thomas or Dickon to close the door so as to shut out the sounds of her argument with Bosley and Sibyl.

Reaching the door, she turned the latch and pushed it open. Warm, stuffy air, smelling of sweat and ammonia, engulfed her like a miasma. Rowena stepped inside, expecting to see the servants. Both Thomas and Dickon had been with her father when she'd left the room earlier that day. Now neither of them was here. Sir Christopher lay alone, looking small and pale in the big bed, a stranger without his spectacles.

His eyes were closed, his hands folded across his chest as if someone had arranged them that way. Rowena leaned over him.

"Father?" she said softly, not wanting to awaken him if he had truly fallen asleep. "I'm here, Father. Every thing is all right with your savage—I left him safely in the stable with young Will."

Sir Christopher made no reply.

Rowena leaned closer, tenderness swelling her heart. "Sleep, then," she whispered. "We can talk when you're awake. I've so much to tell you."

She brushed a kiss across his wrinkled forehead. The skin was as cold as alabaster. Only then did she realize he was not breathing.

"Father!" She seized his hands, shaking them, rubbing them, resisting the awful certainty that crept over her.

No! Sweet Jesus, no... She pressed his lifeless hands to her face, kissing them wildly as she sobbed in helpless grief.

Chapter Nine

Black Otter knew little of white men's ways, but when Rowena did not return to him in the horse lodge, he understood that something of grave importance had happened. Reason told him it could be nothing less than the death of the ancient chief.

He himself had seen the old man fall, and now life in the great house appeared to be in chaos. People had been running in and out like ants uprooted from their nest. He had watched them all evening from the loft beneath the roof, a chink in the wall giving him a view of the yard. Every time the door opened he had strained his eyes for a glimpse of Rowena, but she had not come out.

About midday he had seen the horse-drawn cart depart empty except for its driver. Not long after that, a tall, broad-bodied stranger, richly clad in the color of fading leaves, had walked outside and surveyed the buildings, the yard and the surrounding land with an air of possession. Was this the new chief of the white men? Would he now take the great lodge as his own and Rowena, the old chief's daughter, as his woman?

It seemed a cruel custom, but who could fathom the ways of white men?

The thought of Rowena in another man's arms had tightened a dark knot in Black Otter's chest. He had pressed close to the hidden opening below the thatch, studying the newcomer with appraising eyes. Over the years, he had proven himself a good judge of men. For Rowena's sake, as well as his own, he had searched hopefully for the qualities of a great leader—courage, wisdom, selflessness and integrity. But he saw only weakness in the man's features, laziness and gluttony in the overfed body. And the costume that had first struck Black Otter as splendid now seemed gaudy and ostentatious.

Was this the man who would claim Rowena? This strutting rooster whose belly hung out over his belt? Black Otter willed his fists to unclench. What did it matter? Rowena was nothing to him. He would use her, if need be, to help him leave this place. After that he would put her behind him and never think of her again.

Where was she?

By this time it was past nightfall. Restless, he prowled the loft where the boy, now gone for the night, had indicated he was to stay. Black Otter's mind ticked methodically over the words he had learned over the course of the afternoon. *Horse, house, grass, wagon, walk, man, woman,* and many, many more—all good and useful words. And he had enjoyed the boy's company. He was a bright child, cheerful, and clever in his way of teaching. But Black Otter was already growing impatient. When would he know enough of the language to walk freely in the white man's world? How soon would he have the power to talk his way onto the great boat that would carry him home? One moon? Two? His fingers raked his long hair in frustration.

When he looked outside again, a full moon was rising above the house, flooding the land with its watery light. Thoughts of Rowena stole into his mind once more, despite his efforts to keep them out. Was this the night of her marriage to the new chief? Was he, even now, sharing her bed, knowing the full sweetness of her ripe, sensual woman's body? Black Otter exhaled raggedly, tormented by the image of another man lying between those long, pale legs. It did not matter, he reminded himself once more. Rowena was not of his world. He was not of hers. He could no more love her than a hawk could love a swallow.

Yet, he had touched her—touched her intimately, knowing she desired him as much as he desired her. Now, alone in the darkness, when he should have been thinking of home, the memory of Rowena in his arms was driving him to a frenzy.

He stared through the small opening, across the empty yard to where the dark bulk of the house loomed against the sky. Lamplight flickered through the cracks of the shuttered windows. Now and again, the light was blocked by moving forms. What was happening tonight, inside that labyrinth of rooms?

What had become of Rowena?

Forcing the question aside, he let his gaze move beyond the house to where pools of light and shadow played temptingly across the open moor. The boy had made it clear that Rowena wished him to remain in the loft—wise advice to be sure. There were strangers about the place, and even a brief encounter could lead to his being locked up again. But the restlessness was a fever in his blood. The wind that stirred the clouds and rippled across the moor seemed to be calling his name, singing a sweet song of freedom.

Throwing caution aside, Black Otter descended the ladder to the ground floor of the stable. In the darkness he felt the presence of the horses. He could hear them snorting in their stalls and smell the warm, earthy odor of their dung.

By now he knew the horses well. The nearest stalls held the huge patient beasts that, according to the boy, were used for drawing the wagon. Beyond the two stalls that were empty, the gray female, as delicate as a deer, with large, intelligent eyes, shifted nervously in the darkness. Beyond her, in the last stall, was the fiery, night-black horse Rowena had first shown him—a splendid animal, worthy of the mightiest chief.

Black Otter prowled from one stall to the next, stroking the horses and murmuring softly to them in his own language. What could his people do with such animals? There would be no limits to the lands they could explore, the game they could hunt, the marauding enemies they could vanquish.

He paused, at last, outside the stall of the spirited black. The horse nickered and thrust its petal-soft nose into his palm. He stroked the elegant, tapering head, imagining what it would be like to sit astride the broad back and feel those powerful legs pounding beneath him, devouring time and distance as they outraced the very wind.

It would be like flying...

Black Otter had not planned what happened next, but the temptation was too powerful to resist. Action followed thought as inexorably as the downward plunge of a waterfall.

The stable door was bolted from the inside. He slid back the bolt and swung the door wide. The breeze was sharp with the scent of rain. He took a moment to fill his lungs with its freshness. Then he turned, walked softly toward the black horse's stall and slipped the latch on the gate. The horse snorted warily, its ears pricking forward.

"*Kulamalsi,*" he murmured in his own language, running a hand along the arching neck until his fingers could grip the long, tangled hair of the horse's mane. "*Kulamalsi,* swift one, I will not harm you."

Reassured by his voice, the horse nickered softly and nuzzled his arm. Holding his breath, Black Otter moved back along the animal's shoulder. Then, pushing off from the side of the stall, he flung his weight across the broad, bare back.

For the space of a heartbeat the horse went rigid with shock. Black Otter just had time to swing his left leg over its rump before the startled animal exploded, kicking and bucking, out of its stall. Black Otter clutched the mane with both hands, knees gripping the slippery black sides as the horse spun around, leaped high, then shot like an arrow toward the open door of the stable.

Black Otter's eyes caught the flash of lightning from the direction of the cliffs. Then there was no more time to look or think. He and the horse were flying across the yard, past the fenced pasture and into the wild, dark night.

Rowena tiptoed down the long hallway, past the closed chambers where, at long last, Bosley and Sibyl had retired for the night. She was numb with weariness and raw with grief, her nerves frayed from dealing with the doctor, the vicar, the servants and the two unwelcome guests. It was only toward the end of the nightmarish day that she'd remembered the savage. Hours had passed since she'd left him in the stable, promising to return as soon as she'd seen to her father. Her whole world had crashed into shambles since then, but John Savage was still her responsibility, now more than ever.

Reaching the end of the dark corridor, she started down the stairs. The way was dark, but she had not wanted to risk giving away her presence with a candle. In her arms she clutched a worn but freshly laundered set of clothing she'd borrowed from Thomas. The more John Savage looked like the household servants, the less he was apt to be noticed.

Like the other servants, the big Cornishman still believed the savage was no more than an eccentric Gypsy the master had brought home, but even that much knowledge was dangerous, especially now that Sir Christopher was gone.

She crossed the great hall where Sir Christopher's plain hardwood coffin lay across two trestles. The lid was open, her father's body laid out in his black scholar's robes, ready for burial on the morrow in the small parish cemetery. Rowena averted her eyes as she passed, knowing that to look directly at those waxen features and shriveled body would shatter her tenuous hold on reason. In her father's last moments of need she had been preening before her mirror. Her vanity had caused him to die alone, a sin for which she would never forgive herself.

She hurried through the kitchen, pausing to snatch a loaf of bread from the pantry. Lightning streaked the sky as she crossed the yard. Dark clouds roiled across the face of the moon, drowning its light like the waves of a fierce black sea. Even as she ran, Rowena felt a drop of rain on her cheek. She broke into a sprint, then stopped as if she'd been struck by a lance.

The stable door, which should have been bolted at this hour, was standing wide open.

A boom of thunder split the sky as she rushed inside. "Please...please let him be here..." she murmured. But there was no sign of the savage—and one swift glance confirmed what she'd feared. Blackamoor was missing from his stall.

Frantic, she flung down the bundle of food and clothing and raced to saddle her own palfrey. Mayfair lacked the stamina of the solidly built black gelding, but over short distances she could hold her own. Perhaps it was not too late to catch up with the savage and prevent yet another tragedy.

Spooked by the storm, Mayfair rolled her eyes and whinnied as Rowena slid the saddle onto her back and jerked the cinch tight around her belly. Blackamoor's finely tooled leather saddle and bridle hung where the grooms had left it—nothing, in fact, was missing from the collection of riding gear. Dear heaven, had the savage simply taken the horse without the first idea of how to guide it?

Seizing Mayfair's bridle, Rowena jammed the bit between the skittish mare's teeth and buckled the throat latch. Aye, she should have known John Savage would try something like this. She should have forbidden him to touch the horses, or better yet, left him in the dairy barn or the root cellar—anyplace except the stable!

Thrusting her slippered foot into a stirrup she sprang into the saddle and kneed the mare hard in the side. Mayfair bolted forward, out of the stable and into the stormy night.

Which way should she search? A sense of helplessness swept over Rowena as she galloped her mount onto the open moor. Without a bridle, the savage would be at Blackamoor's mercy—and the high-strung gelding could have gone in any direction. A good pack of hounds, perhaps, might have been able to trail them. But Sir Christopher had not kept dogs for as long as Rowena could remember. The only sport he had enjoyed was falconry, and a hawk would be of no use tonight.

Where would Blackamoor go? Pausing on the crest of a small hill, Rowena surveyed what she could see of the sweeping moor and tried to think like a horse. The gelding's usual inclination would be to return to the stable after a run. But in the tumult of the storm, with a strange rider on his bare back, Blackamoor would be terrified. He could run until he threw the savage to the ground or, in the confusion of darkness, plunge over a ledge and into the sea.

She would head for the cliffs, Rowena resolved. If

Blackamoor was going in that direction, she might at least be able to head him off.

By now the rain was falling in cold gray sheets, plastering her hair to her head and her clothes to her body. She could see no more than a few feet ahead, except when lightning crackled across the sky. By anticipating, she could use the flash of bluish light to scan the open moor before the thunder plunged her back into rainy darkness. With each fleeting interval of light, she strained her eyes for the sight of a man on horseback—or walking, or lying bruised and broken on the ground. But between her and the sea lay nothing but empty vistas of sodden moorland. There was no sign of Blackamoor or the savage.

She could hear the crash of the waves now, intermingled with the hissing sound of rain. Maybe it was time she went back, reason argued. She was so cold her teeth were chattering; and it could be that the savage had not come this way at all—or even that Blackamoor had escaped from the stable without him. Even now, John Savage could be waiting for her in the stable and puzzling over Mayfair's absence.

She paused on the edge of the cliff, the wind whipping through her long, wet hair. What if her supposition was wrong? What if man and horse had gone over the precipice and were lying somewhere below, broken and dying on the sharp rocks? How could she turn and ride away?

Mayfair snorted and rolled her eyes as if sensing danger. With a whinny of fear, she swung back from the edge of the cliff and danced sideways, threatening to bolt.

Rowena felt an odd prickling sensation as the hair

rose on the back of her neck. She heard the mare scream even before the giant thunderbolt struck the ground a mere stone's throw away. The flash split the heavens, blinding her eyes, deafening her ears. Somewhere in the blackness she felt herself flying out of the saddle, into the dark void. For an instant she hung suspended. Then like a fallen bird she struck the rain-soaked ground, shuddered and lay still.

Black Otter leaned forward over the streaming mane, his eyelids half closed against the downpour. The speed of the horse was intoxicating, the feel of motion so heady that he wanted to laugh, to shout, even to weep.

He had given the horse its freedom, not even trying to guide its wildly careening run. In the beginning it had taken all his strength to keep from being pitched off into the darkness. But little by little, as the black hooves pounded across the rain-soaked ground, he had gained a more secure grip and a better sense of balance. He had begun to sense the nature and spirit of the animal he rode, and he had spoken to it, soothing words in his own language. Now they flew over the open moor as a single entity, horse and man, as free as the wind. Lightning danced and crackled across the violet sky. Thunder rolled like the voice of a great medicine drum, and the rain fell around them in stinging silver torrents. Caught up in the magic of flight, Black Otter was scarcely aware of the storm. All his senses were trained on the thrill of motion, and on this wonderful beast that possessed the swiftness of a deer, the strength of a bear and the endurance of a wolf. What would he give to possess such a creature—with a mate, perhaps, to bring back to his people?

The monstrous lightning bolt struck without warning, splitting the sky like the blow of an ax. It struck just beyond the next rise of land so close that the deafening thunderclap seemed to fill the whole universe. The horse shrieked and reared on its hind legs. Black Otter clung to the powerful neck, stroking the animal to calm it as it spun one way then another in a frenzy of confusion.

Black Otter was struggling to turn the massive head in the direction of the stable when, suddenly, a large, pale shape materialized like a ghost from the rainy darkness. Only as it bolted past him did he recognize the gray horse from the stable. It was fleeing from the direction where the lightning had struck.

With a whinny, the black horse turned to follow its stable mate. Both animals had clearly had enough of the storm. But what was the gray doing out here? Black Otter's throat constricted as he realized there could only be one answer to that question. Rowena had come to the stable in his absence. When she'd discovered that both he and the horse were missing, she had taken another mount and gone looking for them. Now she was in trouble, or worse.

Bent on reaching safety, the black horse snorted and broke into a canter. Unable to turn or stop the beast, Black Otter did the only thing he could do— he broke his hold on the running animal, leaned to one side and tumbled off onto the wet ground.

He landed hard, bruising his shoulder, but he ignored the pain and scrambled to his feet. His legs felt unsteady beneath him, strangely alien to the earth after the experience of flying on horseback. Staggering, he raced toward the cliffs.

"Rowena!" His voice was drowned by the roar of the storm. "Rowena!"

He paused, ears straining for an answering sound. He heard nothing but the rain, the wind, and the distant roll of thunder as the storm swept inland.

"Rowena!" He reached the last low ridge before the moor dropped off toward the cliffs. Now he could hear the waves pounding and crashing on the rocks below.

How could he have been so reckless with her safety? He should have known she would come. He should have waited for her.

He reached the precipice and stood staring down at the waves. The dark water churned and roiled, biting at the rocks with angry white fangs. Crouching, he inspected the ground with sensitive fingers. Here…yes, and here, he could feel the large, dish-shaped prints the horse had left. And here the earth was churned where the animal had jumped and wheeled. Rowena could have fallen here. Even now, the ripe, lovely body she had so willingly offered him could be lying down there in the blackness, crushed and bleeding like a broken bird on the rocks.

He remembered her courage that first night, when she'd stolen down the stairs to bring him the quilt and the bread, and again, when he had forced her out of the house with a knife at her throat. That she continued to treat him kindly was a wonder in itself. She was remarkable, this tall, bold, strangely beautiful white woman. If his actions had caused her death—

His thoughts scattered as he glimpsed something

white, pooled in the shadow of a stunted bush. His heart jumped as he saw that it was Rowena's exposed underskirt. She was lying facedown in the long, wet grass, her arms flung outward as if trying to break her fall.

A finger placed along her throat confirmed that she was alive—but barely. Her pulse was ragged, her breathing shallow, her skin as cold as the rain that drizzled from the sodden sky.

She moaned as he checked her body for broken bones, then worked his hands beneath her and gently turned her over. There was a dark welt along her temple, already swollen and tender. Black Otter battled a surge of helpless frustration. Why had she come after him? Why couldn't she have stayed safe and warm inside her enormous house where she belonged?

Carefully he lifted her in his arms. She settled against him with a little whimper. She did not appear to be badly hurt, but who could say how much damage the blow to her head had done? And she was so wet, so cold...

Unbidden, his throat and lips moved in the healing chant of his people. The words were sacred and true, but he had never sung them for one who was not Lenape. Would Rowena's spirit be open to their power? No, his reason argued. She was not of his blood. She knew nothing of his ways. All the same he chanted softly, singing with his voice and with his heart as he strode through the dwindling rain.

Rowena stirred as her chilled body began to warm. Dazed by the fall, she was but dimly aware of being carried across the moor, cradled by powerful arms.

She only knew that she felt safe and secure, as if a soft cocoon were being woven around the bitter core of her grief. She nestled closer, too weary to open her eyes.

The sound of singing, in a rumbling voice that was just loud enough to be heard, penetrated the fog of her awareness. It seemed to come from all around her, quivering through her body.The words—aye, there did seem to be words. Their meaning was a mystery, but Rowena could feel them flowing around her and through her, calming her fears, soothing her agitation. The sound of them was beautiful and strangely familiar, like a forgotten childhood tongue, or a language she had spoken in a place so far away that she remembered it only in dreams. She rose, now, into the magical song, floating, drifting…

The low nicker of a horse summoned Rowena back into the real world. Her body jerked as if she had dropped through the trapdoor of a gallows. The wind was gone and the rain was no longer falling on her face. Her senses swam with the familiar odors of clean straw and horses.

"Kulamalsi." Her feet were lowered to the ground. She stood quivering like a sleepwalker awakening in a strange place. For a long moment she teetered on the edge of wakefulness. Then, the peace of the chant faded and tragic chain of events that had led her here came crashing in like a landslide—starting with the evening her father had brought the savage home, wrapped in a sail, manacled hand and foot and trussed on the flat bed of the dray.

Her befuddled mind recalled the rising conflict between her father and herself, climaxing with the quarrel that had led to his apoplexy. Perhaps, without the savage, Sir Christopher's fragile health would have held out longer. Her precious father might still be alive, and the two human vultures that had taken roost in the house would be gone. Aye, it was as if this man's arrival had brought the curse of discord and death down upon Thornhill manor.

"You!" Reeling with grief and exhaustion, she turned on him. Unreasoned fury blinded her eyes as she flailed at him with impotent fists. "Why did you have to come here and change everything? We were happy, my father and I! He had his work, and I my peaceful life! We were content here until the day he arrived home with you!" The bitter words poured out of her, undammed by logic and the fact that he could understand little of what she was saying. "It was you who brought this calamity down on us—you! By heaven, why couldn't you have *died* aboard that accursed ship that brought you here?"

Horrified by her own words, she broke off and stood staring up at him. The savage could not possibly have understood her, but his expression had darkened. He seized her flailing wrists with a grip like an iron vise.

"Rowena. No." His clasp tightened as she continued to struggle. His black eyes, lit by a flash of faraway lightning through the open door, glittered like anthracite, and for an instant Rowena thought he was going to strike her. Instead, abruptly, he let her go. Caught off guard, she lost her balance and went down in a pile of straw.

When she did not accept his disdainfully proffered hand, he bent down, grasped her upper arms and lifted her to her feet. Only then did Rowena feel the hot, salty tears that were streaming down her face. And only then did she give full vent to the sobs that racked her body.

"Rowena..." He gathered her close, rocking her, stroking her back as if calming a frightened child.

"I'm—sorry—" she gasped against his wet chest. "It's just—my father, lying in there—when he should be alive and working and arguing with me—and those two evil people who've come—they mean to stay. I've no legal authority to throw them out. No court in the land would back me if it meant leaving a woman here alone to run the manor—not when she has a male relative to do the job. Relative, indeed!" Her hands balled into fists. "You should see the way he looks at me! It makes my skin crawl! And that woman—"

Rowena's head sagged against the savage's chest as the outburst died. If only she could make him understand the nightmare that lay waiting inside the walls of the manor house. But what difference could it make? John Savage was the last person who could help her. She could depend on no one but herself; nothing but her own wits, her own resources.

He lifted her chin and gazed into her face, his expression warm and kind. "You go now," he said, nodding in the direction of the house. "Horses—" He pointed to the mare and gelding who stood, coats steaming, under the stable's broad eave, then touched his own chest. He would get the animals inside and care for them, she knew.

"Friends?" He held her lightly by the shoulders, trying out the word he had surely learned from Will, because he would not have picked it up aboard the ship.

"Friends." Rowena nodded through a blur of tears, thinking how much she needed a friend. Her father would be in his grave on the morrow. The servants were her allies for now, but their loyalties were bound to shift to whomever they perceived to be in power. She could not count on any of them, not even Thomas and Dickon. Against all reason, the only person she fully trusted was this unpredictable wild man, so innocent of civilized ways that he did not even know how to bridle a horse.

Heaven help her.

Heaven help them both.

Black Otter watched her go. His gaze followed the glint of moonlight on her wet hair as she fled across the yard to the darkened house. Even after she had vanished, he stood looking into the darkness, his senses holding the sight and scent and feel of her.

It had been all he could do to send her away tonight. Even now his loins ached from holding back all he wanted to give her. She was so in need of loving, this tender, passionate woman. She was so alone, so lost and vulnerable that his heart twisted every time he looked at her.

But he could not allow himself to want her. There was only one thing he truly wanted. That was to go home.

Closing his eyes, he willed his memory to summon the soft, sweet face of Morning Cloud. She had been the best of women, dutiful, submissive and giving. They had spent many good years together, free of the

discord that plagued so many couples. He had loved
her faithfully. But even now, after only a few moons,
Black Otter found that her features were beginning to
blur in his mind.

With a broken sigh, he turned from the open doorway. Morning Cloud was gone. She had died in his
arms on the terrible night that had changed his life
forever. But Singing Bird and Swift Arrow—yes,
their bright young faces were sharp in his mind.
Surely, if they were dead, their images would be fading, too. He had to believe that his son and daughter
had survived the attack on the village, that they were
alive, watching the sea, waiting for him to return.

Whatever happened, he could not fail them. He
could not allow anything—horse or woman—to bind
him to this new land. What he learned of the new
ways, he would use to his advantage, as he would use
any friends and allies he made here. But from the
moment his feet touched the shores of home, he
would once more be Lenape. He would abandon the
language and dress and manners of the white man,
and he would put aside all memories of this hated
land and its people.

Even the memory of Rowena.

Chapter Ten

The tension-filled days had blurred into weeks—each one so fraught with uncertainty that Rowena's nerves had become like frayed bowstrings, constantly on the brink of snapping.

The day after the funeral, Bosley had demanded to see Sir Christopher's accounts. These she had readily handed over. Like many men whose intellect functioned on a higher plane, her father had possessed no head for practical matters. His bookkeeping methods had been so haphazard that Rowena had quietly kept her own, more accurate, accounts.

It had, at least, given her some wry amusement to see Bosley sweating over the heavy ledgers, cursing as he struggled to decipher Sir Christopher's jumbled logic and arcane script. It was only after many days that he'd concluded the same thing Rowena had known all along—there was little money left in the manor's coffers, and almost none coming in. Much of the farmland lay fallow, long since played out. And the income from the tenant farms was so meager that Sir Christopher had not even bothered to collect what he was owed. The good man had cared for little else but his work, which in his old age had brought in nothing.

Bosley had proposed to sell off parcels of the land, but swiftly discovered he could not do so without Rowena's consent, which she steadfastly refused to give. Now matters stood at an impasse while Bosley maneuvered for more power.

And how did he plan to get that power? The answer to that question, Rowena surmised, was evident every time he looked at her. She lived in a state of nervous exhaustion, wondering when his next move would come—surprised, even, that it hadn't come already.

In these days of darkness she had only one corner of warmth and light. She fled there as often as she could escape the confines of the house.

The early dawn sky was opalescent, like dark mother-of-pearl, as she opened the kitchen door, closed it behind her and ran lightly across the yard. The fresh, cool air filled her lungs. She inhaled, savoring the fragrance of summer flowers on the moor and the tang of the sea. Early mornings were her only time of freedom—the only time she could be with John Savage.

He was waiting for her under the eave of the stable, his costume of common russet made elegant by his stature and easy grace. His hair, which despite Rowena's urging he had refused to cut, was tied back with a thong of knotted leather. His skin gleamed like polished mahogany in the pale morning light, the line of birds a brilliant blue across his forehead. Even starved and ill he had been a fine-looking man. Now, in full possession of his health, he was a kingly figure, as handsome as a blooded stallion.

My Lord Savage. The phrase slipped through her mind, even though she had long since ceased to call him by that title.

"Good morrow, Rowena." John Savage's swift mastery of English had earned his young tutor a princely sum. He still spoke haltingly, with an odd lilt that recalled his native tongue, but his progress with the new language had come in leaps and bounds, perhaps in part because he had spent so long a time hearing it spoken aboard the ship.

How long could she justify keeping him here at the manor? Rowena asked herself yet again. How long before she would be forced to set him free, like an injured bird that had regained the use of its wings?

"The horses—they are ready." As was customary, he had saddled and bridled the mare and the gelding. These morning rides across the moor were the only joy that remained in Rowena's life. She treasured them like jeweled beads on a fragile thread, knowing that one day they would end.

"Shall we get the falcons?" she asked him, and was rewarded by the flash of his smile. John Savage had come to love her father's birds almost as much as he loved the horses.

They mounted and rode quietly out of the yard. Bosley and Sibyl, as was their habit, had played whist late into the night and would not likely rise until midday. But there was always the danger one of them might wake up and look out of a window. So far Rowena had managed to keep the savage out of their sight. But the thought of what Bosley might do if he

knew the true identity of John Savage had cost her
many sleepless nights.

The mews had been erected long ago in a small
copse beyond the stable. Only two falcons remained
in the high pens—the elegant little kestrel Rowena
had raised and trained herself, and Sir Christopher's
great silver-white gyrfalcon, a bird of the northern
tundra that had blown south in a winter storm. Still
mounted, Rowena and the savage donned the heavy
left-hand gauntlets, captured the birds by their jesses
and threaded the thin, braided tethers through the slits.
Then, with the hooded birds on their gloves, they
nudged their mounts and cantered out onto the open
moor.

At first they rode in silence, their eyes scanning the
dawn-silvered sky. Rowena's gaze flickered toward
the savage's rough-chiseled profile. He was leaning
forward in the saddle, the wind sweeping tendrils of
ebony hair back from his face. At times like this he
looked every inch the warrior he was, as fierce and
proud as the gyrfalcon that rode on his gauntleted
hand. But like the great bird, she knew, he was tethered and hooded, a restless captive in this place, with
longings she had no power to ease.

He had never spoken of their searing encounter in
the hollow. Nor had he touched her since that wild,
stormy night on the moor, or even so much as glanced
at her with the look of desire. They had settled into
a warm, quiet friendship, which was just as well, Rowena supposed. Heaven knows she needed a friend
badly. Still, there were times when she looked at him
and ached for what might have been—times, even,
when it was all she could do to keep herself from

reaching out and running her hand along his shoulder or brushing a fingertip down the sharp slant of his coppery cheek.

"Your face is a storm cloud, Rowena." Even in a foreign tongue, metaphor seemed a natural way of speaking for John Savage. "It is bad in the big house?"

"Aye." Rowena guided her mare around a thick clump of hedgerow. "Bad and bound to get worse."

"What does the fat *chingwe* do now?" It had amused Rowena to learn how the savage had once thought her father to be chief of all the white men and Bosley to be his successor. He knew better now, and Bosley had been demoted from the new chief to the fat bobcat.

"He does nothing. Least of all any useful work." Rowena fell silent, pondering her own answer. Aye, that was most troubling of all—Bosley doing nothing. He seemed to be biding his time of late, watching her with slitted, hungry eyes, like a hyena waiting for its prey to weaken and stumble. What was he plotting? Surely not her death—it was common knowledge that if she were to die without legal issue, Thornhill Manor with its surrounding lands would revert to the Crown. No, Bosley could only profit by keeping her alive and cooperative. All he required was the means to control her.

"*Chingwe* would make you his wife?" John Savage echoed her own thoughts, his words more of a declaration than a question.

"I fear he may try."

"And can he do this thing? Force you?"

Rowena shook her head vehemently. "The law is

on my side. He was married to my mother's sister. Even though we have no common blood, we are considered relatives. Any marriage between us would be condemned as incest.'' All quite true. Henry VIII had forged the law himself, as grounds for divorcing Catherine of Aragon, his brother's widow. But there were always ways in which the law could be twisted, perhaps with the help of a few pounds slipped to a local magistrate. Anything was possible with the right connections. Bosley would know that.

"My people, too, have such laws." John Savage narrowed his eyes as he scanned the sky. "Some people break them. Then bad things happen. *Chingwe* could break the law, Rowena."

"I know. But there is nothing the man can do that would force me to marry him. I would sooner die!"

"I could fight him and kill him." He spoke the words as emotionlessly as if he were offering to saddle her horse. "*Chingwe* is not of my blood. To me he is nothing."

"No!" Rowena started so suddenly that the kestrel on her gauntlet flapped its wings, lifted into the air and was jerked upside down by the pull of its jesses. The small falcon hung, squawking for a moment until it managed to right itself and clamber back onto the gauntlet.

"Kill a man, any man, in this country and you would be hunted down and hanged, John Savage!" Rowena exclaimed. "You would never see your children in this life! You must not even think of such a thing!"

Ignoring her reaction, he stared at the sky. "There," he said softly, pointing. "Tell me."

Rowena squinted at the soaring black shape. *"Ahas!"* she answered, giving him the Lenape word for crow. She knew how much it pleased him when she tried to speak his language. *"Kumhokot,"* she added, sweeping her arm across the clouded sky. *"Kshaxen.* It is cloudy and windy."

"Cloudy and windy," he repeated dutifully, both of them relishing the exchange. She had learned a considerable number of Lenape words and phrases on these morning rides. She had even learned his Lenape name and taught him its English meaning. She had also learned many things about the savage's homeland—Lenapehoken, as he called it. He had struggled with words to describe the verdant forests, teeming with birds and animals and stretching all the way from the great ocean to the place where the sun sank behind the earth.

He had told her, as well, about his people, the Lenni Lenape, who lived in dome-shaped bark lodges, wore clothing made of deerskin and lived by hunting, fishing and farming their small patches of open land. Only when she'd pressed him had he admitted that he was a powerful chief—a *sakima,* among them. In turn, she had done her best to describe for him the complexities of English life and customs. Most of her explanations had left John Savage shaking his head in wonder and dismay.

Now she saw him stiffen, peering far ahead at something her less-practiced eyes could not see. Silently he lifted the gyrfalcon's hood and slipped its tether. At once the great bird spread its powerful wings and soared into the air. Rowena watched it circle, its keen eyes scanning the moor. Suddenly it stooped, diving like an arrow. There was a flurry of movement in the gorse as its talons struck a hare. The impact knocked the timid creature off its feet and sent it rolling. By the time Rowena and the savage rode up, the gyrfalcon was crouched atop its prey, waiting to be taken back onto the glove.

They hunted until the sun had risen well above the moor, bagging several partridges for the kitchen, as well as some smaller doves, taken by the kestrel, which would go to feed the two falcons back in their mews. As was their custom, they spoke little while the birds were aloft. Much of the time the savage seemed one with the great silver falcon. His spirit seemed to mount the sky as the bird soared upward to wheel and circle, then dive on its prey in a blinding blur of speed. Rowena could almost feel his thoughts—the longing to take wing and fly far out over the sea, all the way to his homeland.

Soon, with or without her help, he would leave this place. And even if she were able, Rowena knew she could not hold him back. If John Savage were forced to stay in England his heart would surely break.

"Over there—" She turned her palfrey toward a jagged recess in the line of the sea cliffs. "Years ago, as a girl, I found a hidden cave below these ledges. It became my secret place. I never told anyone about it until now."

"The cave is still there?" he asked, his interest aroused at once.

"Aye. The way down starts right there." She pointed to a spot on the edge of the cliff. "The climb is a steep one. It's a wonder I didn't fall and break my neck on the rocks below."

He nodded, then glanced eastward. Following his gaze, she saw that the morning had flown. The sun gleamed high through a scattering of clouds. Soon now, Bosley and Sibyl would be awakening in their chambers, setting the household on edge with their shrill demands. Then they, or the servants, would surely be looking for her.

The gyrfalcon was already on the savage's gauntlet, leashed and hooded, but the little kestrel was still aloft. As they watched, it hovered for the space of a heartbeat, then stooped and dived—inexplicably—toward a flock of large black crows.

Rowena groaned as the tiny falcon struck one of the crows in midair, knocking it off balance. Over and over they tumbled, struggling in the air. The kestrel was clearly taking a beating from the much larger bird, but its talons were locked firmly into the crow's feathery back, and Rowena knew the falcon's predatory instincts would not allow it to let go.

The two birds hit the ground hard. As they tumbled in the long grass, Rowena flung herself out of the saddle and raced toward the spot where they had gone down. The crow exploded upward, almost in her face. Its back was bloodied where the talons had pulled loose, but it took readily to wing, screeching and cawing as it spiraled upward.

Spent and battered, the kestrel lay on its side in a clump of weeds. Its beak was gaping and, as she dropped to her knees, Rowena could see a spreading stain of crimson where one wing curved against its body. With a little cry, she gathered up the bird in the folds of her skirt, wrapping it gently and nestling it against the curve of her waist. John Savage watched her from the back of the gelding. The gyrfalcon on his gauntlet prevented him from helping her, but he watched with concern as she climbed awkwardly into the saddle, using only one hand.

"How bad?" he asked as she settled herself astride.

"Truly, I don't know," Rowena answered, choking back the fear that the little falcon could be badly hurt, even dying. "Let's get back. After you've penned the gyr, you can help me examine him."

They spurred their horses and galloped back across the moor where, a furlong behind the house, the low grove of trees sheltered the mews. Rowena could feel the heat of the kestrel's body through the fabric of her skirt. She could feel the thready beating of its jewel-size heart and the damp seepage of blood from its wing. It was only a bird, she reminded herself as tears blurred her vision. Only a bird, indeed. But she had pampered, fed and trained the little creature. She had watched the heart-stopping beauty of its flight and thrilled to the lightning swiftness of its strikes. Now the tiny warrior lay beneath her hand, crushed, beaten and in pain.

The savage returned the gyrfalcon to its perch, gave it one of the pigeons and latched the door of the pen. Then, slipping off the heavy gauntlet, he cupped his hands to receive the wounded kestrel.

Rowena had long considered herself an expert with birds. But it took only a few seconds for her to realize that John Savage's knowledge far surpassed her own. He cradled the small falcon in his warm, brown palm, stroking it gently and murmuring to it in his own language. The words and tones took on a caressing rhythm that flowed around and through Rowena like

clear, soothing water. She felt the peace in his voice—
the same peace she had known on that stormy night
when his arms had carried her home across the moor.

She held her breath as his fingers probed the small
feathered body. The kestrel had stopped struggling,
soothed, perhaps, by the sound of the chant. It lay
still now, staring up at him with fierce golden eyes as
he lifted the injured wing. What gentle hands he had,
Rowena observed. Most men she'd known flaunted
their strength like bragging schoolboys. But the
greatest strength lay in gentleness—the kind of gentleness that could cradle a wounded bird and soothe
its spirit with a song.

Her gaze shifted to his craggy profile, lingering on
the taut, sensitive line of his mouth. She remembered
kissing that mouth, the earthen, salty taste of him, the
searing heat of his touch.

Sweet heaven, she loved this man she realized—
loved him as she had never loved anyone in her lonely
life—loved him as she would never love again.

"I am sorry, Rowena. I could not save him." The
sound of his voice startled her. She bit back a cry as
she looked down and saw that the kestrel's eyes had
glazed and its elegant little head had fallen to one
side. "His spirit has gone," the savage said.

Without a word he dismounted and, still cradling
the bird, found a sharp stone and began scraping out
a hollow at the base of a gnarled oak. Fighting tears,
Rowena slipped off the mare and joined him, scooping out the dirt with her hands where the stone had
scraped it loose. By the time the hole was deep
enough, her fingers were raw, the nails broken and
dirt-caked, but the savage did not try to stop her. This

task was the last she would do for the small creature she had loved.

She paused and met his sad black eyes with her own. Nodding he laid the kestrel in the hole, smoothed its feathers and covered it with leaves. "A warrior's grave," he said softly.

Together they filled in the dirt, smoothing it out and laying the stone on top. Rowena paused long enough to pluck a miniature bouquet of bluebells and lay it across the stone. Then they mounted in silence and rode back toward the stable.

Rowena sat rigidly in the saddle, her agitated fingers twisting the reins into tangled knots as she cursed her own foolish innocence. For a few moments she had almost believed the savage could save her little falcon. But he was an ordinary man, not a miracle worker—and miracles, like happy endings, only occurred in stories.

She glanced back toward the sea, where, on the heels of a glorious morning, ugly black clouds, heavy with rain, were scudding in from the west. She was getting too old to believe in fairy tales, she lectured herself. The fact that she loved John Savage held no promise of joy. Destiny had already decreed that she would lose him, as she had lost the falcon, as she had lost her father, as she had lost her own bearings in a world that had turned as treacherous as the sea.

A leaden rain was falling by the time they reached the stable. They entered through the rear door, which could not be seen from the house. Rowena felt the savage's eyes on her as she slid wearily out of the saddle and bent at once to unfasten the cinch.

"I can do that," he said. "Leave it, Rowena."

"No, I can do it—" Her fingers were bleeding; she felt awkward and perversely stubborn. The cinch was tightly drawn, and the mare was restless. A sudden movement twisted her hand, tearing a fingernail. The sudden sharp pain brought a freshet of tears to her eyes. She turned her face toward the mare's flank so the savage would not see them.

"Rowena—"

He touched her shoulder, the light contact radiating warmth and aching need through her body. Gently he drew her upward, turned her toward him, and then, suddenly, she was in his arms.

She gave a little sob as he caught her close. Then her arms flew around his neck, and she clasped him tightly, holding him, loving him, feeling his solid strength as the rain drummed against the walls of the stable. She clung to the moment as she clung to him, knowing all this must end, knowing their time was running out and she needed to let him go.

His breath caught sharply as his body responded to her nearness. His hands grew bold, seeking her breasts, her hips, pressing her exquisitely against the hard ridge of his desire. Rowena felt her own body go liquid, felt the hot, wet swell of her own need. Heaven, how she wanted this man, wanted all of him, here and now…

"Well, now, what a pretty picture this is! The prim and proper Mistress Thornhill cavorting with a common stable hand!"

Rowena felt the savage freeze against her. She spun around as his arms fell away, and her heart dropped to her shoes.

Edward Bosley stood in the open doorway of the stable, rain dripping from his ginger-colored beard. Beside him, simpering under her green umbrella, was Sibyl.

Chapter Eleven

Rowena's first impulse was to protect John Savage, but it was he who stepped forward now, placing himself between her and the intruders. He stood like the warrior he was—tall, proud and fiercely majestic, a man that no one but a fool could mistake for a servant. She saw Bosley take a half step backward. Sibyl was staring at the savage's splendid body, all but licking her lips in delight.

"Why do you speak like an empty wind?" he demanded calmly. "Rowena has done nothing to bring shame on her own head or on this house."

Bosley drew himself up, recovering a measure of bravado. "That's high-and-mighty talk for a servant," he snarled. "Remember your position, knave, and my own. I could have you flogged and dismissed for such insolence."

"Oh, if you mean to flog him, do give him to me, Edward!" Sybil purred. "I have my own delicious ways of flogging a man."

"Enough!" Rowena pushed forward, fearful that the savage's pride would expose him for what he truly was. "The man is a foreigner—a gypsy. He's quite wonderful with horses, but he knows little of English customs and manners."

"Then perhaps it's time I taught him a lesson. Might there be a whip in that wagon?"

"Even if there was, I would not give you leave to touch him with it!" Rowena snapped. "Despite your posturing, Edward Bosley, you are not master here. The servants are my domain, not yours."

"So I see." Bosley's slit-eyed gaze flickered toward the savage, then back to Rowena. "All the more reason to be mortified by your conduct this morning, mistress. Sneaking off with a stable hand like a common whore! By the crown of our blessed queen, I've a mind to—"

He raised his hand and would have struck Rowena hard across the face if the savage's hand had not flashed out and seized his wrist. Bosley's face whitened with the pain of the bone-crushing grip as his arm was twisted back behind his shoulder.

"Touch her and I kill you." John Savage spoke in a quiet voice but there was no mistaking the cold anger behind his words. No one who heard those words could have doubted that this man meant what he said. "Go, Rowena. Take the small woman to the house. This fat *chingwe* needs a lesson in respect."

"No." Rowena held her ground, fearful for the savage's safety. "Let him go, John, this man is not worth the harm that could come to you!"

He hesitated, then his obsidian eyes flashed and, with a contemptuous gesture, he shoved Bosley away from him.

Bosley stumbled and fell, landing on his knees in

a pile of stable sweepings. He staggered to his feet, brushing flecks of straw and manure off his hose, his face florid with rage.

"By the hounds of hell, I'll see you hanged!" he snarled at the savage, then whirled on Rowena. "I'm sending a boy for the local midwife to examine you. If this…this *animal* has despoiled your virtue, so help me—"

"There'll be no midwife and no examination!" Rowena retorted, glaring at him in cold fury. "And I'm not despoiled, Edward—not that it would be any of your business if I were. You've no rights here— not to the house, lands and vassals, not to what little money there is, and least of all to me!"

Bosley's flushed face had deepened to the hue of a boiled beet. He inhaled, puffing himself up like an imperious toad. "That may well change soon," he snapped, "perhaps much sooner than you expect. Now, are you coming back to the house under your own power, Rowena, or must I drag you?"

Rowena stood in silence as thunder from the re- treating storm echoed across the moor. She had no choice except to obey him, she realized with a sinking heart. If she forced Bosley to lay a hand on her, the savage would be at his throat.

Avoiding any contact with the savage's burning black eyes, she walked swiftly past him, out through the stable door and into the rain-puddled yard. Her throat ached. Her eyes were raw with unshed tears, and she knew that the leaden weight in her stomach would not go away. The savage—her savage—was in more danger than his innocent mind could fathom. Perhaps it was time she sent him away. The jewels her mother had left her as a dowry would surely buy passage on a ship for the New World.

But no, John Savage was not ready for such a voyage. The dangers of his being murdered by some unscrupulous captain, sold into slavery in the Indies or forced into a lifetime of servitude aboard the ship were too great. To release the savage now would be to seal his doom.

"Wait, Rowena!" Sybil caught up with her halfway across the yard. She clutched her lace-trimmed petticoats above the mud, her breath coming in ladylike gasps. "My dear, you must tell me about that glorious man! Where did you ever find him? Who'd have thought that you, a creature so plain and shy—" She broke off, then bent intimately close to Rowena's ear. "I know you were forced to say what you did to Edward, but you can tell me the truth. What is that beautiful man like in bed, eh?"

Rowena had been striving to ignore Sybil's lascivious comments, but the final question triggered a burst of bitter annoyance. "Leave me alone, Sybil," she said, gazing straight ahead. "The man's not what you think, and neither am I."

"O-oh!" Sybil cooed. "I do believe I hear jealousy talking. Are you afraid I'll take him away from you? I could, you know, very easily."

Rowena lengthened her stride, swiftly leaving the irritating woman behind to wait for Bosley. Sybil was not worth her anger, she admonished herself. The woman was nothing but a malicious tart, stirring up trouble for the sake of her own amusement.

So why, then, did the woman's taunts hurt so

much? Was it because they contained just enough truth to penetrate and sting?

It didn't matter, she told herself, walking faster. If John Savage was fool enough to be taken in by a woman like Sibyl, then good riddance to him. As for herself, she had better things to do than pine over a hopeless love that could never be fulfilled.

Rowena raised her head proudly, hoping at least for a dignified retreat. Alas, it was not to be. Her toe struck hard against a stone, the impact spurting hot pain all the way up her leg. She stumbled, nearly going down on one knee before she managed to right herself and lurch to her feet.

Behind her, Sibyl's mocking laughter rang out across the yard. Half blinded by pain and tears, Rowena clenched her fists and, without a backward glance, stalked toward the house.

Black Otter watched the three of them go. The fat *chingwe* slogged through the mud, his head lowered so that the folds of his chin rested on the dingy white ruff of his collar. A dangerous man—all the more so for his stupidity. He wanted the house and the land around it. He wanted the power that a marriage to Rowena would give him. And it was clear that he would destroy anyone who stood in his way.

The pale-haired woman walked just ahead of him, balancing her umbrella with one hand and clutching her skirts with the other as she minced among the puddles. He would call her *Sangwe,* the weasel, Black Otter decided. The name suited her dainty stature and the sharp, predatory look in her eyes. Her gown was very fine, much more so than Rowena's plain, dark mourning costume. Clearly the weasel thought herself beautiful, and perhaps, by white men's standards, she was. But he sensed no warmth in her, no trace of the deeper, richer beauty he had found in another.

Black Otter's eyes lingered on Rowena until she passed silently into the house—so proud, so beautiful and so sad that he ached for her. In his own land it would be a simple matter to challenge *Chingwe* to fair combat, kill or disgrace him before the council and take Rowena as his woman. Here in England everything was different—how different he was still in the process of learning.

For two moons now, while those in the great house slept, he had spent his time exploring the countryside. Sometimes he would go on foot, moving like a shadow over the moonlit moor, slipping along the edge of the sea cliffs or blending into the wooded hollows like the wild creatures who lived there.

Now and then he would come upon a small farm with rude stone outbuildings and a house no bigger than the lodges of his own people. Quieting the dogs with soothing words, he would steal close to the windows and hear the talk of the men, women and children inside. Once, by accident, he had come across a man and woman tumbling together on a bed of straw. He had stolen away and left them to their panting and moaning, but the ache of his own loneliness had lingered into dawn.

Another time he had come to a crossing of two roads, marked by a gnarled and leafless tree. From one thick branch, the putrefying body of a man had hung swaying in the night wind, a rope looped tightly about his neck. Black Otter had known by then that

this was one way the English punished their crimi-
nals, but the horror of it had made him so sick that
he'd returned straightaway to the stable and ceased
his roaming for the next three nights.

Now and again he would mount the black horse
and ride to a village or town. There, with the horse
secluded in a nearby wood, he would walk the streets
like an ordinary visitor. Thus it was he knew much
more of the English world than either Rowena or the
boy had taught him.

He knew that in this land of wonders there were
people poorer and hungrier than the most unfortunate
members of his own tribe. He knew that certain drinks
had the power to turn men into mumbling, staggering
fools, and that those with a taste for those drinks
would do anything to get them.

He had learned that life in the towns revolved
around the getting of money—those small, useless
gold and silver disks that carried the queen's portrait
and functioned much as wampum shells did among
his own people. He had watched men toil, gamble and
fight for money. He had seen women offer their bodies to strangers for money, and he had learned that
without the accursed little metal circles, virtually
nothing was possible.

One night when the full moon shone brightly across
the moor he had galloped all the way to the sprawling
town that lay where the river opened its mouth to the
sea. There he had wandered the docks, staring up at
the tall ships with a mixture of admiration and loathing. There were sailors about, and he had spoken with
a few of them, but always the question of which ships

might be bound for the New World had been met with a shake of the head or a shrug of the shoulders.

"Only fools and pirates would venture so far from port," one grizzled old man had told him. "But, now, if ye want to see Lisbon or Malta or even Alexandria, there'd sure be a place on any deck for a strong laddie like yourself. And who could say, in years to come, where the sea might take ye?"

Black Otter contemplated the prospect of years at sea, the rolling decks, the sickness and the misery, coupled with the odds that he would never reach home, and his spirit had darkened. "I wish to go only to the New World," he'd insisted, "and to one place, a river that I would know on sight."

The old man's rheumy eyes had narrowed. "In that case, me lad, ye'd have no choice except to charter a vessel. Such a grand thing would take more gold and silver than the likes of ye or me will see in a lifetime."

Money was the key again, as he should have known it would be. He had thanked the old man and gone dejectedly on his way.

Now, as he watched the three figures vanish into the house, Black Otter once more considered the possibility of running away to the sea. Now that *Chingwe* had caught him with his arms around Rowena, every day would be fraught with peril. For all Rowena's protests, he knew that the man had great power to harm him—to have him killed or lock him up where he would never see his children again.

It would be an easy matter, he knew, to make his way to Falmouth by night and sign onto some departing vessel. But Black Otter had already weighed the odds of reaching home this way and found them too dismal to consider. He had seen what life was like for men who served aboard a ship—the lash, the miserable food, the backbreaking toil, the sickness—and he wanted no part of it. Now, however, he found himself in danger, and the sea was his only real avenue of escape.

Last night he had dreamed of his children. He had seen them clearly this time, standing on the misty shore, thin and ragged, their eyes red from weeping. They had held out their small hands, and he had struggled through the fog of the dream, straining to reach them. Finally, with the last of his strength, he had succeeded in touching their fingertips—the flesh that was his flesh. For the space of a heartbeat he had known the peace of coming home. Then the mist had swirled up and around them. Swift Arrow and Singing Bird had disappeared, lost to him once more.

He had awakened in torment.

Somewhere beyond the ocean, his children and his people were waiting for him. He ached to go to them by any means—to hack out a canoe and paddle it across the great vastness, to swim like a fish or fly like a bird, to gather his courage and take a chance that a ship, any ship, would one day set his feet on that beloved shore where the *Mochijirickhicken,* the great tidal river, joined the sea.

Every instinct called him to leave this place. So what was holding him back? Fear? Surely not. How often, as a *sakima,* had he been first to explore an unknown river or to claim a new hunting ground? How often had he struck the first blow against an enemy or aimed the first arrow at a charging bear?

He had proven his bravery countless times. Why then, against all reason, did he find himself so hesitant to go?

Black Otter's gaze took in the great house, lingering on the one high window that, he knew, opened into Rowena's chamber. Even now the memory of her stricken face tore at his heart. The very thought of leaving her to the mercy of her predatory houseguests...

A shudder of tightly reined anger passed through his body. There was little he could do for her, he reminded himself. He had no power in this land, no influence, no money. Except for the strength of his body, he had no means of protecting her. But his heart told him that Rowena needed him—and as long as that need existed, he knew could not turn away from her.

In this cold, alien place Rowena had warmed him like a flame. She had reawakened his spirit to life... and to love.

He owed her his very soul.

As soon as she entered the house, Rowena had raced for her chamber. She was in the act of locking the door when Bosley shoved it open with a force that sent her stumbling backward.

"Not so fast, mistress!" he snapped, looming above her where she had fallen against the bed. "If you think you won't have to answer for your shameful conduct, you're quite mistaken. Neither of us is leaving this chamber until we get to the bottom of this disgraceful business. Who is that man? What is he doing here?"

He made a move to close the door, but Rowena was on her feet at once. She lunged for the opening, but he caught her wrist and spun her back into the room. Only Sibyl's arrival in the corridor stopped him from bolting the door and doing her untold harm.

"Why, Edward, you naughty boy!" Sibyl leaned against the door frame, cocking her head like a curious fox. "Did I interrupt something interesting? Do continue. I promise I shan't make a sound."

Bosley exhaled like a winded bull, giving Rowena a chance to gather her wits. Why not tell him what he wanted to know? she reasoned. He could easily learn as much from questioning the servants.

"The man in question is called John Savage," she said, measuring each word. "My father found him in Falmouth, newly off a ship, and with no place to go."

"And you've kept him all this time?" Bosley asked suspiciously.

"Why not? He's a fine hand with horses—we had need of such a person. Young Will is too small to handle the beasts, Dickon is too slow-witted, and Thomas is busy with other household matters."

"And you—" Bosley leaned so close that his spittle sprayed Rowena's cheek. "How long has he been tumbling you like a common slut? How many times has the scoundrel been under your petticoats, eh?"

Rowena's face paled. Despite her resolve to remain calm, she felt a dizzying surge of anger. "None," she replied coldly. "And I'll thank you to save your vulgarities for the alehouse!"

Bosley's florid color deepened. "That won't work, mistress," he hissed. "Trying to hide your sin behind

a show of self-righteousness! I know what I saw with
my own eyes out there in the stable!''

"Indeed you do not!" Rowena flared. "My falcon
had just died. The man was consoling me, nothing
more. On my father's grave, I swear it! John Savage
is not my lover!''

Sibyl tittered. "In that case, my dear, you're an
even bigger fool than I judged you to be!''

Bosley rocked back on his heels, one hand scratch-
ing at his buttocks. "Very well, I accept your story,
Rowena. But all the same, I should have the insolent
wretch flogged for daring to lay hands on my future
wife.''

"What?" Rowena felt the blood drain from her
face. She clutched at a bedpost for support as her
knees buckled beneath her. "If this is your idea of a
jest, Edward Bosley, then it's a poor one. The Crown
forbids such marriages—and even if that were not so,
I would sooner die than become your wife!''

"Henry's so-called law is easily dealt with," Bosley said. "Even now, my lawyer is drawing up the
documents invalidating my marriage to your late aunt.
She was a cold woman, if the truth be told, and no
true wife to me ever—the absence of children will
support that claim.''

"Well and good!" Rowena countered. "Nothing
could make me happier than to have you out of the
family once and for all!''

"That's where the beauty of timing comes in, my
dear." Bosley's upper lip curled in a smirk. "The
annulment will not be final until the day of our wedding. Meanwhile, as your only living relative, I will
continue to run Thornhill Manor as I see fit.''

As your only living relative.

The words echoed strangely in Rowena's mind as she sank, reeling, onto the bed. Where had she heard them before, and when? Why did they strike her now like a hammer blow to the temple?

"Ah, my dear!" Sibyl spread her arms in a mockery of affection. "Just think of it! We're to be sisters! Perhaps I can take you in hand, teach you how to dress, how to entertain, how to refurbish this drab old barn of a house!"

"Out!" Rowena's hard-won self-control shattered. In despair, she seized a pewter ewer from the dresser and charged the invaders, swinging the heavy utensil like a war club. "Out of my chamber! Out of my house!"

Startled by her wild behavior, Bosley edged toward the door. Sibyl, still laughing, retreated deeper into the hallway.

"Out!" Rowena swung the ewer with all her strength. The blow glanced off Bosley's cheekbone, breaking the skin and leaving a thin trail of blood.

"You hellcat!" he gasped, staggering backward over the threshold. "I'll show you who's master here—"

Rowena slammed the door hard in his face, throwing her weight against the thick planks as she slid the bolt home. From the hallway she could hear his curses echoed by Sibyl's mocking laughter. Then the sounds faded into blessed silence.

Shaking, Rowena sagged against the wall. In days to come, would this be her only defense—feigning madness? Would she be driven to screeching and frothing at the mouth to protect herself from Bosley's advances?

A bitter smile tugged at a corner of her mouth. Madness, feigned or real, would gain her nothing. Bosley would simply lock her up somewhere and, as her only living relative, take over all the affairs of the manor.

As her only living relative.

Again the phrase pierced her awareness, probing the furrows of her brain, searching for the connection that her conscious mind had yet to make.

…her only living relative…

Rowena sank to the floor with a groan as her memory cleared, transporting her back to that day—the most terrible day of her life.

Bosley had startled her in her chamber, she recalled now, and they had argued over his plan to stay and take over the running of the manor. Aye, he had declared it his right—as her only living relative.

Rowena broke into a cold sweat as she remembered coming upstairs from the moor to the sound of arguing in her father's sickroom. She remembered Sir Christopher's sonorous voice all but ringing through the walls—certainly not the voice of a dying man. Yet, minutes later, when she had broken away from Bosley and hurried to her father's chamber, she had found him lying white and still, his hands crossed as if he had already been laid out for burial.

…your only living relative…

Edward Bosley had spoken those words. He had spoken them as if he already knew Sir Christopher was dead.

* * *

Black Otter had cut short his nightly roaming, lacking, for once, the spirit to be abroad. The waning moon was still high when he crested the last low hill and paused for a moment, gazing across the moor toward the silent house.

Worry gnawed at his innards. What was happening behind those forbidding walls? Was Rowena safe? Had he been wrong to let her go back inside without him?

His hands clenched into fists as he fixed his gaze on her darkened window. For a long moment he fought the temptation to scale the outside wall of the house, using chinks in the stones to hold his weight until he reached her window. He would stay only long enough to make sure she was safe, then leave as he had come.

But, no, the risk was too great. If discovered, his presence in the house would only confirm *Chingwe's* suspicions and make trouble for them both. Rowena was better off without him—that he knew in his mind. But his heart ached to hold her, to feel her close against him, slim and vital and needing, trembling in his arms as he protected her from danger.

He sprinted the remaining distance, finding some release in physical exertion. As always, the heaviness of his English boots made him long for moccasins, but that was just one more thing he could not change right now. He would go inside and try to sleep. Perhaps with the dawn Rowena would at least show herself outside to let him know she was safe.

Reaching the stable, he saw that the back door was open. Black Otter stopped in his tracks, his pulse leaping. Had he forgotten to close it? No, he remembered fastening the latch as he always did when going out. Someone else had opened the door—someone who might still be there waiting for him.

Cautiously he slipped inside. The stable was dark and still, all four of the horses standing quietly in their stalls. Likely as not the unknown visitor had already gone.

Had it been Rowena? His heart contracted at the thought that she might have come looking for him, seeking help and comfort, and he had not been there for her.

"Rowena?" he called softly, but there was no answer. By now his eyes had grown accustomed to the darkness. He inspected the stalls and the space beneath the wagon to make sure no one was hiding there. A startled mouse squeaked and scurried across the toe of his boot, but he found nothing else. Perhaps his memory was playing tricks on him, and he had not latched the door, after all.

Wearily he climbed the ladder to his bed in the loft. He would not sleep, he knew. But if Rowena returned he wanted to be in the one place where she could not fail to find him.

The loft was warm, redolent with the familiar smells of hay and horses. Nothing seemed amiss here, but as he reached the top of the ladder, Black Otter sensed something else in the air—a sweet, musky, almost cloying aroma, as if someone had just emptied a large basket of stale flowers.

"Rowena?" The blanket where he slept was in deep shadow. He could just make out the form that huddled there, stirring now at his approach.

"Who's there?" He leaned close, his heart almost

stopping as two pale arms reached upward from the darkness, entwining like twin serpents around his neck.

"Where have you been for so long?" a lusty female voice whispered. "I thought you would never get here. Come, my Gypsy stallion. Show me how sorry you are for making your Sibyl wait."

Chapter Twelve

The voice galvanized Black Otter to full alert. Whatever the weasel's purpose for coming here, he knew her presence meant only one thing: trouble.

Her fingers twined and tangled in his hair, pulling him down toward her. Her breath smelled, not unpleasantly, of fermented cherries. "You needn't be so shy," she whispered, giggling. "We both know what you want. All you have to do is take it."

"Is this the way of all white women?" he asked, remembering Rowena's sweetly awkward offering of herself on the moor. "Can they not wait for a man to decide he wants them?"

The weasel laughed again, freeing one hand to reach down and grope his crotch. Her body moved, uncoiling in the darkness, and he realized she was naked on the quilt that served as his bed, her pale hair artfully fanned on the dark fabric. In spite of his distrust Black Otter felt his loins stir and begin to harden. *Indeed, why not take her?* temptation argued. It was only mating after all—a brief tumble and a pleasant release, like the coupling of two animals. He cared nothing for this woman, just as surely as she cared nothing for him. There was no risk of involvement here—certainly not the kind of risk that had kept him from making love to Rowena.

The thought of Rowena now, alone and afraid in the great, dark house was enough to cool his simmering blood. At once he was contrite. He pulled away from the weasel and sank back onto his heels.

"Get your clothes and go," he said gently. "It is not a good thing, your being here now."

The weasel's breath hissed outward as she worked her way up onto her elbows. Through a chink in the roof, a shaft of moonlight gleamed on one perfectly formed ivory breast.

"What *is* the matter with you?" she demanded, glaring up at him. "You want me, you ill-bred lout! I know you do—I felt you myself! There are men who'd give a king's ransom for an hour in my arms— indeed, there are men who've paid that dearly for the pleasure! And now you, a mere peasant—"

"Here." He found her bundled clothes and thrust them toward her. "Go back to the house. No one must know you were here."

"Not until you give me an explanation!" she snapped. "It can't be Rowena, that big, stumbling chestnut mare, so awkward she can barely give a man the time of day—not unless you're after her fortune, of which, I can assure you, she has very little! Why would you refuse an offer from a woman most men would give their very lives to possess?"

"You would not understand." Black Otter shook his head, not certain whether he understood fully himself. He only knew that anything happening between himself and this woman might ultimately be used to hurt Rowena, and he could not allow that to happen.

"You'll be sorry!" She snatched the bundled clothes out of his hand, clutching them against her as she struggled to her feet. "One day, by God, you'll beg me for what I offered you tonight! And when that time comes, you ingrate, I will spit…in your…face!"

Her hand struck him resoundingly on the cheek. Black Otter took the stinging blow without flinching. He understood why she was angry. The women of his own tribe were not so different in this respect. But there was nothing he could—or would—do.

"You insolent Gypsy pig!" she hissed as her feet fumbled for the hanging ladder. "You'll pay for this insult—you'll pay for the rest of your miserable life!"

He sat quietly, listening as she clambered downward in the darkness. There was a breath of silence, then the sound of her falling off the bottom rung of the ladder, which ended at knee height above the floor. She thrashed in the straw, cursing as vividly as the sailors he had heard on the ship. A moment later he heard the creak of the stable door opening. Then the dark stillness closed around him, broken only by the sigh of the wind and the restless shifting of the horses below.

Too agitated to sleep, Rowena huddled at her window, staring down into the moonlit yard. Was her savage there in the shadows below, as restless and worried as she was? Did she dare steal out of her chamber and go to him? No, she banished the thought as quickly as it had come. She could not risk letting Bosley catch them together again, especially at night.

She would have to rely on someone else, young Will most likely, to let him know she was safe.

Her heart stopped as the stable door nearest the house inched open, just far enough to accommodate a slight, pale figure. Rowena gasped out loud as she recognized Sibyl, stark-naked except for the trailing bundle of clothes she clutched against her chest.

As the shock penetrated, a leaden lump of misery congealed in the pit of Rowena's stomach. It had not taken long for Sibyl to make good her boast of that morning—nor for John Savage to take advantage of what was offered. The two of them had met only that morning. Now it appeared they were lovers.

Her mind flew backward to that reckless day on the moor when she had flung herself into his arms, determined to lose her virtue. Over time, she had dared to hope that he'd rejected her because of his own moral code, or perhaps out of concern for her. What a fool she had been! The truth, as she faced it now, was that he simply had not wanted her. She was not the sort of woman who appealed to him. Sibyl clearly was.

Her spirits, already low, plummeted deeper as she closed the shutters and turned away from the window. What would she do with "her" savage now that she could no longer endure the sight of his face? He was still her captive, her responsibility. But how could she hold him as her friend when every glance, every touch or word from him would remind her of what had taken place tonight?

In the stillness beyond the bolted door, she heard the swift patter of Sibyl's footsteps along the corridor and the opening of her chamber door. Rowena bit back the urge to weep with rage. She had thought she had one true ally in this place, one friend she could trust unconditionally. But John Savage had betrayed that friendship—and her love.

How could she face the two of them tomorrow? How could she look at either one without imagining them coupled in the loft, their splendid bodies gleaming with sweat and lust?

But what did it matter? she reminded herself bitterly. She had other, more pressing concerns now. If Bosley and his alleged half sister had truly murdered her father, she needed to find proof. Only then could she notify the constable and have the pair taken away to pay for their crime.

Sinking onto the edge of the bed, she buried her face in her hands and forced her reeling mind to concentrate. She would have to plan carefully. And she would have to work in absolute secrecy, trusting no one—least of all the man to whom she had foolishly given her heart. He was one of the enemy now. She could count on no one but herself.

True to habit, neither Sibyl nor Bosley had risen early that morning. At first light, Rowena had unbolted her door and cautiously checked the corridor. From behind Bosley's door, loud nasal snoring had proclaimed to all within hearing that he was sound asleep. As for Sibyl…aye, her chamber was tightly closed. She, of all people, would be weary enough to sleep like a stone.

Returning to her chamber, Rowena had hurriedly pulled on her clothes and pinned up her hair. Now she was ready to take full advantage of her time alone.

Taking the heavy key ring, she stole down the hallway to her father's chamber at the far end. On her own orders the room had been locked as soon as Sir Christopher's body was removed, and no one had been allowed to visit it since. If there was evidence of murder to be found in his chamber, it would still be there.

Bracing herself for a wave of emotion, she turned the key in the lock. It had been more than two months since her father's death. If Bosley and Sibyl had not been here she would have come in much sooner to put things in order—but then, perhaps, if not for them, Sir Christopher might still be alive.

For the space of a breath she lingered with her hand on the latch, preparing herself for the sight of well-loved objects—the spectacles on the bedside table, the well-thumbed books, the quills and inkwells, the faded dressing gown, the nightcap, stretched to the broad, flat shape of her father's skull. She knew she would want to cry, but this was no time for tears.

Swallowing hard, she opened the door, stepped over the threshold, then stopped as if she'd run into a brick wall.

The room had been thoroughly cleaned—the bed stripped of linens, the carpets rolled and stacked against one wall, the floor swept and scrubbed. The wardrobe that had held Sir Christopher's clothes stood open and empty.

Frantic, she darted around the room, inspecting the cabinets, pulling open doors and drawers. Everything had been emptied and cleared. It was as if Sir Christopher Thornhill had never occupied this room—almost as if he had never existed.

Racing downstairs to the kitchen, she found
Thomas still hunched over his breakfast of porridge
and milk. He glanced up, his big slab of a face furrowing as he saw her.

"Mistress?"

"My father's chamber—I gave orders that the
room wasn't to be touched!"

"Aye, mistress, that ye did."

"Then why has the place been stripped to the bare
walls and floors? Where are my father's things?"

Thomas stared at her, clearly bewildered. "But,
mistress, 'twas on your own orders the room was
cleaned, and the master's things put away in the cellar."

"On *my* orders?"

"Aye—or so Master Bosley told Hattie and me. 'E
said ye were in too much of a state to bear the sight
of the chamber as it was and wanted it cleaned. 'E
gave us a few farthings extra to do the job right,
then." His bland, blue eyes gazed at her over the
bowl of porridge. Dear, innocent, trusting Thomas.
Bosley had probably taken everything of value from
the room and sold it on one of his infrequent trips to
Falmouth.

"When was this done?" she asked.

"Why, just a few mornings after Sir Christopher
passed on. Master Bosley said ye were out on the
moor and wouldn't want to watch—" He broke off,
looking stricken. "Ah, mistress, we meant no harm."

"Aye, I know that." Rowena sighed and turned to
go, then swung back to face him. "Thomas, where
were you when my father died?"

"When I heard ye shout I was 'ere in the kitchen,

fetchin' some broth for Mistress Sibyl. She'd gone to one of the guest rooms to lie down—claimed to be feelin' faint.''

"And so Bosley was alone with my father?''

"Aye." He returned her gaze blandly. "The old master seemed well enough when I left. But the doctor said such attacks as 'is could come with no warnin' at all.''

"And what about Dickon? Where was he?''

Thomas blinked. "Why, I don't know, mistress. 'E could've run off. A flighty fellow, Dickon is. And 'e's not been back since that day. Young Will claims 'e's not feelin' right.''

Rowena nodded, choosing to not express her suspicions. "When I came upstairs that day, I heard what sounded like an argument. Can you tell me what it was about?''

"Argument?" Thomas blinked. "To be honest, mistress, I can't say as I recall. True, Sir Christopher wouldn't have been happy to see Master Bosley. But if they quarreled, 'twasn't till after I'd left the room.''

"I see." She studied the big Cornishman's earnest, freckled face. Had Bosley won Thomas to his side, or was the big Cornishman simply incapable of distrust? Either way, she could not risk confiding in him.

"In the future, Thomas, please remember you take your orders directly from me, not from Bosley, is that clear?''

"Aye, mistress.''

"And if he questions you about me or about any of the affairs of this household, you're to come and tell me at once.''

"Aye." He gazed down at his calloused hands, so

large that they dwarfed the knife and spoon he held.
"Mistress?"

Rowena had turned once more to go, but the urgent
undertone in his voice halted her at once. "What is
it?" she asked.

"Master Bosley did ask me about John Savage."

She felt her heart miss a beat. "When?"

"Yesterday. After ye'd gone upstairs. Mistress
Sibyl was with him."

"And what did you tell them?" Rowena braced her
knees to keep them from buckling. The familiar
smells and sounds of the kitchen seemed to freeze
around her, as if the earth had stopped in its motion.

Thomas shrugged. "Only what I've seen and
'eard—that the old master brought 'im back from Falmouth on a dray, and that the man was mad from
fever the first few days."

"Anything more?"

"Mistress Sibyl asked about the tattoos. I said 'e
was a Gypsy fellow, most likely a Turk or a Portugee,
an' that the marks were a custom of 'is people. Gyp-
sies 'ave odd ways about 'em, no doubt."

"And that was all."

"Aye, that was all." Thomas looked dismayed.
"Ah, mistress, don't ye frown at me so. 'Tis no secret
the man's a strange one. Young Will has naught but
good to say about 'im, but 'e keeps apart from the
rest of us."

"Aye, that's his way," Rowena said, realizing
Thomas was trying to spare her feelings. Gossip traveled fast among the servants. They doubtless knew
that Bosley had caught her in the savage's arms yesterday. And it wouldn't surprise her to learn that

someone had also seen Sibyl coming or going last night. Servants were the eyes and ears of a household. Day or night, few things escaped their notice.

"Did I do wrong, mistress?"

"No, Thomas." She touched his shoulder in a rare show of affection. "These are difficult times, that's all."

She left him to finish his breakfast, her thoughts churning as she mounted the stairs. Edward Bosley might be boorish and presumptuous, but he was not stupid. Given time and access to the papers he'd taken from Sir Christopher's room, he would no doubt discover John Savage's true origin and be swift to exploit his worth.

The savage had no legal rights in this country. Some people would even argue that he was less than human. Bosley could take him prisoner and exhibit him like a dancing bear, in war paint and feathers, or simply sell him to the highest bidder. Either way, John Savage would never see his home or his children again.

There was no time to be lost. She had to get him away from the manor while she still could.

She hurried upstairs, pausing outside Bosley's and Sibyl's closed doors to make certain no one was stirring. Once more the image of Sibyl, traipsing naked across the moonlit yard after her tryst, flashed through Rowena's mind, stabbing her heart like a shard of ice. It made no difference, she told herself, thrusting the memory aside. As the legacy of Sir Christopher's folly, the savage's welfare was still her responsibility. She could not rest until she had repaired, in some part, the great wrong her father had done.

Inside her chamber, she bolted the door, then dropped to her knees and withdrew the carved cedar wood chest from beneath the platform that supported her bed. Carefully, almost reverently, she placed it on the floor in front of her and raised the hinged lid.

There, nested on the dark blue velvet lining, lay Rowena's legacy from her mother—the only dowry she possessed. Tenderly she lifted the necklace of fine gold filigree set with garnets and held it up to the ray of morning sunlight that streamed through her window. True, the stones were not costly, but the workmanship was exquisite, and the gold was real—as were the garnet earrings made to be worn with the necklace and the flawlessly matched pearls in a strand as long as her arm.

There were bracelets, also, one of plain gold, the other of silver with insets of lapis, as well as three rings of excellent quality. Rowena knew she would never wear this jewelry. Such baubles were for pretty women—on her they would only look ludicrous. But they carried the memory of her mother, and for that she treasured them.

Would the pieces fetch enough money to charter a vessel for the New World? Rowena massed them in her hands, her mind spinning with questions—how to get the jewelry to Falmouth without arousing Bosley's suspicious; where to find an honest buyer and a reliable captain.

But first things first. Getting John Savage out of danger was the most urgent part of her plan. The rest would have to wait until that was accomplished.

Resolutely she closed the chest and slipped it back into its hiding place. Yes, her mother would approve of this wild venture. Lady Marian Thornhill had been a kindly woman with a fierce love of truth and justice. She would want her husband's wrong made right at any cost.

Rowena opened her chamber door a cautious crack. Seeing no one about, she slipped into the corridor and locked the door behind her. Then she hurried down the stairs, skirted the far side of the great hall and slipped out the front entrance, where the servants would be less likely to notice her.

By the time she reached the front stoop, her heart was pounding. Her ribs jerked with tension beneath the constricting stays of her corset as she scanned the open country to the road and beyond. Seeing no one, she circled outward across the moor, then, running full-out, she cut back toward the stable. When she reached the rear entrance she collapsed against the door frame, gasping for breath. Dear heaven, how she dreaded facing John Savage, dreaded the sight of those dark, earnest eyes. How could she bear to look at him, knowing what he and Sibyl had done last night?

Thrusting her own pain aside, she opened the door and stepped inside. For a moment she stood blinking in the warm darkness, surrounded by the familiar aromas of clean hay and fresh manure. It was not until her eyes became accustomed to the dim light that she saw him, standing just a few paces away in Blackamoor's stall, currying the gelding's coat to an ebony sheen.

"Rowena." He whispered her name. The metal comb dropped to the straw as he moved out of the stall, never once taking his gaze off her. The relief and trust in his black eyes appeared so genuine that she might have been taken in if she had not witnessed his betrayal with her own eyes.

"Are you all right?" His voice held such concern, such tenderness. Merciful heaven, how she hated him!

"I had no sleep last night, for fear he had hurt you." He reached out, as if to take her in his arms, but she backed away, possessed by a cold fury she could scarcely contain.

"What is it?" His expression had darkened. "Did he—"

"No." Rowena edged backward. *He wasn't the one who hurt me!* she wanted to scream at him. *It was you—you who hurt me!*

"Come here," he said softly. "Let me look at you."

Rowena stumbled backward against the wagon. "Don't touch me!" she whispered, despising her own wildly churning emotions. "I only came to warn you that you're in danger. If Bosley finds out who you are—and he may have found out already—you'll never be free again. We have to get you out of here—now!"

He gazed at her in consternation. "What did he do to you?" His voice was a menacing rumble. "If he—"

"No!" Her words lashed out at him. "Bosley did not touch me! Certainly not the way you touched—" She broke off, wanting to flee from the stable and leave him to his wretched fate, and knowing she could not abandon him. He was her charge, her responsibility.

He stared at her in sudden comprehension. "Rowena, I did not—"

"No, don't try to deny it!" she fumed, knowing that his denial was the one thing she desperately wanted to hear. "I know what I saw, and there's naught to say about it. What you choose to do with a woman is none of my—"

"Rowena!" He caught her shoulders, his powerful hands gripping so hard that she winced. His black eyes burned into the depths of her wounded soul.

"What you saw," he spoke slowly and deliberately, forcing each word. "It was not what you think. She came to me, naked as you saw her. I sent her away very angry, so angry that she did not even stop to put on her clothes."

"You refused her?" She stared up at him, still fearful that he might be lying.

"I refused her, as I refused you. But not for the same—" He fumbled for the word, then abandoned the search with a shrug of exasperation. "Not the same as with you."

"Not the same how?" she pressed, despising the fact that it mattered so much. Nothing should matter now except getting this man to safety, as much for her father's sake as for his own. Her private feelings were of no importance.

But she had asked him, and now she saw that he was struggling to explain. John Savage had learned English well enough to deal with tangible objects and situations, but the deeper world of mind and heart, of man and woman, still lay beyond his grasp.

"You—she—" The rest emerged as a furious out-

burst in his eloquent native tongue that left Rowena
staring at him in confusion.

"You do not understand?" he asked, clearly frustrated.

"No." She shook her head, still held fast by his
iron grip on her shoulders. "But it doesn't matter
now. We've got to get you to a safe hiding place, and
then—"

She gasped as his arms jerked her hard against him.
His lips closed on hers with a power and sweetness
that moved the earth beneath her feet. She responded
like tinder to a torch, abandoning all reason except to
feel his nearness…all purpose except to give him her
soul.

Black Otter knew the danger. He knew she had
warned him that they must leave. But he also knew—
as he had known from the instant Rowena walked into
the stable—that he could not go without holding her
one last time. Without letting her know, beyond all
doubt, that she was a beautiful, desirable woman,
more than worthy of love.

Now it was as if he held flame in his arms. He
could feel the heat of her response searing his body,
igniting his own flesh and blood to a fever pitch of
need. He molded her against him, vainly willing their
maddening English clothes to dissolve like dust in
summer rain, willing their bodies to be as naked and
open to one another as their spirits.

"I love you—love you," she whispered, her frantic
lips devouring his mouth, his cheeks, every part of
him she could reach. "Whatever happens—never,
never forget—"

Black Otter's aching throat would not allow him to

answer, but his heart swelled to overflowing. In the hellish prison of the ship, he had believed his life was over. Even here, in England, it was as if his soul had withered like a frozen tree, never again to feel, to laugh, to love. Then this strong, tender woman had awakened him like a fresh spring wind. She had blundered her way into his life, offering him all she had to give.

Rowena.

Her memory would warm him through all the lonely times to come.

"I have a plan," she whispered, still holding him with all her strength. "Hide in the cave—you know where—I can meet you there tonight, with the horses. We'll ride to Falmouth, where I can sell my mother's jewelry to get you money for a ship."

"No."

She stared up at him.

"Not your money," he said. "You need it to get away from *Chingwe*—or to fight him for what is yours."

"But you—"

"I have been many times to the town you call Falmouth. I can go there alone, get work on a ship—"

"And go where?" she stormed at him. "It's a miserable life—you'd be no better than a slave! You were on a ship! You saw how it was!"

"Aye," he said slowly. "That I know. But I am a man, Rowena, a warrior. I will find a way to do this thing." His arms tightened protectively as he thought of leaving her in this unhappy place, with so much danger to face alone. "You must not stay here," he said. "Go where you can be safe."

She shook her head fiercely. "This is my home. I'll die before I let a monster like Bosley force me out!"

"Then what will you do?" He pressed her close, torn to the point of anguish. How could he leave her alone and exposed? Yet what could he do for her if he stayed? She needed the help of someone with power and influence, someone with a knowledge of English law. He could offer her nothing but the strength of his body. And that, he knew, would not be enough.

"Ssh!" She stiffened abruptly against him, listening. Black Otter held his breath, then he heard it, too—the sound of heavy footsteps approaching the stable door.

Chapter Thirteen

"**R**un!" Rowena broke away and shoved the savage toward the rear door, but at that instant the door exploded open as if it had been kicked. Two burly peasants, whom she recognized as troublemakers from a nearby village, burst into the stable. One of them was armed with a heavy wooden club. The other brandished a small, vicious-looking dagger.

"This way!" She caught the savage's wrist, but then, like a scene from a nightmare, the other door swung open. A third village thug barged in gripping an ax. Behind him, brandishing a ridiculously large broadsword, strode Edward Bosley.

Bosley's eyes flickered toward Rowena. "Get out of the way," he growled. "It's not you we've come for."

Without warning, Rowena flew at him. She struck like a mythical fury, kicking and clawing. She knew she was no match for his size and strength, but this brief flurry of distraction was her only hope of giving the savage a chance to escape.

She felt the wetness of blood where her nails raked

Bosley's cheek. Cursing, he caught her wrist and
flung her to one side. She spun into the corner post
of a stall, striking her head. Stars exploded and faded
into darkness as she went down.

Moments later Rowena's vision cleared. Her heart
sank as she saw John Savage struggling against the
three village toughs. They had backed him into a corner, but he had wrested the club from one of them
and was keeping them at bay with blows of bone-
shattering power. Bosley hung back like the coward
he was, gripping the sword awkwardly as he watched
for an easy opening.

The sword! Gathering her strength into a crouch,
Rowena lunged for it. Her low, hurtling body struck
the back of Bosley's legs, causing his knees to buckle.
As he flailed for balance she strained upward and
caught the weapon by its hilt. For an agonizing instant, she thought she had it, but then he twisted it
away. The blade sliced into the flesh at the base of
her thumb. Blood oozed freely, dripping onto the
straw.

"Hellcat!" Bosley cursed, using his leg to shove
her out of his way. "You, Watson! See to her! Don't
let her interfere again!"

At Bosley's command, the man who had lost his
club to the savage backed out of the melee, seized
Rowena by the shoulders and dragged her beyond the
wagon. She clutched her maimed hand, stanching the
blood with a fold of her petticoat. She had drawn one
man out of action, but the odds against her savage
were as fearful as ever.

Her heart seemed to stop as she watched him feint
and dodge, plying the club with a warrior's ferocity

and skill. If the men had worked as a team they might have been able to overcome him by sheer numbers, but at such close quarters the two husky peasants were struggling at cross purposes, blocking each other's blows. And Bosley was still hanging back, sweat making a dark, wet stain down the back of his doublet.

The thick hardwood club cracked down solidly on the wrist of the man holding the knife. He yowled with pain, dropped the weapon and stumbled backward, cradling his arm. Now the savage was pitted one on one against the largest of the village thugs, the one with the ax. With more room to maneuver, the hulking peasant was already bearing down on him, swinging the ax in a deadly arc. The heavy blade whistled through the air, slicing the savage's shoulder as he leaped to one side. Rowena cried out as blood spurted from the gash, but the rough, salty hand that clamped over her mouth, muffled the sound.

By now the savage's blood was flowing in a crimson river down his arm. Even so, he reacted swiftly to the blow that had wounded him. Before his adversary could land another blow, he swung the club. The thick, knotted end of it struck the hulking peasant solidly across the temple. The ax blade wavered in the air as the big man reeled and staggered backward. Another blow from the club—he buckled like a sack of wheat and went down. Suddenly the savage had an opening.

Run! Rowena would have screamed the word if she'd been able to speak. *Get away now! It's your only chance!*

A silent groan quivered in her throat as she saw

the savage hesitate and realized that he was not strong
enough to escape. He had already lost too much
blood. His arm still held the club aloft, ready to strike
any attacker, but Rowena, who knew him so well,
could see the beads of sweat that had formed along
his upper lip. She could see the glazed eyes and the
underlying gray pallor that tinged his bronze skin.
Aye, it was all he could do to stay on his feet.

Only now did Bosley attack. His sword was so
large and gaudy that it looked like a stage prop—as
it likely was, or had been, at least. But the blade, in
its present condition, had been sharp enough to slice
Rowena's hand like a razor.

She watched the savage, praying under her breath.
He was conserving his strength now, using the club
to parry Bosley's sword thrusts while he waited for a
chance to strike. He would strike to kill, she realized.
Only when Bosley was dead would she be free to
send him back to his homeland.

"You should have listened to me the first time,
Gypsy!" Bosley said with a sneer. "I warned you not
to go near my woman! Now you'll pay for your insolence with your manhood!"

Rowena's stomach contracted. Bosley did not appear to have discovered the savage's true identity, but
John Savage was in no less peril. A man who had
committed murder would be more than capable of
castrating the alleged lover of the woman he claimed
as his own.

She struggled and tried to cry out, but her captor
held her firmly, his ugly hand clamping her jaw so
that she could not bite him. She could only watch in
horror as her warrior swayed dizzily on his feet. The

hulking peasant who'd gone down earlier had recovered his ax and was up and moving in beside Bosley. Even the man with the broken wrist had bound his injury with a kerchief and come forward now with his knife in his good hand. The three of them circled the savage like slinking hounds waiting for a great stag to fall so they could leap in for the kill.

Bosley turned back to Rowena, a smirk on his evil face. "So, my dear, what's it to be? Do you wish to stay and watch us unman your Gypsy lover, or should I have Watson, here, take you back to the house and lock you in your room?" His eyes flickered toward Rowena's captor, who uncovered her mouth so she could answer.

"Let him go, Bosley!" she pleaded. "The man is not my lover! I swear it on the graves of my parents!"

"You're lying, my dear. You'd swear on anything to save him."

"I'm *not* lying!" Rowena argued vehemently.

"But you *would* lie, I'll warrant. What else will you do to save this black-eyed bastard, Rowena?"

She felt her knees buckle beneath her. "Anything," she whispered. "I'll do anything!"

"Anything?" Bosley's eyes narrowed. His tongue slithered wetly over his full, red lips.

"But only if you bind his wound and set him free. Harm him, and so help me, I'll kill you with my own hands!"

Bosley glanced around him, clearly enjoying the dramatic tableau he'd created—Rowena, frantically pleading in the arms of her captor; the savage, pinioned to the wall in helpless fury by the two peasants;

the horses watching from their stalls, innocent witnesses to the horror that was to come.

He turned back to Rowena. "You'll become my wife, in the fullest sense of that word?"

"Aye." She stared down at the straw, unable to look at him, or at the savage.

"You give me your word?"

"That I do. Now allow me to bind the Gypsy's wound before he faints. If he dies, any promise I've made you dies with him!"

"As it may well die when and if I set him free." Bosley ruminated a moment, then turned to the two men who held the savage against the wall. The savage's face was the color of potter's clay. Only the eyes were alive. They burned in their deep sockets like two smoldering coals.

"Take the wretch to the house and have Bessie tend to his wound," Bosley said. "Then haul him down to the cellar—ask her the way. There you'll find a cell and a set of irons. Here are the keys." He reached into his pocket and drew them out. "When he's shackled and locked away, come to me and I'll pay you what I promised."

"No!" Rowena jerked and twisted against the peasant who restrained her, kicking his shins in a futile effort to get free. "You gave me your word, you slimy toad! You promised you'd let him go if I agreed to wed you!"

"And so I shall. On the morning after our wedding, when your wifely body and worldly goods are safely mine, the swarthy bastard will be run out of the county, free to go where he will. But if you cross me..." Bosley's eyebrows knit in a menacing, theatrical scowl. "One false move from you, my dear, and your Gypsy will spend the rest of his miserable life pissing through a straw!"

The two husky peasants were dragging the savage toward the door. He hung between them, deathly pale, unable to stand on his own. Blood—so much blood—soaked his sleeve and streamed down his arm.

"Let me go with them and tend the wound myself!" Rowena pleaded. "Bessie knows nothing about such things. He'll get blood poisoning and die. Then where will you be?"

Once more Bosley savored the dramatic pause, the grim tableau with himself as the centerpiece. "I might consider it," he said, pausing to prop the glass-encrusted hilt of his sword against a stall. "As a newly betrothed man, I'm in a mood to be generous. But only for a price—one kiss from your sweet lips."

Rowena stood like a stone pillar as the rough peasant hands released their hold on her arms. Her gaze shifted to the savage where he sagged between his captors, more dead than alive, the precious seconds of his mortality slipping away with his flowing blood.

When she turned back toward Bosley her eyes blazed hatred. "Damn your soul to hell!" she said in a low, shaking voice.

Bosley smirked and opened his arms.

She hesitated, then flung herself at him with the speed of desperation, praying for a quick retreat, but Bosley was ready for her. With a predator's gusto he enfolded her, his wet, red lips smothering in their ardor. She struggled in his embrace, grunting in vehement protest as his free hand roamed her body, kneading her breast, then sliding lower to cup her hips and pull her in against his unmistakable erection. Rowena could feel the heat in the stable, feel the animal lust that emanated from the watching peasants, feel the helpless rage of John Savage and her own wild, hot fury.

After what seemed like an eternity, Bosley released her. He was breathing like a stallion, his lips slimed and swollen, his eyes twitching beneath heavy lids. Dizzy with loathing and revulsion, Rowena stumbled backward. She wanted to be sick, or to bare her talons and fly like a falcon at his face. But only one thing really mattered now—the life of her savage.

Without a word she turned and strode away from her betrothed. Only when she reached the men who held the savage did she trust herself to speak.

"We've got to get him to the house. Hurry, for the love of heaven—*hurry!*"

Black Otter was a boy again, running like a fawn through the mossy depths of the forest. Light and shadow played on his naked brown skin as he slipped among the trees, his leather moccasins scarcely touching the forest floor. The warm air sang with the aromas of pine, alder and damp, rich earth.

As he ran his sharp young eyes glimpsed his brothers, the wild animals of the forest, hiding among the leaves. Laughing, he called out to them—to the squirrel, "I see you, xanikw, you can't hide from me." To the fox, "Don't be afraid, okwes, I'm not after you today!" Always he addressed them with courtesy. These were the children of Mesingw, the lord and protector of the forests, who would only allow the Lenape to hunt game if they behaved well.

But he was not hunting game today, only running for pure joy as the forest called to him, leading him ever deeper along the branching trails. A cloud of white butterflies flitted across his path. An unseen woodpecker drummed a happy rhythm on a towering sycamore. All around him there was nothing but peace and beauty.

The overhanging branches were so thick that he could not see the gathering clouds in the sky. He was not aware of the coming storm until it burst down upon him in full fury. Wind lashed the trees, howling like an evil monster. Rain streamed down in cold, stinging torrents, plastering his long black hair to his shoulders. Black Otter staggered through the storm, scratched and beaten by the whipping branches.

Just ahead, in his very path, lightning struck an ancient tree, splitting the trunk like the blow of a huge ax. The shock knocked him flat on the ground. Time stopped as he lay there, dazed and trembling. Through the gathering darkness he could hear the hiss of the rain and, not far away, the scream of a puma. Blinded by terror, he scrambled to his feet and began to run.

Brambles clawed his skin as he bolted through a heavy thicket. He pushed ahead through the high undergrowth, wanting only to escape. One step, another—and suddenly there was nothing beneath his feet. He crashed through the brush and fell spread-eagled and screaming, down, down, as if he had tumbled off the very edge of the earth.

He felt the treetops at the foot of the ledge jabbing, tearing his skin as they broke his fall, then the sudden shock of landing on solid earth. He whimpered once,

*like a small, lost wolf pup before darkness closed
around him and he lay still.*

*Time and distance blurred. He sensed that the
storm was gone, and that he was being lifted upward
by giant arms—arms that cradled his broken body
with infinite care. He felt motion, the rhythm of im-
possibly long strides as they carried him, with the
lightness of a swallow's flight, across a vast and mysterious distance. Strangely, he was not afraid.*

*He willed his eyelids to open, but they would not
obey. Perhaps that was just as well, for Black Otter
knew without doubt that he lay in the arms of Mesingw, the great and benevolent forest god who possessed the body of a giant warrior and the flat,
scarred face of an ancient sage, thus encompassing
all strength and wisdom. A feeling of bliss crept over
the boy as he felt his injuries begin to heal. The sensation was one of pure light, pure love and trust; and
as he lay with his eyes closed, the voice of Mesingw
spoke like a rushing wind, not to his ears but to his
spirit.*

*"Do not be afraid, my son... You will live to be-
come a great* sakima *among your people... You will
lead them in the strength of your young manhood and
in the wisdom of your old age, and the trials you
suffer now will save them from the storms to come..."*

But how? *Black Otter felt the question but knew he
had not spoken.* Show me the way.

*"That I cannot do," Mesingw sighed. "You must
find your own path and learn from those you meet.
And all the while you must search for the stranger
from a far land, she who will walk the path with*

you..." His voice faded, even as the wind fades at the end of a storm.

"Wait!" the boy cried. "Tell me more! I have so much to learn!"

But the great forest god had gone, leaving him alone on a soft bed of moss and leaves.

Black Otter opened his eyes in utter darkness. For a moment he lay still, drifting in the dream of Mesingw's arms and voice. Then his body jerked in a reflex of awakening. He felt the cold, chafing weight of the iron bands around his wrists and ankles, heard the jarring clink of the heavy chains, and he remembered.

He had come full circle, back to the dark hole beneath the great house, where the three ruffians had flung him after Rowena had bandaged his wound. And this time, he knew, there would be no release. He was the captive of a man who would never let him leave this place alive.

For the space of a breath he closed his eyes, straining to recapture the dream and the sweet, peaceful voice of Mesingw.

...Search for a stranger from a far land, she who will walk the path with you...

But the words and the voice fled as he opened his eyes to the darkness around him. Had the words been true, or was he dwelling on the ramblings of his own unconscious mind? Mesingw could not save him in this miserable place. And the stranger he would have chosen to walk at his side was as much a prisoner as he was.

He moved his left shoulder and felt the stinging

pull of the stitches Rowena had made in his flesh. He
had drifted in and out of consciousness during the
process of cauterizing and closing the wound, but he
remembered the sight of her long, white hands, trembling as they worked the needle. And he remembered
her solemn eyes, gazing at him with so much love
and fear that it tore at his heart.

Seeing her in the arms of the monster he'd called
Chingwe had pained him more than any wound of the
flesh. He had all but screamed out loud as the man
kissed and fondled her.

Black Otter had understood enough of their conversation to know that she had given herself to save
him, and that after their wedding Bosley had promised to let him go free. But he knew the promise was
as worthless as dust. As soon as Rowena was his wife,
Chingwe would have his captive swiftly and secretly
killed. He would never see Lenapehoken or his children again.

Lying still to conserve precious strength, he battled
fear and despair with the only weapon he still possessed—anger. For two moons now he had submitted
himself to learning the white men's language and customs. But no more. He was a warrior, and his enemies, the white people, had shown him nothing but
treachery. For whatever time remained, he would fight
them with all he possessed—with the returning
strength of his body, with the craft of his mind and
with all the hatred that had slumbered in his heart
these past moons. If he was to die, he would die a
warrior, ringed by the bodies of his slain enemies. Oh,
Great Mesingw, what he would give for a bow and
arrows, or even a knife—

A small, scurrying sound reached his ears, scattering his thoughts and causing his stomach to lurch with a fear that was deeper than reason. He braced himself for the onrush of bodies, knowing, by now, there was little he could do to hold them back.

The rats had found him again.

"Please!" Rowena gazed up at the hulking brute Bosley had hired to guard the entrance to the cellar. "Just for a moment. I've a gold sovereign in my pocket. It's yours if you'll just turn your back or go off to the privy for a short time."

The man, tallest of the three village toughs who'd taken the savage prisoner, blinked down at her with his nearsighted little mole eyes. "Nay, mistress, I've my orders. Master Bosley'd 'ave me drawn and quartered if I was to let you down there. Can't do it."

"Ah, not even for a kiss?" She glanced coyly up at him, thinking that kissing this smelly lout could not possibly be worse than kissing Bosley had been.

He belched and licked his lips nervously, then shook his head. "Faith, 't would be a pleasure, mistress, but ye be pledged to the master. 'E'd flay me like a bloody 'erring for such a thing!"

"Then for the sake of Christian charity!" Rowena pleaded, catching the peasant's arm in desperation. "A man is suffering down there in that awful darkness! If you'd just allow me a few moments to—"

"What's this?" Bosley's angry voice thundered down the long, dim corridor. "Rowena, you've been ordered not to go near that blasted Gypsy!"

"I know," she said, detesting him. "I only wanted to check his shoulder and make sure the stitches aren't

festering. Grant me that, at least, if you've a shred of
decency in you.''

''Why should I care whether the stitches fester or
not?'' He swaggered down the hallway, conscious of
the absolute power he held over her. His thrusting
belly bounced slightly as he walked. He had eaten
well in her kitchen these past two months.

''It's in your best interest to keep the Gypsy in
sound health,'' she replied, reining in her temper. ''If
he dies you have no more control over me.''

Bosley scowled down at her. ''From all reports, the
bastard's as healthy as a horse,'' he snapped. ''But if
I catch you trying to sneak downstairs again, your
Gypsy will pay for it. There are plenty of ways to
punish a man without killing or castrating him. An
ear…a finger…an eye, perhaps…'' He took his time,
letting the implications sink in.

Rowena shuddered, knowing he would do exactly
as he'd threatened, or worse. She had hoped, at least,
to speak to John Savage, even smuggle him a key or
at least a knife. But she could not take the terrible
risk Bosley had laid out before her.

''You can't get to him in any case,'' Bosley said.
''I put a new lock on the cell, and the only key to his
shackles seems to be the one I found on your father's
nightstand—''

''When you helped yourself to the things in his
room!'' Rowena turned on him, unable to hold her
tongue. ''You had no right—''

Her words ended in a gasp as he seized her arm
and whipped her around to face him. ''No right?'' he
rasped, his breath reeking of ale. ''You're quite

wrong about that, my dear. I've a right to anything I want in this house, including you!''

He twisted her arm behind her back, arching her upward against him. His mouth came down on hers, lips thick and wet, tongue deeply probing, all but choking off her breath.

He released her with a rough laugh. ''Soon you'll be mine, Rowena. As soon as my lawyers finish drawing up the annulment papers and get a ruling from a magistrate—''

''One who's no doubt in your pay!'' She spun away from him and, without waiting for a reply, stalked up the passageway toward the great hall.

As soon she was out of sight, she began to run. By the time she reached the top of the stairs she was out of breath. Heart pounding, she fumbled for the key on the ring at her waist. These days she never left the room without locking the door behind her. Even then she feared that Bosley or Sibyl might come across a spare key somewhere.

Now, as the door swung open, she stumbled across the threshold and slammed the bolt into place. Only then did she give way to fear. Her knees buckled beneath her as she slipped to the floor where she sat quivering like a leaf, furiously wiping Bosley's kiss off her lips.

She was trapped—she knew it and Edward Bosley knew it. If she wanted John Savage alive and whole, she had no choice except to do whatever the vile man demanded of her.

How soon would he demand her in his bed? In truth, she was surprised he hadn't done so already. What was stopping him? Had his lawyers advised him

to leave her alone until all legalities were in place?
Had her efforts in eluding him—making sure there
were servants about whenever she left her room—
been successful? Or was Sibyl filling his carnal needs
for the present? Rowena pressed a hand to her aching
head. If that woman was really Bosley's half sister,
then cows had wings!

Taking a deep breath, Rowena willed her heart to
stop galloping. Slowly she worked her feet beneath
her, rose and walked across the room to the open
window.

It was full summer now, and the open moor swept
down to the sea in a tapestry of rich greens, golds
and browns. The seabirds wheeled and dipped above
the cliffs, their cries recalling the day of the albatross—the day Sir Christopher had brought the savage
from Falmouth chained and lashed to the dray.

What if she could bring that day back again? Rowena wondered idly. What would she do differently?
Could anything have prevented the awful chain of
events that had left her father dead, the savage a prisoner and herself pledged to a man she despised?

Never mind! She wrenched herself away from the
window and began to pace the room like a caged
animal. She had to stop Bosley and somehow set the
savage free. But how? She had racked her brain night
after night, grasping at straws and rejecting them one
by one.

Prove Bosley had murdered her father? She had
certainly tried that solution. She had grilled the servants and searched every inch of her father's chamber, but so far she had found not a shred of evidence.

Enlist the help of the servants? Rowena shook her

head in frustration. The servants were sheep, willing to follow whichever bell jingled the loudest. They were looking out for their own welfare and treated Bosley as if he were already master.

Seek out legal help or the counsel of some powerful family friend? This idea had merit, especially since she had long questioned Bosley's right to come in and take over her affairs. But Sir Christopher had become almost reclusive after his wife's death. He had distrusted lawyers and their ilk, and never made the kind of friends who might be helpful now.

Kill Bosley? Poison, perhaps? Her mouth twisted in a bitter little smile. That was a fantasy, nothing more. Even if she thought she could get away with it, she was not capable of murder. No, there had to be another answer.

Rowena sank onto the edge of the bed, desperately searching every corner of her mind. The most urgent thing was to get the savage out of the cellar before he died there. The rest…aye, the rest could wait.

At least Bosley did not appear to know the savage's true identity. He still referred to him as "the Gypsy," or as her lover. If Bosley had come across the bill of sale among Sir Christopher's papers, he had given her no sign of it…

But where were her thoughts wandering now? Rowena leaped off the bed, her heart slamming as the idea struck her—an idea so preposterous that she could scarcely believe she'd thought of it.

It would work—it *had* to work. But to carry out her audacious plan, she would need a new and very unlikely ally.

Heart fluttering, she opened the door and slipped

out into the hallway, taking care to turn the key in the lock. The door to Sibyl's chamber was ajar, a hopeful sign that the maid had delivered her breakfast tray and the irritating woman would be awake.

"Sibyl?" Rowena rapped cautiously on the door.

"Yes?" Sibyl's throaty voice was rough with the remnants of sleep and last night's ale.

"May I come in? It seems I have a favor to ask of you."

"A favor? That could be amusing. Come on in and tell me about it."

Rowena opened the door to find Sibyl propped against the pillows, her hair mussed, her kohl-smudged eyes and pale mouth giving her a ferret-like appearance. The breakfast tray, porridge and eggs still untouched, lay across her lap as she eyed Rowena warily. "Well?" she asked.

"Remember the day Edward announced his intention to marry me? You were there, Sibyl. You said we'd be sisters, and that you'd help me cheer up this gloomy old house."

"I remember." Sibyl yawned, the sleep still lifting from her mind.

"I've been thinking about what you said. And you're right. The place does need livening up—with good food, music, games, stimulating conversation..."

A spark of life flickered in the depths of Sibyl's bloodshot blue eyes. "Are you saying what I think you are?"

"Aye." Rowena seized her hands, playing her part like a seasoned actress. "I want you to help me give a party, the likes of which this county has never seen!"

Chapter Fourteen

Sybil reacted exactly as Rowena had hoped she would. Bored to the point of ennui by country life, she pounced on the prospect of a party like a cat on a slice of fresh liver. Even Rowena's insistence that the affair be held within a fortnight did not dampen her enthusiasm.

"We will have to buy everything locally, alas, and depend on the servants to cook it. There'll be no time to send to London for fine wines or to hire a proper meat and pastry cook, but that can't be helped. For a cultural backwater like Cornwall, we can do well enough, eh?" She brushed her tousled hair back from her face, her eyes glittering. "I'll see to the menu and the entertainment—oh, dear, what shall we do for music on such short notice?"

"There's a tavern in Falmouth that employs traveling musicians. Leave that to me," Rowena volunteered, thinking that a trip to town could serve her purpose well, especially if she could get away alone.

"The great hall and all of the rooms will need to be cleaned," Sibyl said. "There'll be no time to order new hangings for the walls—a pity, since the old ones are moldering on their rods, but—'' She shrugged prettily. ''And I suppose we'll just have to make do with what we have in the way of linens.''

''There's a trunk full of table linens in the attic,'' Rowena said. ''As long as the mildew hasn't gotten to them, they should be adequate. And there'll be no need for bed linens. We'll invite only those neighbors who live near enough to come and go the same day.''

''What about dishes?'' Sibyl asked.

''There's a fair supply of platters and goblets in one of the kitchen cupboards. The Thornhills were sociable folk a generation ago, not solitary creatures like my father and myself. Nothing's been thrown out.''

''Splendid!'' Sibyl caught Rowena's hand, pulling her downward until she was sitting on the edge of the bed. ''And if we could set up a canvas pavilion out-doors—''

''I do believe there's one stored in the stable.'' Rowena's careful mind was, by habit, already ticking off what the party would cost. Even a modest feast would drain the meager resources of the manor. She shuddered to think what the cost might be if Sibyl were given more time to arrange things. But then, what did it matter? There were more urgent things at stake here than money.

''I must insist you give me free rein with the servants,'' Sibyl was saying. ''You're much too easy on them. They've become quite slipshod, and there's really no excuse for it. Didn't your mother teach you anything about the proper way to run a house?''

Rowena chose to ignore the question. ''I'll instruct

the servants to follow your orders,'' she said. ''Now as to the guest list—''

''Ah, but that must be *your* responsibility, since I don't know the neighbors. Can I trust you to restrict the list to people of quality?''

''Of course.'' Rowena breathed deeply, willing her racing pulse to slow.

''No common sorts. Dear Edward will be making his first social appearance as the future lord of Thornhill Manor. It will be to his advantage and to yours, Rowena, if he can make some influential friends. Do you understand?''

''Certainly.'' Rowena bit back the caustic retort that had sprung to her lips.

''Now about the invitations. We must get them out as soon as possible. Can I trust you to see to that?''

Rowena hesitated, then sighed. ''Aye, somebody must do that task, I suppose. If you can keep the servants occupied, I'll write the invitations today and the stable boys can deliver them tomorrow.'' She spoke lightly, her manner belying the tension that quivered through every nerve. The invitations were the key to her entire plan. It was imperative that she write and send them herself.

''All that scribbling! Such a dreary job, my dear, but well suited to your scholarly nature.'' Sibyl's delicate fingers tightened around Rowena's wrist, the nails as sharp as the talons of a shrike. ''When you're married to dear Edward, we'll have parties every season! The gaiety of it—the gowns, the wines, the music! I'll invite all my friends down from London! You can't imagine what—''

''I really should start on those invitations.'' Rowena pulled away and scrambled awkwardly to her feet. "Is there anything in particular you'd like me to write?"

Sibyl pursed her unpainted lips. "The usual, I suppose. 'Mistress Rowena Thornhill requests the honor of your presence in a celebration of her betrothal to Mister Edward Bosley on—'"

"I can hardly say that," Rowena interrupted. "Your brother's lawyers are still working out the legalities of such a betrothal."

Sibyl gave a little huff of dismay. "Oh, bother! I suppose you're right. Well then, you'll just have to think of something else. You're a clever woman— certainly you can come up with something suitable to say."

"Aye, it shouldn't be too difficult. If I need any help—"

"Of course. Feel free to come and ask me anything at all! I'll be downstairs organizing the servants!"

Rowena made her excuses and hurried back down the hall to her own chamber. Her trembling hand could barely work the key in the latch. She had what she wanted—manipulating Sibyl had been almost shamefully easy. But the next step would plunge John Savage into danger. The risks were frightening, the stakes so high that the savage himself might hesitate to gamble. But there was even more risk in doing nothing.

She bolted the door behind her. Then, seated at her small writing desk, she found a sheaf of paper, filled her inkwell and sharpened a usable quill. How did one write a social invitation? she wondered. Dear heaven, had she ever even received one? What was the proper phrasing? Should she go back and ask Sibyl?

No? Well, never mind, then. With a mental shrug, Rowena dipped the quill into the ink and poised it above the first sheet of paper. The impact of the message, she hoped, would make up for any lack of propriety in the words.

Taking a deep breath, she touched quill to paper and with desperate haste began to write.

Black Otter lifted his head as the sliver of light appeared at the top of the stairway. He willed himself to keep still as the door creaked open, widening the light to a pale rectangle. Was it Rowena this time? His heart leaped, then dropped like a stone as he recognized the lumpy outline and plumed cap of Bosley, who no longer merited even the appellation of *Chingwe.* Trailing at his heels with a torch was one of the three coarse men who served him as bodyguards and jailers.

In the silent darkness of the cell, Black Otter waited, giving no sign that he was aware of his visitor. Bosley had come down twice before, for no apparent purpose except to torment his captive. Now Black Otter turned his back on the bars, determined to not give him the satisfaction of a response. As the torchlight pooled around him, he sat cross-legged in the center of the floor, his wrists and ankles chafed by the weight of the heavy iron manacles, his body splotched with festering rat bites. As before, he fixed his thoughts on a distant dream—a sunlit wood beside a sparkling river, a clearing where fresh, clean wood smoke curled from cook fires among the lodges, where the air rang with the songs of birds and the laughter of beautiful, black-eyed children…

"So you're still alive, eh, Gypsy?" Bosley stood outside the bars, waiting for the reply that did not come.

"You'll never see her again, you know," he continued, prodding for pain. "Rowena is mine now, in every sense of the word, and we're to be married as soon as my lawyers finish the arrangements." He paused, testing the impact of his words. "She loves me as she never loved you. Why, just last night, after everyone had retired, she crept into my bed. Ah…such a wanton! I was in her so many times I could scarcely walk this morning. I fear that by the time we're lawfully wed, she'll by carrying my babe in her belly."

Black Otter tried to close his ears to the taunts, but he could feel the words and images eating into him. Lies or not, the thought of Rowena in another man's bed was exquisite torture. Even though she had never been his—and could never be—she had filled the emptiness in his heart and made life bearable in this hostile land. A woman such as Rowena deserved the noblest of husbands, not this cowardly glutton whose body reeked of liquor and unwashed sweat.

Worst of all, for Black Otter, was the knowledge that Rowena had given herself to save him. Such a loving sacrifice, all for this! It would have been better to die as a warrior, fighting for his life, than to rot away here in the darkness. Better, even, to bleed to death—which he surely would have done if they'd cut away his manhood—than to lie here in filth and chains, knowing Rowena had given up her own freedom and happiness for nothing. Bosley had no intention of allowing him to leave this place alive.

"We're planning a banquet for all the landed gentry in Cornwall," Bosley was saying. "Mistress Rowena wants to make sure I'm properly introduced into society. There'll be a grand feast with music and dancing, as well as billiards, archery and bowls. Pity you can't be there, Gypsy. You could wash platters in the scullery or stable the horses. But even that won't be your good fortune. We can't have the likes of you running loose, despoiling our sweet English virgins, can we now?"

Black Otter did not reply, but for all his efforts to remain calm and detached, he could feel the anger building in him, heating to a molten fury. He would use that anger, he vowed. He would feed his rage, fuel his strength with hatred until the one weak moment when escape was possible. Then he would take his vengeance on this English race for his village, his wife, and the precious children he would never see again. He would die as the Lenape warrior he was, surrounded by the dead and bleeding bodies of his enemies.

As for Rowena, so warm and passionate and giving, he could only hope that such a death would, at last, set her free.

"What the infernal devil is *this?*" Bosley clutched the crumpled paper, his face engorged and throbbing.

Rowena studied him quietly from the opposite side of the table. She had left the scrolled invitation beside his dinner plate and then, though she usually took meals in her own chamber, sat down to watch his reaction. Her own pulse was jumping so violently that she could feel the blood vessels twitching in her wrist, but she did not stir. It was critical to her plan that she remain absolutely calm.

"This is your doing, isn't it, you witch?" His hand crashed against the tabletop, upsetting a goblet, as he flung the paper down in front of her. "How can you justify such a lie?"

"Because it's not a lie at all," Rowena said in a calm voice. "Every word of it is true."

She glanced down at the rumpled paper, an exact copy of the twenty-three invitations young Will and his brother Henry had delivered the previous week. A quick glance confirmed the words, written in her own mannishly large, but graceful hand.

Mistress Rowena Thornhill
requests the pleasure of your company
at a banquet honoring Master John Savage,
a chieftain of the Lenape tribe from the shores
of North America, brought to England
by the late Sir Christopher Thornhill...

The details of time and place blurred in her vision as Bosley sprang to his feet, jarring the dishes and upending his chair. Striding around the table, he seized her shoulders and jerked her upward, bringing her face to within a hand breadth of his own.

"How could you do this?" he rasped. "How could you betray me like this?"

Rowena met his eyes coldly. She could almost feel Sibyl's avid gaze taking in the scene from the far side of the table.

"If I betrayed you, it was only with the truth," she said. "The man you have locked and chained in the cellar is no Gypsy. If you'd taken more care in going through my father's papers, you might have found the bill of sale from the captain of the ship that brought him to Falmouth. Now it's too late for you to threaten him with harm. Everyone of importance in the entire county knows the savage is here, and they'll all be wanting to meet him."

Dead silence hung in the great hall. Then Sibyl began to laugh.

"I fear you underestimated your little bride, Edward! She's got you in a box! If you don't produce John Savage, hale, hearty and intact, the most distinguished families in Cornwall will be clamoring for your head on the block! And once word gets out, everyone from the queen on down will be flocking to see him!" She erupted into laughter again. "Rowena, my dear, I salute you! I couldn't have come up with a more clever plan myself!"

"Traitor!" Bosley turned on her, his face grotesquely livid. "This ruins everything! What are we going to do now?"

Sibyl raised one exquisitely drawn eyebrow. "I don't know what you are going to do, Edward, but I'm going to enjoy one of the most interesting social affairs I've seen in years!"

Rowena's victory was far from complete. Bosley, with the help of his three village ruffians, still ruled the manor, and he had flatly refused to let the savage out of his cell until the day of the banquet. But the threat of bodily harm had lifted for the present, and with it a measure of Bosley's control over Rowena. For the present, at least, there was no more talk of marriage.

For Rowena, the change was like a breath of air to a drowning victim, but there was much to be done before she could rest in the knowledge that her savage was safe.

The most urgent matter now was to speak with John Savage and prepare him for what was to come. Arranging this would be easier now that she no longer feared the consequences. The entire household was in an uproar with Sibyl's preparations for the banquet. With so much going on—so many people edgy and distracted—it was easy enough for Rowena to fill a dish of pudding from the pantry, lace it with an herb she had ground in the laboratory, and order the little scullery maid to deliver it to the night guard. The herb was harmless, but when mixed correctly it had enough power to render the husky peasant as drowsy as a milk-fed babe.

Anxiously she waited for darkness to fall, and after that for Bosley and Sibyl to finish their interminable game of whist and retire for the night. Only when she was certain the entire household was asleep did she venture to light a solitary candle, slip out of her room and move like a shadow down the stairs.

As she had hoped, the cellar guard was asleep, sprawled like a tired child in the corner between the wall and the door, the empty bowl lying beside his outstretched legs. Rowena stepped around him and, holding her breath, unlocked the door.

As she pushed it open, the creaking hinges raked her taut nerves. For a terrifying moment she feared the sound would wake the guard, but he slumbered on as, with even greater care, she closed the door behind her and, shielding the guttering candle with her palm, edged down the stone steps into the black pit of the cellar.

Her mind recalled an earlier time—creeping down these same steps in her nightdress, clutching the quilt and the loaf of bread as she approached the lurking savage. How frightened and unsure she had been, but no more. Now she moved with purpose, her heart leaping with anticipation at the thought of seeing him, touching him and bringing him hope.

Candlelight flickered over the clutter of boxes, crates and barrels and glinted on the cold iron bars of the cell. Now, dimly, she could see the dark outline of the savage's head and shoulders against the pale stone wall. Why hadn't he moved or spoken? Surely by now he had recognized her.

She reached the foot of the stairs and, heedless of the filth and clutter, rushed forward and all but flung herself against the bars. She saw him fully now—the rigid shoulders with the ax wound still scabbed and sore, the impassive face, the rat bites that mottled his bare chest and arms. Bosley's thugs had not done him further harm, but there had been no need for that. The savage had spent nearly a fortnight in this hellish darkness, cold, alone and without hope. His expression was that of a trapped animal waiting for death.

Heartsick, she stood outside the bars and willed him to look at her. She had come bringing good news, but perhaps even now it was too late. Every instinct told her that the man she had rescued, nurtured, schooled and loved was gone.

Black Otter gazed impassively through the bars, his emotions in a state of war—on one side fear, anger and despair, on the other side hope, love and trust. Once he had bowed to this woman's will. He had learned the white men's language and manners, dressed as they dressed, eaten as they ate—all of this as much for her sake as for his own. Now it was as if an ocean lay between them.

Not that he blamed Rowena. None of his misfortune was her fault. But the time alone in the rat-infested darkness had brought him back to his true self. He was a Lenape warrior. He belonged in another place, and he could not, would not, continue to live in her world.

She pressed against the bars, her very silence pleading with him. Part of him ached to go to her and take her in his arms, to feel her close against him, kissing her through the bars until desire flamed to exquisite torment. He wanted to lose himself inside her, to love her until the heat of passion consumed all pain and regret.

But still the wide and terrible distance lay between them, and he knew that she sensed it, too.

"Why did you save me?" Pride and pain lashed out in the coldness of his voice.

"How could I not save you?" she demanded. "It was my father who had you brought to England. In his absence, it was my duty to see you safe."

"And do you see me…safe?" The icy edge in his voice was so sharp that she flinched. "Go back upstairs and save yourself, Rowena. Your friend Bosley will never let me live. I ask only one thing—bring me a knife. When they come to kill me, I want to die fighting.''

For an instant she looked flustered. Then her anger exploded, the force of her words making the candle flame dance. ''So you've given up, have you? Without even hearing what I've come to tell you? You proud, vain fool!''

He stared as she related her fantastic scheme. Her resourcefulness touched and amazed him. But even as hope flooded his being, fear and distrust warned him to be cautious.

''I am to mix with these people? Talk to them?''

''Aye, just for the afternoon.'' The excitement of it had caught her and she was beautiful, her eyes glowing in the golden light. ''You'll have nothing to fear. They'll be curious, but no one will wish you harm. You've met the worst of the English in Bosley and the men on the ship, but these will be good people. If you allow it, some may even become your friends, your protectors—''

''And then?'' he asked, grasping her intent. ''What will happen when they go? Will I be chained like a dog, to be brought out only for visitors?''

''No!'' She pressed closer to the bars again, her face so eager and lovely in the candlelight that his throat tightened with sadness. ''Bosley will never be able to touch you again! Everyone who hears about you will want to meet you—even the queen! Don't you see?''

Black Otter nodded to please her, but he was beset with doubts. He saw too much, that was the trouble. And he had come too far to be chained like a wild animal and paraded before every curious pair of eyes in England.

"And will the queen send me back to Lenape-hoken?" he asked.

The slight hesitation in her voice told him more than her words. "The queen has the power to do anything she wishes. Perhaps in time—"

"But not soon?"

Her gaze dropped for an instant, then she met his eyes once more. "I fear not. You'll be much too valuable for that. But one day you may be sent back as a guide—"

"You mean, I can only return as a traitor to my people?"

"Don't think of it that way!" There was a catch in her voice, as if she were on the verge of tears. "Think of *now!* You'll be out of this terrible cell! You'll be safe from Bosley! You'll have the means of making powerful friends and perhaps one day become a voice for your people in this place!"

My spirit is dying in your England, Rowena. My heart is dying here. He did not speak the words. She had gone to such lengths to help him, and he could not bear to wound her again. He would do as she asked, but his appearance at the feast would be no more than an empty show. His eyes and ears would be alert for any chance to escape, and when that chance came, he would seize it at once and make for Falmouth. There was the matter of money, but somewhere on the docks there was bound to be a ship's captain that would hire him as a crewman. He would, at least, be free to take his chances.

And then what? What would happen to Rowena?

"This is the only way I could save you," she whispered, reaching out to him through the bars. "Please understand. Please use this gift."

Black Otter took her hand and pressed the palm to his cheek. Her soft white skin was as smooth as the petal of a wild rose, and for a moment he allowed himself to imagine a life as her husband—the sweetness of lying beside her every night, filling her lovely, ripe belly with his seed, protecting her, providing for her and for the children he would give her, watching the seasons pass and seeing every sunrise in the light of her luminous golden eyes...

Loving Rowena would be a dream. If he bowed to fate and learned to live as an Englishman, such a dream might even be his. But without Swift Arrow and Singing Bird, the dream would be a mockery of all he held dear. Rowena had brought him hope and he was grateful. He loved her for her warmth, her passion, her courage. But he could not allow himself to think of anything except getting home to his children. He could not rest until he held them in his arms, touching their hair, their cheeks, hearing their childish voices, filling his senses with the clean, smoky, innocent smell of their young bodies. The thought of never returning to them was bleaker than death itself.

"How soon?" he asked, still clasping her hand.

"In three days. Bosley won't let you out until he's forced to. You'll be given a bath and new clothes—"

"And a weapon? Even a knife? Can you get me something, Rowena?"

She withdrew her hand, her eyes suddenly wide and fearful.

"Even the small knife would do," he pressed her,

"the one I took from the big room with the windows. I lost it in the straw when the men took me from the stable—"

"No." She shook her head vehemently. "No knife. I won't have your death on my conscience, nor anyone else's!"

"Rowena—"

"I said no!" As if afraid he would succeed in changing her mind, she spun away from him. The candle flame flickered wildly as she plunged up the stairs. Black Otter's throat moved as he swallowed the urge to call her back, knowing a shout could alert the guard and bring calamity upon them both.

His gaze followed her until she vanished behind the closed door, leaving him alone in darkness.

Chapter Fifteen

Sibyl had done her work well. Within and without, the crumbling old manor swarmed with life and color. Sunlight danced on summer gowns of bright damask, cambric and sarcenet and richly trimmed doublets of brocade and taffeta, flashing vivid hues of willow, tawny, flame and primrose. The lively notes of lute and gittern floated across the moor, their music mingling with the sounds of laughter and conversation, the snorting of horses and the playful shouts of children.

It was Rowena who, over Sibyl's objections, had insisted on inviting the youngsters along with their elders. They scampered among the grown-ups, dodging boots and farthingales in an endless game of tag. The dogs had joined in at first but now, in the muggy afternoon heat, most of them had retreated to doze in the shade of the carts and wagons.

All the landed families within a three-league distance were here, as well as a few carefully chosen merchants, doctors and scholars. Earlier that afternoon they had feasted on roast beef and ale with kid-

ney pie, summer vegetables and fresh-baked bread,
followed by a rich, black plum pudding laced with
thick country cream. Now, with the meal still heavy
in their bellies, they strolled, danced, gamed and mingled on the moor or lounged in the shade of the
shabby but serviceable pavilion.

"My dear, I don't suppose you remember me, do
you?" The plump matron, showing damp gray curls
beneath her partlet, clasped Rowena's hand. "Lady
Osgood. Your mother was a dear friend of mine. Such
a pity her going so young, and now your father, as
well—ah, how ever do you bear it?" She dabbed at
her eyes with a linen kerchief. "That's my husband
over there, the one in blue, conversing with
your...Indian." She nodded toward a squat man in a
pale blue doublet, one of a score of guests who stood
around the savage, plying him with questions.

Rowena studied the savage covertly through the
haze of her mourning veil. He had done himself credit
at the banquet, quietly imitating the table manners of
the other guests. But now she sensed his constraint
was beginning to crumble. He stood at bay against
one of the poles that supported the pavilion, looking
for all the world like a tethered eagle beset by a
swarm of gulls. His desire to fly was so strong, so
tangible, that Rowena, who knew him so well, could
sense it easily across the distance.

His appearance was truly majestic. Rowena had
personally chosen the simple leather doublet with a
white linen shirt beneath, worn with breeches and
hose of fine dark brown wool. He had balked at the
velvet cap she'd selected, finally agreed to wear the
thing, then promptly lost it. His leonine head, with its

gleaming mane of blue-black hair, rose above the crowd, the tattooed line of flying birds emblazoned across his forehead. He was as regal as any monarch, and Rowena felt her heart swell with pride whenever she looked at him.

But had she done the right thing, bringing the savage out into society? Had her bold act saved him, or, in the end, would it only compound his miseries?

"My dear, have you heard a word I've been saying?" Lady Osgood's sharp voice jerked Rowena's thoughts out of their reverie. "I was commenting on what a ferocious-looking creature that Indian of yours is. Those strange tattoos—and those untamed eyes! Quite uncivilized, the way he looks directly at you, as if he could see right through your clothes!"

"I think he's delicious!" A woman about Rowena's age, her belly big with child, had joined the conversation. "All the girls are atwitter over him! Look at those shoulders! Why he makes our English gentlemen look like a flock of strutting pigeons! If I were single again and not swollen like an overripe plum, I'd be hot after him myself!"

"Really, Arabella!" Lady Osgood huffed. "I'd be fearful for my virtue around such a creature!"

"With all respect, my lady, virtue is valued far too highly!" Arabella giggled and patted her tummy. "I, for one, miss mine not at all! And with such a man..." She gazed at the savage with undisguised lust.

Lady Osgood huffed her disapproval and turned to Rowena. "What a fortunate thing you had Master Bosley nearby to protect you! And his charming sister! How blessed you were, my dear, to have them appear like angels at your time of greatest need!''

"Yes,'' Rowena muttered absently. Her gaze flickered toward Sibyl, who was holding court under the far side of the pavilion, surrounded by callow young bloods who hung on every word that issued from her dainty, heart-shaped mouth. The bored expression on her face was visible even from a distance. Clearly she had hoped for richer pickings. A dozen yards away Bosley had been cornered by the doctor's wife, a plump, gushy woman who never seemed to stop talking. As her chatter washed over him, his glowering eyes scanned the crowd, darting furtively from Sibyl to the savage, then to Rowena, who pretended to not notice.

Bosley had been in a foul temper since the revelation that the party was little more than a ruse to free the savage. He had stormed and sulked, threatening to have the affair canceled, but Sibyl had been adamant—everything had already been arranged, the invitations delivered, the food ordered, the musicians paid half their fee. There was going to be a party whether he liked it or not.

Whatever was going through Bosley's mind, Rowena knew it would be ugly and dangerous. Aye, he had been far too silent today. Too docile. Too resigned.

And Sibyl—was her manner too cheerful? Her eyes too desperately bright? Was the whole heretofore pleasant gathering about to explode like a powder keg with a smoldering fuse?

Extricating herself none too skillfully from the conversation with the two women, Rowena edged closer to the group of men who clustered around the savage. These, she noted gratefully, were the very ones she had hoped would take an interest in him—wealthy traders, scholars and noblemen who wished to profit from the vast, untapped wealth of the New World.

"You say your people own no land, Master Savage?" a baron with large holdings in Cornwall asked incredulously. "How is that possible?"

The savage glanced down at him and spoke as one might speak to a backward child. "Can a man own the sky or the rain?" he asked. "Can he own the moon or the sun? The earth is our mother. For a man to say that any part of her belongs to him and no one else—" He shrugged, implying that the very idea was ridiculous. It was an honest answer, she knew. But her heart sank as she noticed the avaricious glints in the eyes of some of the men. All that land, and no one claiming to own it!

"Would your people be open to trade?" a merchant asked.

"What kind of trade?" The savage raised one ink-black eyebrow.

"Say, furs, for example. Your people trap beaver and mink. They give us the pelts and we give them things they can use—blankets, dishes, bolts of cloth."

"I know what trade is. But my people have all they need," the savage replied. "What would they do with cloth and dishes?"

"Do your people believe in God?" a local vicar cut in before the merchant could respond. "Would they be open to accepting baptism in the name of the Father, the Son and the Holy Ghost?"

The savage frowned. "We believe in a great spirit

and in other spirits, as well. Could it be that your gods are the same, only called by different names? As for your baptism, why should we need something we do so well without?"

"Humph!" The vicar's ruddy face deepened in hue. "Where do you stand on the doctrine of original sin?"

The savage looked puzzled, and the vicar hastily retraced his steps. "What do your people view as mortal sins?" he asked, speaking each word slowly and loudly this time.

"Sin?" Sunlight glinted on the savage's long, black hair as he shook his head. "I am sorry, but I do not know the word. If you would explain—"

"Listen one and all!" Sibyl had broken away from her ring of gangling suitors to resume her duties as unofficial hostess. "Time for the archery contest! The target is set up on the moor, and we've spare bows aplenty for any man without his own. The winner claims a kiss from the lady of his choice!"

Rowena felt the dampness of sweat beneath her somber dress as relief swept over her. It would have been unthinkable to not invite the vicar to this gathering, but he was a fanatical man, apt to make too much of John Savage's heathen state. He might have felt it his duty to press for immediate conversion and baptism, a crusade that would have run headlong into the savage's stubborn contempt for the white man's religion.

"Do you shoot?" The baron had fallen into step beside the savage. "I hear your people are remarkably skilled with the long bow."

"Aye. I shoot."

"Then by all means, join us," said the baron. "There are spare bows and arrows on that rack. Take your pick."

Rowena saw the savage's interest quicken as he strode toward the wooden rack, selected a long bow and strung it with an easy twist of his hands. As he tested its strength, the words came back to Rowena, striking her like the blow of a mailed fist.

... a weapon? Even a knife? Can you get me something, Rowena?

She gulped back the urge to cry out as he selected four arrows, his eyes checking the straightness of each shaft, his fingers touching the deadly sharpness of each barbed steel point. Dear heaven, she'd thought she knew this man. But the time in the cellar had changed him. What would he do with a deadly weapon in his hand? Rowena already knew the answer to that question. And she knew that if he succeeded, he would end his life at the end of a hangman's rope.

Somehow she had to stop him.

A shouted warning would be premature, even dangerous. She could only watch, her heart in her throat, as the savage made his final choice of arrows, and then, with the weapons lightly balanced, strode with a terrible, panther-like grace toward the group of competitors.

Black Otter stood back and watched as the first man stepped up to the line, drew back his bow and aimed his arrow at the painted circle. Such contests were nothing new to him. Lenape warriors enjoyed testing their skills in much the same way. But why was the target so large and placed such a short distance away? In Lenapehoken this would be a contest for small boys, not for men!

The bow felt solid against his palm, the string satisfactorily taut. It was not so strong or fine as the bows made by his own people, but the arrows were amazing, their razor-sharp steel heads far superior to the points the Lenape chipped from flint. Black Otter's imagination took wing and soared. If his people had such arrows, and if they had horses to carry them wherever they wished...

But no—he wrenched his thoughts back to earth. It would be foolish to change the ways of his people too swiftly. There was no way of knowing how a change meant for good could, in the end, lead to disaster.

Black Otter turned his attention back to the bow. He had no doubt that it was strong enough to drive a steel-headed arrow deep into the wooden target—or, if need be, through the chest of a man. It would be a useful weapon, if he could manage to keep it.

He had long since made up his mind to slip away from the festivities and make his escape. Unfortunately, since his release from the cell that morning he had been constantly surrounded by white people. Their rancid odors, pointing fingers, chattering voices and staring eyes had triggered a rage akin to panic in him. Only the reminder that he was a Lenape warrior, expected to endure all things, kept him from shoving them aside and bolting for the peace of the open moor.

Bosley's three ugly watchdogs were there, as well, the stoutest one with his broken wrist still encased in

splinted wrappings. Black Otter sensed their eyes on
him as he toyed with the bow, testing the balance of
rigidity and give that lent it strength. Bosley was
watching him as well, his badger-like eyes glittering
with ill-disguised fear. Aye, the man was no fool. He
knew.

How easy would it be to simply turn, send the
death arrow into Bosley's chest, and then escape in
the melee that followed? The odds would be against
him, Black Otter knew. But at least, whatever the final
outcome, he would be leaving Rowena safe and free.

His eyes found her on the fringe of the crowd,
shrouded like a ghost in the veil that she wore pub-
licly as a sign of mourning for her father. The sight
of her, so alone and, like him, so ill at ease in the
noisy crowd, stirred an ache of longing in him. If this
were Lenapehoken instead of England he would make
her his woman. She would share his lodge, his bed
and his life as he surrounded her with his strength
and with the happy laughter of their children—children who would be as beautiful and brave and intelligent as their mother.

The dream caught him for an instant—lying on the
furs beside the glowing fire with Rowena in his arms,
her skin naked against his own, his love filling her,
warming her...

But no— He brought himself up short. This was
England, not Lenapehoken, and as for Rowena, he
was nothing but a burden and a danger to her. The
only thing within his power to give her was the death
of the man who had made her life a waking nightmare.

Could he escape? Perhaps. He would be hunted,

surely, but by now he knew every path, stream, wood
and hollow of the surrounding countryside. And he
knew about the hidden sea cave, Rowena's cave,
where he might be able to hide until the furor faded
enough for him to make his way to the docks by night
and hire onto an outbound ship.

"Master Savage, 'tis your turn to shoot." Black
Otter felt a tentative nudge from the man behind him
and realized that a silence had fallen over the crowd.
Everyone was watching him, waiting.

Taking his time, he selected an arrow, fitted notch
to string, then paused. Should he kill Bosley now or
send the arrow flashing to the center of the target?
Winning such a contest would mean nothing, and as
for the foolish prize... A wry smile tugged at a corner
of Black Otter's taut mouth. He would never humiliate Rowena by kissing her in public. So why waste
a precious arrow on a kiss when he could strike now,
boldly and surely, for her freedom?

Outwardly he appeared as calm as a frozen lake in
winter, but his pulse thundered in his ears as he
glanced back to check Bosley's whereabouts, then
raised the bow to shoulder level. If no one moved, he
would have a clear shot at the man. First he would
aim at the target, then, with one swift motion, he
would swing the bow around, release the deadly arrow and make his escape.

His peripheral vision caught the image of Rowena
standing among the crowd of watchers. Her mourning
veil had blown back, revealing wide eyes in a pale,
worried face. Had she guessed what he would do?
Never mind, it would be over in a few heartbeats. He

would be gone and she would be free. It was the last, best thing he could do for her.

I love you, Black Otter whispered silently. Then he turned his full attention to the task.

Once more he glanced backward to make certain Bosley was in his place, fully exposed and unaware. Then slowly, quivering with tension, he drew back the bowstring. *Now!* his nerves screamed. *Do it now!*

His body swung the bow toward Bosley, but then, before he could release the arrow, the air was shattered by the most unearthly cry Black Otter had ever heard.

The cry was birdlike in its shrillness, the voice barely discernible as a woman's. When Black Otter, with everyone else, jerked his gaze in the direction of the sound, he saw that it was Rowena. She had fallen to the ground where she lay, rigid and staring, her lovely face contorted, her limbs thrashing and jerking spasmodically.

The crowd had closed in front of Bosley, but Black Otter had forgotten him. It took all his strength of will to keep from running to Rowena and gathering her in his arms. Others could, and would help her, he reminded himself harshly. His touch, in this public place, would only expose her to shame and ridicule.

People pressed close as Rowena continued to jerk and twitch. Black Otter recognized the symptoms of the falling sickness, which sometimes came upon his own people. But how could that be? Rowena had never shown signs of suffering from such an affliction, nor had she mentioned it to him. The sight of her now seemed somehow unreal, like a scene from a nightmare.

"Lapich knewel!" Her tortured voice screamed the words—puzzling words until the truth struck him—she had just cried out in Lenape.

Suddenly he realized what was happening. This wild and audacious performance was Rowena's gift to him—a ruse to create the distraction he needed to escape. In a language only the two of them would recognize, she was telling him everything he needed to know.

She was telling him goodbye.

A swift glance around the crowd confirmed that everyone's eyes were on Rowena. Black Otter paused for an instant, his heart bursting with love and gratitude. *"Lapich knewel,"* he whispered. Farewell, my rescuer, my heart, my life.

Moving with long, easy strides that would not draw suspicion, he made for the corner of the house and slipped out of sight. The way was clear except for an elderly man hurrying from the direction of the outdoor privy behind the stable. Distracted by the noises coming from the archery field, the arthritic old fellow hobbled past Black Otter without a glance. Holding his breath, Black Otter sauntered past him, then, with the old man safely out of sight, he made for the stable.

Flattened against one sheltering wall, he took a moment to collect his thoughts. A horse perhaps—he would not want to take one of Rowena's precious animals, but the guests had left plenty of others hobbled and grazing in the pasture. Mounted, he could travel far and fast. His gaze swept over the score of horses clustered beyond the fence as he weighed the possibilities. No, he concluded, taking a horse would not be wise. Horses were noisy, unpredictable creatures, and his escape would require the utmost stealth. He would be better off taking his chances on foot.

He was slipping past the rear door of the stable when he remembered the knife—the small one, so exquisitely sharp, that he had lost in the straw during the fight with Bosley's thugs. Such a knife would serve him well, as both a tool and a weapon. If the stable boys hadn't swept the floor and discovered it, the knife could still be there, buried by scuffling feet. He would take a few precious seconds, no more, to look for it.

The familiar odors stole over him as he entered the stable. With all the horses out to pasture, the place was so quiet he could hear the rustle of a mouse in the hay. Long fingers of sunlight poked down through the thatch, making a bright patchwork pattern on the floor, and he saw at once that the straw was dusty and matted, as if it had not been changed in many days.

Hopeful now, he found the spot where he had stood against Bosley and his thugs. The straw was still spattered with blood from the shoulder wound he had suffered in the fight. Surely, then, the knife would still be here.

Dropping to a crouch he ran a cautious hand through the straw, mindful of the sharp blade. Finding nothing, his fingers became bolder, more desperate. He groped a wider field, scattering straw in his haste. But the knife was nowhere to be found and he was running out of time.

"Well, what have we here?" The laughing, feminine voice, emerging from the far end of the stable, nearly stopped his heart. Black Otter's head jerked up, his dazzled eyes staring at the delicate figure who stood in the open doorway, silhouetted against the blazing sunlight.

"We appear to have come full circle," *Sangwe* said. "You. Me. This place. But what's this, Master Savage? Why aren't you at the archery contest, winning a kiss from that long-faced Rowena? Don't tell me you're thinking of leaving us so soon!"

Without taking her eyes off him, she closed the door behind her and slid the bolt. Now that the glare was gone he could see *Sangwe* more clearly. Her face wore a cold, sly smile, and her hands carried a small riding whip. Her fingers toyed with it as she spoke.

"How clever of Rowena, staging that fit so you could slip away unnoticed. But neither of you counted on little Sibyl. I've got you, Master Savage. Now all I have to do is scream, and you'll be back in that cell before you can say cheese and biscuits! And don't think you can silence me with one of those arrows! By the time you draw your bow, I'll have made enough noise to summon every able-bodied man in half a league. You'll be caught and hanged on the spot!"

"What do you want?" He edged backward toward the rear door, which stood slightly ajar.

"What do you think?" Her laughter rang out in the darkness of the stable. "I said I'd have you on your knees before me one day, and so I shall. But this time it will be for my pleasure alone, not for yours. Put the bow and arrows down. Now."

Tensely Black Otter complied. He had no doubt that *Sangwe* would carry out her threat to scream for help. And what then? Could he outrun—or even outride—a mob of mounted men, horses and dogs in hot pursuit?

"Come here," she teased, lifting her skirts. "Right here on your knees, Master Savage. And while your tongue is giving me pleasure I shall punish you with this little whip on your back. Who knows, you may find you like such punishment. The Duke of Buckingham loved it!"

Black Otter hesitated, weighing his choices. Should he meet her demands or simply turn and go, leaving her to do her worst? Both courses were fraught with peril.

"What are you waiting for?" she demanded, pouting like a spoiled child. "Now! On your knees, Savage, or I start—"

A sudden pounding on the door interrupted her words. "Sibyl!" Bosley's voice thundered through the thick wooden planks. "Don't play games with me, I know you're in there, and not alone! Now open this door before I force my way in and break your whoring little neck!"

For an instant Sibyl turned toward the door, distracted. That was all the time Black Otter needed. With the speed of a bounding puma he was out the rear door of the stable, running as only a Lenape could run—running for his freedom and his life.

Rowena lay on a quilt in the shade of the pavilion, surrounded by clucking women and doing her best to look pale and exhausted. The exhaustion was real. She had carried on her energetic performance for as long as she dared, inwardly praying the whole time that the savage would have the good sense, and the good luck, to get away while he could.

Beneath the layers of anxiety, grief lay like a heavy weight in her heart. Heaven willing, she would never see her savage again. He would be free to sign onto a ship and, perhaps one day, find his way home. Whatever the final sum of her dreary life, she would never forget him or stop praying for his safety and happiness. *"Lapich knewel,"* she whispered. "Farewell and Godspeed, my dearest love."

As she lay with a damp linen cloth across her forehead, her half-closed eyes searched the crowd around her. She did not see the savage, praise heaven, but Bosley was there at the fringe of the crowd, a long red welt marring his left cheek. At the sight of that mark Rowena's throat tightened in a spasm of fear. Something had gone wrong. But what?

As if in answer to her question, a rending scream shattered the air. It had come from the direction of the stable.

Abandoning all pretense, Rowena clambered to her feet.

"My dear, you mustn't get up so soon!" Lady Osgood protested, but Rowena was already plunging toward the sound of the screams, pushing aside all hands that reached out to hold her back.

The stable, though not far, seemed an endless distance away as she ran, her limbs churning, stretching impotently like the motion of a runner in a nightmare. An eternity seemed to pass before she came around the house and saw the woman who had screamed in such terror. It was Bessie, the cook. She was standing outside with two of the guests, sobbing hysterically.

"Bessie!" Rowena sprinted into the stable yard, her heart pounding. "What is it? What's happened?"

"Ah, mistress!" The woman's jowly face was ashen. "Lor', don't go into that stable! Thee mustn't look, mustn't see—"

But Rowena was already rushing past her, flinging the door wide.

For the first moment her sun-dazzled eyes saw only shadows. Then, there on the stable floor, she saw what Bessie had seen.

Sibyl lay sprawled faceup in the dirty straw, her skirts bunched around her hips, her bare legs awkwardly spread. Her head lay oddly twisted on the ivory column of her neck, the lips gray, the eyes open, staring, lifeless.

Next to her body lay a bow and three arrows—the same weapons the savage had selected for the archery contest.

Chapter Sixteen

Darkening clouds as fine as cobwebs streaked across the deep night sky. Where they veiled the face of the waning moon, pools of inky shadow moved like living creatures over the silvery moor. The long grasses waved and rippled, stirred by a lusty wind that smelled sharply of rain.

Laden with a rolled quilt and a pillowcase stuffed with food from the pantry, Rowena crept out through the kitchen door and closed it stealthily behind her. Scarcely daring to breathe, she stole along the side of the house, breaking into the open only where she knew she could not be seen from any of the windows.

Beneath the shadowed eave of the barn she rested a moment, her breath coming in tense gasps. The wind whipped her long, loose hair across her face as she glanced back toward the house to make certain all was quiet.

The horror of the afternoon still haunted her, rank with the memory of Sibyl lying broken and violated on the dirty straw. Bosley had raved like a madman all afternoon and evening. To avoid being alone with him, Rowena had kept with the guests and servants while she could. Then as the house emptied she had bolted herself inside the sanctuary of her chamber while he'd raged and stormed outside the door.

"The devil's own curse be on that filthy, rutting savage! The curse be on your father for bringing him here, and on you for staging that ridiculous banquet and pulling Sibyl into it. You used her, you conniving witch! You used us all to get that murdering animal out of the cellar, and now look what's happened!"

Rowena had pressed against the wall, trembling in spite of herself as he'd ranted, swore and pounded on the door. The man was an accomplished actor, she knew, and likely a murderer, as well. But her own role in the tragedy added a sting to his words. If she had not manipulated Sibyl into helping with the party, perhaps the poor woman would still be alive.

What had really happened out there in the stable? Rowena's churning mind had conjured up and discarded one idea after another. Had Bosley murdered Sibyl in a jealous rage? Had he lured the savage into the stable to frame him? Had he stolen or found the bows and arrows? Only one certainty loomed like a rock out of the murky sea of speculation—she had to find the savage.

The swelling wind lashed her gown as she stumbled along the path that skirted the cliffs. The distance from the house to the sea cave was more than a mile, and it would have been far easier to take a horse. But a mounted rider could be seen and heard much more readily than a woman on foot, and tonight secrecy was vital to her mission.

Would the savage be there? Rowena had no way

of knowing. Only instinct, spurred by hope, drove her now through the gathering storm—the same instinct that told her John Savage could not possibly be a murderer.

Below the path, the sea flung itself wildly against the rocks, the impact sending up drops of salt spray that Rowena could taste on her lips. A flash of lightning revealed, just ahead, the cleft that marked the entrance to the hidden cave. It was so close that, in her blind haste, she could have easily stepped over the edge and fallen into the sea.

The descent to the cave would be perilous, especially in the tearing wind. But she had no other choice if she wanted to find the savage. Even if he was there, and even if she shouted at the top of her lungs, he would never hear her over the sound of the waves and the wind.

And what if he was not there? What then?

Rowena thrust the question from her mind as she tucked her bundle beneath a sheltering rock and, hands free, began the downward climb. The cliff was wet with sea spray, every shift in position fraught with unknown peril. Far below she could hear the waves, hissing and snapping, clawing at the cliff as if daring her to fall.

Inch by inch, wind ripping at her skirts, she moved down and across the ledge. The way had seemed so easy when she was a child. Tonight it was an exercise in terror. Her wet slipper groped for the last toehold before the drop to the cave entrance. Where was it? She could not—

A cry burst from her throat as she lost her hold and plunged downward. She could feel the sea reaching up to take her, then, at the last possible second, strong hands caught her wrists, swinging her upward, into the safety of the cave.

"Oh—" She gasped as the savage pulled her into the haven of his arms. Unable to say more, she simply clung to him, losing herself in the warm strength of his body, the hard rasp of his breathing and the drumming of his heart against her ear. "Thank heaven, you're safe!" she whispered, finding her voice at last. "Oh, I feared I would never again see you in this life!"

He lifted her face in the darkness, his fingertip tracing the contour of her cheek, her jaw, her mouth. Catching his hand she turned it and pressed her lips into the hollow of his palm, as if to leave the imprint of her kiss there forever.

"They were all out there looking for you today," she said, still out of breath. "The men with their horses and dogs. I knew you had to be here. Otherwise they'd have found you."

"I heard them. They passed up there, on the cliff, before my false trail led the dogs away."

Rowena nodded, her head nested against his collarbone. Once, on the moor, he had shown her the trick of doubling back on one's own trail to throw off pursuers. That trick had served him well today.

"They'd have hanged you if you'd been caught," she said. "Your bow and arrows were found in the stable. Everyone thinks you killed her."

"Killed her?" He had gone rigid.

"Aye. Killed Sibyl." She told him what had happened. He listened as she described the scene in the stable. His honest surprise and dismay only strength-

ened her certainty that he'd had nothing to do with
the murder.

"And you, Rowena?" he asked when she had finished. "Do you believe I did this thing?"

"No." She shook her head vehemently. "It was
Bosley. It had to be."

"He was there, outside the door." The savage told
her about looking for the knife, about Sibyl and the
whip. Rowena listened in horror, remembering the
welt on Bosley's cheek.

"I heard him and I ran," the savage said. "I left
the bow and the arrows. But the knife—there was no
time to find it."

"The knife would not have been there," Rowena
said sadly. "After Bosley's men took you that day, I
found it and put it back in my father's laboratory. If
I'd trusted you to have it, there'd have been no need
for you to go into the stable." She gazed up at him.
"So much of this is my fault. Can you ever forgive
me?"

"Forgive you?" His muscles hardened beneath her
touch. Sensing the tension in his body, she braced
herself for an outburst of anger.

"Forgive you?" His voice was like thick, rough
velvet. He gripped her shoulders, his gaze burning
through the darkness. Outside, lightning forked across
the horizon. The sea crashed violently against the
rocks, shooting white spray up the side of the cliff.
But here, inside the cave, it was so quiet that Rowena
could hear the frantic pounding of her own heart.

"John, please," she whispered.

"Not John Savage—never again. My name is
Black Otter." He glared down at her for the space of

a long breath—then suddenly caught her close, his arms crushing her against his chest, his mouth seeking, devouring her own.

"Forgive you?" The words rasped between kisses. "You are my life, Rowena... You are my heart, my spirit...I live because of what you give me..."

Her clasping hands caught his hair, tangling in its rich, thick blackness as she pulled him down to her. The heat that had been smoldering in her from the moment she touched him burst into sudden, searing flame. She wanted his hands on her breasts—no, sweet heaven, she wanted them everywhere; his lips, everywhere, on every part of her body. She wanted to have all of him, here now...as she would never have him again.

A flash of lightning flooded the cave with blue-white light. Thunder crashed across the roiling sky as the rain began to fall, streaming like a curtain over the rocky entrance. Only then did Rowena remember the bundle of provisions she had brought with her.

"What is it?" he asked, his lips brushing her temple.

"Up there—I left some things for you. No, wait, don't go now. It's too dangerous—"

But he was already swinging upward, moving with strength and sureness in spite of the streaming rain and slippery rocks. Rowena stood looking up at the spot where he had disappeared, feeling suddenly cold and alone. It would be like this after he had gone, she thought, only a thousand times more devastating. How would she build a new life for herself, knowing that the man who had filled her lonely soul with love was gone forever?

She would have nothing except the memory of their time together unless, heaven willing…

Warm color suffused her face as she pondered the new possibility. The rightness of it filled her like a song. Aye, perhaps, with the help of nature and providence, there was a way to keep and hold a part of her love forever.

Aching with anticipation she waited for him to return.

Black Otter tucked the rolled quilt and the bag of provisions under his arm, sheltering it from the rain while he stood for a moment, gazing out over the ocean. He remembered the first time he had stood on these cliffs, the sense of hopelessness that had swept over him as he saw the watery barrier that separated him from his homeland. Now he saw the sea differently, not so much as an obstacle as a path—the only path his heart could rightly follow.

Somewhere beyond those restless gray waters his people waited. His children waited. The way would be long and dangerous, with many false twists and turns, but it was open. He had gained enough knowledge of the white man's ways to get him onto the deck of a ship. Nothing could stop him from leaving now.

Nothing…

An aching tightness rose in his throat as he thought of Rowena waiting for him below. Her love had given him strength and life. How could he leave her? How could he send her back to deal with Bosley and all the other dangers at the manor? And how could he face the days and seasons to come, knowing he had held her in his arms for the last time?

Balancing the bundle on his shoulder he eased his way down the cliff. He had no choice except to go, he reminded himself harshly. At first light, dogs and horsemen would be combing the moors for him. If they captured him, he would end his life with a rope around his neck, just like the man at the crossroads. Even if he chose to stay, his presence could only implicate Rowena in the crime. The longer he stayed, the more dangerous it would be for them both.

The storm would be the measure of the time he and Rowena had left, he resolved. When it ended they would go their separate ways. Their farewell would tear out his heart.

He climbed steadily downward, his strong limbs and fingers supporting the weight of his body. As he dropped to the floor of the cave where Rowena was waiting, another lightning bolt split the sky. They held each other close as the thunder boomed around them. There was no question of what would happen next. They were safely alone, trapped by the storm, and her every touch told him that her desire burned as hot as his own.

"There's a candle and a flint in the bag," she whispered. "Let me light it. I want to fill my eyes with you."

He unrolled the quilt and spread it on the dry floor at the back of the cave. When she struck the flint and lit the candle, the soft yellow glow made their shadows dance on the rough stone walls. Tendrils of Rowena's damp chestnut hair caught the light, framing her face in warm radiance. She had never looked happier or more beautiful.

"Wendaxa," he murmured. "Come here. I want to touch you. All of you."

They undressed each other slowly, savoring each touch, each sweet new discovery. Black Otter was grateful Rowena had left off the body-constricting corset and petticoats she so often wore. Her damp gown and chemise fell away under his eager hands. She lowered her eyes, trembling as he marveled over the petal softness of her skin, the ripe, perfect breasts, their nipples as pink as wild spring raspberries. She moaned out loud as he bent and kissed them, brushing them with his tongue until the puckering sensation quivered downward into the warm, pulsing core of her need.

His own body held few surprises for her. She had nursed him as he lay nearly naked, burning with fever. But she had never known him like this. Her touch was tender, almost reverent, as she ran a fingertip along the scar that crossed his flank. "My warrior," she whispered, her fingers growing bolder. "My Lord Savage…"

She gasped as her fingers found his aroused manhood, exploring, then fiercely clasping him. How could something be so petal-soft, yet as hard as steel? "Do I surprise you?" he asked, gazing down at her. "Your eyes are like a child's."

"Then make me a woman." She strained closer to him. "Leave me with your child, Black Otter, that is the only parting gift I would ask of you."

His eyes darkened. "Such a gift can only be given

by the great spirit,'' he murmured, moved almost to tears. "But we will ask, as a man and woman ask..."

Sweeping her up in his arms he lowered her to the blanket. She lay beneath him, quivering with need as he loomed above her, so beautiful in the golden light. Beautiful, as surely their child would be. He was her savage, her only love. "Now," she whispered, her body wet and throbbing. "Please..."

He brushed one swollen nipple with the tip of his tongue. "Soon, my heart," he murmured, tracing a line of nibbling kisses down her belly. "Soon..."

His fingers hovered lightly above the soft nest at the joining of her thighs. He was barely touching her, but the anticipation sent a hot ache surging upward through the needy core of her, so that when he began to stroke her she exploded beneath his hand. Her eyes closed as the sensation took her. Her head lashed back and forth on the quilt. Sweet heaven, she wanted him—every part of him—the taste of rain and sea spray on his skin, the searching fingers, the tender, teasing mouth...

Candlelight flickered on his golden body as he leaned above her, his black eyes liquid with tenderness. "I love you," she whispered as he glided into her so smoothly that she scarcely felt the slight tearing. She was lost in the wonder of their joining, the heaven of his body filling her, the powerful male thrusts, each one carrying her to new heights of ecstasy. Her legs clasped him close, binding him to her as they soared together like two falcons, up, up until they passed beyond the limits of the sky and became one.

* * *

"When will you go?" she whispered as they lay in each other's arms, listening to the drizzle of the rain and the shattering of the waves against the cliff.

"As soon as it is safe. But you must leave when the storm ends." His arms tightened around her. "No one must see you near this place."

She nodded wordlessly and buried her face in the hollow of his shoulder, filling her senses with the warm, salty aroma of his skin, wishing she could freeze time right here and spend the rest of eternity in his arms.

"How can I leave you like this, my heart," he whispered, "alone here, with no one to protect you?"

"Hush." Her finger touched his lips. "Bosley wants Thornhill Manor. If anything happens to me, the property will revert to the Crown. He may threaten me, but my life will be safe enough. And meanwhile I will fight Edward Bosley in my own way, with the power of English law. The man will pay for all he's done, never fear."

And pay he would, she vowed. An idea had come to her as she'd crossed the moor on her way to the sea cave. An old friend and former suitor of her mother was now a respected judge, living in Plymouth. She would make the journey there and beg his help for the sake of her mother's memory. With luck, especially if she could bring evidence against Bosley, the judge would open his home to her and guide her to an able lawyer who would take her case. Otherwise she would find her own lodgings and hire the best lawyer she could find on her own. Either way she would need the only resource left to her, her mother's jewels.

But there would be time enough for planning when she was alone. Now, while she lay beside Black Otter, every moment was precious.

"I worry for you, too," she whispered, her lips brushing his golden skin. "The world can be an evil place, and you have so much to learn."

"I know enough to find work on a ship. The rest..." He shrugged, implying that he would just have to take things as they came.

Rowena held him tightly, tortured by questions. Should she tell him that most ships' captains were unscrupulous rascals who would take every advantage of an innocent man? That his fellow crewmen would challenge and test him again and again? That with the Spanish enemy controlling so much of the New World, his chances of reaching America on anything but a pirate ship were so small as to be nonexistent? No, she decided, there was no time, and the dashing of his hopes would change nothing. He could not remain in England another day.

"If only we could send word to each other," she said, but even as she spoke she knew it was an impossible wish. The savage had learned to speak remarkably good English, but no one had taught him to read or write. Once he was gone, she would never hear from him again.

His arms drew her closer. "Listen," he whispered.

Rowena held her breath, but even then her straining ears heard nothing but the sound of the sea. Then her heart contracted as she realized the rain had stopped.

"No!" she cried, clinging to him. "Not so soon!"

"You must go," he murmured, his hand caressing

her tangled hair, then moving downward to stroke the curve of her bare back. "Be careful. Promise me."

"Aye, I promise." She felt him rise and harden against her, and she prayed there would be a little time left. "But first, may we petition the great spirit once more, as a man and a woman?"

His breath caught in a little gasp of anguish as he drew her into the heaven of his loving.

The sky had begun to clear by the time she left him. The waning moon floated above the western horizon, clear and bright now, etching each grass blade in stark black and silver.

Rowena held her head high, but her eyes were blind with the tears she had held back while she was with him. Their lives would take separate paths now. She would never know if her savage had reached America safely. He would never know if he had given her a child.

She trudged toward the road, willing herself to not look back. If she saw him standing there, at the edge of the cliff, she would never be able to walk away. If she did not see him, her heart would shatter.

He had helped her gently up the face of the cliff. Then they had held each other for a long moment. *"Lapich knewel,"* he had whispered, releasing her. "Farewell, my heart." Too overcome to answer, she had simply turned and stumbled away. It was over.

As she trudged across the moor, the shifting clouds in the east revealed an iridescent gleam, like the inner surface of an abalone shell. Soon it would be the dawn of a new day, a day of decision and change. She had to look ahead, to the tasks that loomed ahead of her—first getting out of the house with the jewelry and some suitable clothing, then saddling a horse and riding like the wind for Plymouth, and after that—

But there was one thing she wanted to do before she went into the house. It sprang into her mind as she saw, just ahead, the moonlit copse where the falcons were kept.

The kestrel's small pen stood open and empty. Only the gyrfalcon was here now. Young Will had been caring for the bird, cleaning its pen, changing its water bowl, and bringing it mice from the stable. But the great silver bird had not been taken out to hunt since the terrible day when the kestrel had died and Bosley's thugs had taken the savage prisoner.

Rowena heard the gyrfalcon stirring as she slipped the thick glove off its hook and thrust it onto her left hand. Its cry, a harsh *kek, kek, kek,* echoed through the trees as she unlatched the door and reached behind the bird, allowing it to step back onto her gloved fist. Catching the leather jesses with her thumb, she found the tiny plumed hood and slipped it deftly over the falcon's head.

The next part would be the most difficult. Working mostly by feel, she pulled and twisted the jesses loose from the leg bands, first one, then the other, until the falcon sat untethered on her fist, restrained only by the hood over its eyes.

Carefully she removed the hood. The great bird shifted on the glove, hesitating for an instant. Then its powerful wings began to beat, and it soared upward with the speed of an arrow. The falcon was free, just as Black Otter was free.

Only she remained earthbound.

Rowena's eyes followed the falcon's flight as it circled higher, a speck of white against the darkly iridescent dawn sky. *"Lapich knewel,"* she whispered, echoing Black Otter's farewell to her. "Godspeed."

Gulping back the lump in her throat she turned once more toward the house. Bosley had been drinking the night before. With luck he would still be in his chamber, dead to the world. But she would not breathe easily until she was well away from this place.

In the dim light, her tear-blurred eyes failed to see the root in her path. She stumbled forward, and would have gone sprawling if a pair of large, thick hands had not caught her elbows from behind.

A scream caught in her throat as she tore loose and spun sharply around, her hands raised to strike and claw at any attacker.

But the tall, bulky figure that loomed against the morning light did not attack. He merely stood his ground, arms hanging at his side, staring at her with the innocent eyes of a child.

Chapter Seventeen

"Dickon!" Rowena's knees weakened with relief at the sight of the simple young man.

"Mistress?" He blinked at her, his gaze as bland as an infant's.

"You startled me, Dickon. What are you doing here at this hour?"

"Walking. I see things when there's no one about. Birds. Hares. Why did you let the falcon go, mistress?"

"It was time for the falcon to go home." Rowena gave him a sad smile. "Why haven't I seen you at the house?"

Dickon's gaze dropped to his brogans. A lock of wheaten hair tumbled over his low, flat forehead but he did not reply.

"Something frightened you? Was it Master Savage?" she asked, remembering his ordeal in the cellar.

Dickon's only response was the tightening of his mouth and the dogged thrust of his lower lip.

"Well, no matter. Come up to the house with me,"

she said, thinking it might be a good idea to have him with her. "It's a bit early for Bessie to be about, but we can surely find you some leftover pie in the pantry." Then, seeing his hesitant look, she added, "There's nothing to fear. Master Savage is gone from this place, never to return." Speaking the words twisted the knife in her heart, but they forced one more small degree of acceptance.

"Come, now." She tugged at his limp arm. "The savage is gone, I tell you. There's no one about the place but a few servants and Master Bosley, and after so much drink last night, he's more than likely—"

She broke off as she saw Dickon's pale blue eyes widen in stark terror. He took a step backward, as if he were about to bolt like a terrified animal. Only then did she remember when and where she had last seen him. It had been at her father's bedside on the day of Sir Christopher's death.

She gripped his wrist so hard that her fingernails made crimson moons in his flesh. "What did you see in my father's chamber?" Her voice rasped with urgency. "Tell me, Dickon! You must!"

He was trembling now, tears trickling down his baby-pink cheeks. "'Twas Master Bosley. 'E and the old master, they were quarrelin', carryin' on somethin' fierce. You'd told me to stay in the room, but I was afraid, mistress, so I 'id behind the curtain." He wiped his streaming eyes, struggling to control himself. "They fought some more, and then Master Bosley, 'e took a pillow, and shoved it down on the old master's face. Oh, mistress, I wanted to 'elp your father, but I was afraid...so afraid—" He broke into blubbering sobs.

"There…" Rowena stroked the heaving shoulders, reeling inwardly as she imagined the horror of what Dickon had witnessed and the fear that had kept him from going to Sir Christopher's aid. But this was no time to relive what could not be changed, she reminded herself. Her father was gone, and her best hope now was to bring his murderer to justice.

"Listen to me, Dickon!" She seized his plump red hands, gripping them hard. "You've no need to fear. You were right to stay in the room with my father as I ordered. But now there's one last thing you must do for me and for your master. Do you promise you'll do it?"

"Aye, mistress." His fingers trembled in her clasp but his eyes were clear and earnest. "What must I do?"

"Only this. Run and find the constable—Simon Butler. You know where he lives, do you not?"

"Aye. On the mill road, past the 'angin' tree."

"Find him as quickly as you can, and tell him everything you just told me. Then tell him he must come here at once with enough men to capture Bosley and lock him up. Do you understand?"

"Aye." Dickon's cherubic face shone with joy at the chance to redeem himself in Rowena's eyes.

"Then tell him, also, that I believe Bosley killed Mistress Sibyl yesterday. Is that clear?"

"Aye, mistress." He was as eager to please as a puppy. Still she worried as she watched him take to his heels. Would he be clever enough to find the constable? Would he remember all he had to say? Most important of all, would he be believed? She could only hope for the best and trust in divine justice.

Her gaze followed Dickon's flaxen head until it vanished through the trees. As she turned back toward the house, it occurred to her that her desperate war against Edward Bosley could be coming to an end. Meeting Dickon had been an incredible stroke of luck. If her luck continued, she would have little more to do than wait for the constable and his deputies, lead them to Bosley's chamber and stand back while they arrested the murderer in his bed. If Bosley could also be forced to confess to the crime against Sibyl, Black Otter would be cleared. They would both be free.

She stood for a moment beside the empty mews, watching the dawn light creep into the sky and imagining how wonderful that freedom would be. She could race to Falmouth on horseback, arriving in time to stop Black Otter from leaving. Then, when all was in readiness, she could sell the jewels, charter a trustworthy vessel and make the journey with him. The very thought of seeing America, perhaps even building a new life there with the only man she would ever love—

But she was daydreaming now, and this was no time for such foolishness. Any one of a hundred things could go wrong. Dickon could wander off or fail to return with help. Bosley could refute the young man's story—he was, after all, an accomplished actor. Black Otter could be intercepted on his way to Falmouth with no chance to prove his innocence, and, as a man with no rights under English law...

Rowena's hands twisted the folds of her skirt as she battled for self-control. Standing here and thinking of all the awful possibilities, she could go quite mad. She had to act, but not impulsively or recklessly. Now, of all times, it was essential that she plan every move.

What to do next? Ride and find Black Otter? No, if there were searchers about, she could lead them right to him. Better to go inside and see to the safety of the jewels and to her own appearance. Dickon had been too innocent to make anything of her damp, disheveled clothing, her tousled hair and the faint but unmistakable aura of last night's lovemaking. But the constable's men and her own servants would be more observant. If they were to guess she'd spent the night in a cave with the savage, anything could happen.

Rousing herself to action, she strode toward the house. There was no danger in here, she reassured herself. Bosley had been roaring drunk last night, and on similar occasions she had never known him to wake up before noon the next day. As for the servants, aye, they would soon be busy about the place. Bessie could already be bustling about the kitchen preparing breakfast while her helpers brought in fresh milk and eggs from the barn. There would be safety enough in their company until the constable and his men arrived.

And what if the constable did not come?

Rowena thrust the question aside as she skirted the house and entered by the front door where the servants were less likely to see her coming in. She would wash, change her clothing, and wait until the sun was a hand breadth above the horizon. If no one had appeared by then, she would pack the jewelry into a roll beneath her skirts, saddle Blackamoor and ride straightaway for Plymouth and the house of her mother's friend.

As she passed along the side of the great hall, she was struck by the utter silence of the place. She could hear no rattling of pots and pans from the open kitchen, no buzz of conversation or shouting of orders. Even the familiar aromas of steaming porridge and salt pork were absent this morning. Perhaps the servants had overindulged in leftover food and drink after the ill-fated banquet. Well, never mind them. They would be along later, bleary-eyed and sheepish, expecting to be scolded. Right now she had more pressing concerns.

Dismissing a prickle of apprehension, Rowena mounted the stairs on silent feet. All the better the servants weren't about, she told herself. If any of them were to see her, the gossip in the kitchen would be as hot and delicious as Bessie's beef and onion stew.

The corridor was empty, the doors to the chambers and the laboratory all closed as she had left them. Her heart lurched, however, as she slid the key into her own lock, gave it a turn, and realized she had just locked—not unlocked—the door. Could she have forgotten to lock it before stealing out of the house last night? A foolish oversight, but understandable. She had been so worried at the time.

Glancing up and down the corridor once more, she twisted the key in the lock and felt the mechanism click open. Relief washed over her as she turned the knob. Here, at least, she would find a measure of rest before danger and uncertainty came crashing in on her again.

Stepping over the threshold she paused to close the door behind her. Only when she turned forward again did her shocked eyes take in the heart-stopping devastation.

Her entire chamber had been ransacked, the doors torn from the wardrobe, the rear panels smashed, her gowns slashed and strewn on the floor. Drawers and cabinets had been overturned, the contents flung helter-skelter around the room. Her writing desk lay on its side, the drawers splintered as if someone had stomped on them. The inkwell had shattered against the wall, ink spilling like black blood down the whitewashed plaster, speckling the torn writing papers, the destroyed notebooks. Feathers from slashed quilts and pillows floated through the air.

Rowena looked toward the bed, and her breath stopped as if someone had jerked a garrote around her throat.

Edward Bosley lay sprawled facedown on the torn mattress, the clothes he had worn to the banquet stained, rumpled and smelling of stale beer. A blubbering snore escaped his lips as his back rose and fell in the rhythm of deep slumber.

Scattered around him on the bed, like a child's discarded toys, were the pieces of her mother's jewelry, the brooches, the rings, the splendid rope of pearls—everything.

A single garnet, set in a gold ring, glowed like a tiny blood-red sun where it caught a beam of morning light through the open window. Rowena fixed her eyes on it as she fought back a rising tide of panic. Bosley was dead to the world. If she moved swiftly and silently, it would still be possible to snatch up

the jewelry and flee from the house before he awakened.

Holding her breath, she crept to the side of the bed.
Her fingers closed on the garnet ring. Her heart hammered as she slipped it into her pocket and reached
for the filigreed necklace, which lay against Bosley's
inert arm.

As she leaned closer, an image flashed into her
mind—Bosley standing over a helpless, bedridden old
man, taking the pillow, pressing it down, holding
it…holding it. The rage that swept over her was dizzying in its power. Why settle for the jewels when
she could avenge her father's murder here and now?
It would take only a moment to slip into the laboratory next door and find one of Sir Christopher's small
dissecting knives. A single judicious cut to a blood
vessel—she knew exactly which one—and Bosley
would wake up in hell where he belonged.

Rowena hesitated, then drew back, shaking her
head. She was no executioner. All she truly wanted
was justice and freedom for herself and Black Otter.
To secure those things she would need the jewels.

Thrusting everything from her mind but the task at
hand, she reached for the necklace. Her fingers caught
it, tugged at it. Only then, as she felt the slight resistance, did she realize the clasp of the necklace had
caught on a thread of the gold embroidery that dec-
orated Bosley's sleeve. Distracted, she bent closer to
free it.

She was twisting at the clasp when she felt Bosley's huge hand close around her arm.

Black Otter stood at the edge of the wooded hollow, his lithe brown body blending with the leafy

shadows. His eyes scanned the moor, coming to rest yet again on the silent manor house.

He knew it would have been wiser for him to stay in the cave. The sun was already flooding the land with light. Soon mounted men with their keen-nosed dogs would be scouring the land for him, hunting him down like a wild animal. He had long since made up his mind that he would not be taken alive. But his own safety meant nothing when Rowena was in danger.

Restlessly he shifted to a closer vantage point, his gaze never leaving the house. She had assured him that she would be safe, his beautiful, brave Rowena. But she had seemed almost too brave, too certain that all would be well.

Light and shadow flowed across the glistening moor as the sun began to rise. By now the servants should be busy in the barn and the stable, milking the cows, gathering the eggs, turning the horses out to pasture. In the kitchen the cook and her helpers should be scurrying to prepare breakfast, feeding the banked coals of the fire, boiling the porridge, spitting the meat for the midday meal. Smoke should be curling upward from the great stone chimney, its silvery spiral catching the light of the coming day.

Black Otter's eyes narrowed as he studied the house. There was no smoke coming from the chimney, no sign of life anywhere except for a flicker of motion in the window of the room he knew to be Rowena's.

It could have been nothing, he told himself—a trick of light, or a simple movement made by Rowena herself. He waited, hoping to see her face through the glass, measuring time by the beating of his own pulse.

As seconds crawled past and she did not appear, the certainty grew. She was there and she was in trouble.

His danger instincts blazed, exploding into action. Rowena was alone in the house with no protection against a man who had already raped and murdered one woman. The law could not help her. The servants could not help her. Only he, Black Otter, could help her, and if he did not reach her in time he knew she would die.

Heedless of his own safety he broke cover and raced across the open moor, praying to all the spirit powers he would not be too late.

Rowena lay supine on the stripped, slashed mattress, her arms and legs stretched and tied to the bedposts with her own spare stockings. She had fought like a tigress—Bosley's swollen left eye and the bloody scratch marks on his cheeks attested to that. But as they struggled, he had slammed her against the wall with enough force to knock her cold. She had awakened like this, lashed to the bed, with Bosley standing over her, gloating.

"If you have the least bit of common sense, you'll untie these knots right now," she said, clenching her teeth against the pain. "The servants will be along any minute, and they won't take kindly to your treating me this way."

"I gave all the servants the day off," Bosley said. "They're not to come near the place today, on pain of dismissal. And while you were still waking up, I took the liberty of barring all the doors to the house. You see, my dear, I wanted you all to myself."

Rowena glared up at him, masking her fear, knowing her only chance of rescue lay in stalling him until

Dickon could arrive with the constable. "Exactly what do you plan to do with me?" she demanded. "If I die without legal issue, the manor reverts to the Crown. You'll be homeless within the week!"

"A pox on the manor!" His bruised and bleeding face twisted in contempt. "What do I want with this crumbling heap of stones now that Sibyl's gone? It was for her, you big, clumsy cow! All for her!"

Rowena stared up at him, bewildered and suddenly terrified. Only a supreme effort of will kept her voice calm. "Would you care to explain that?"

"It was all for Sibyl, all for her..." He mumbled the phrase as if he had spoken it a hundred times since her death. "When her lover, the Duke of Buckingham, abandoned her for a younger woman, she was lost. She had no money and no place to go. I..." His eyes took on a faraway look. "I had worshiped her for years, and now I saw my only chance. I promised her a fine, permanent home and all the money she required if she would have me as her lover."

"A permanent home? And that was Thornhill Manor?" Rowena forced herself to laugh incredulously. "You were plotting to wed me just so your mistress would have a roof over her head?"

"Not my mistress—she made it clear that I wasn't to touch her until I'd made good on my offer. And in the meantime she forbade me to lie with any other woman—even you—until the manor was lawfully mine."

"But you couldn't live up to your promise, could you?" Rowena taunted, goading him to keep up the narrative.

His small, greenish eyes smoldered with hate. "I thought it would be easy, that you'd welcome a man in your bed, someone who could look after the estate and provide you with an heir. Such a simple thing— I didn't even demand that you love me. But no, you had to go and spoil it all! You and your damned, filthy, rutting savage!''

The silence in the room became dark and heavy. Aye, he would kill her, she realized. And in the end her only satisfaction would lie in the hope that her beloved savage was safe and free.

As he moved toward her, Rowena made haste to speak again. ''Is that why you murdered Sibyl? Because of her and the savage?''

Bosley stopped as if he had walked into a wall. He stared blankly for a moment, then exploded into a paroxysm of rage. ''I kept my vow to her! I was as chaste as a bleeding monk, though it came near to driving me mad! But that little she-cat in heat—she made a game of teasing me about the savage. And yesterday, when I caught them together in the stable...'' Emotion choked off his words. He stared down at his own hands, his shoulders quivering.

''It's finished,'' Rowena said quietly. ''Dickon saw you kill my father. I've sent him for the constable. They should be arriving here at any moment.''

''Dickon? That idiot boy?'' Bosley was swift to recover his aplomb. ''No one will believe a word he says! And even if they do, you know I can talk my way out of it. Nobody can prove I killed anyone, not even you.''

His eyes narrowed. They were predator's eyes now, hard and vicious. Showing fear for the first time, Rowena cringed and began to struggle uselessly against her bonds. He stood over her, a cold smile on his battered face as he dangled a weighted leather pouch before her eyes.

"Imagine this scenario, my sweet Rowena. I leave the doors barred downstairs until after I've taken my pleasure with your body and dispatched you to join your dear, departed father. Then I hide this bag of jewels while I go down to greet the constable and tell him that, unfortunately, you were foolish enough to let the savage take refuge in your chamber, and that sometime around dawn he ravished and murdered you, ransacked the room and made off with whatever suited his heathen fancy."

His hand slid up her bare leg, causing her to writhe in helpless revulsion. He grinned demonically as he tossed the jewels aside and fumbled with his codpiece. "See how simple it is, my dear? Your jewels will buy me a new start anywhere I choose to go. And everything that happens here will be blamed on the sav—"

The rest of Bosley's utterance died in his throat as the window casement behind him burst inward. Glass flew and shattered as Black Otter vaulted into the room.

With the swiftness of an attacking puma he leaped at Bosley, striking him with the full force of both feet. Bosley was a large man, well over twenty stone. The savage's hurtling weight failed to topple him, but it did knock him off balance. He reeled backward, stumbling over a broken drawer and crashing heavily into the wardrobe.

Black Otter was on him in a flash. The savage was unarmed, but the fists that pummeled Bosley's face were brutal, crushing flesh and bone. Rowena twisted and strained against her bonds, desperate to get loose.

Reeling backward, Bosley righted himself, then lowered his head, bellowed like a bull and charged. His weight and momentum shoved the savage backward, all the way to the far end of the room. Black Otter staggered, catching his balance against the door, giving Bosley enough time to yank a long, wicked-looking dagger from the fullness of his sleeve. But instead of attacking the savage with it, he turned and sprang toward Rowena. Seizing her by the hair he pressed the blade to her neck.

"Let's see how brave you are now, you filthy Indian!" he snarled. "One step closer and I slit your doxy's lying, white throat!"

Rowena's head swam with the stench of him—sweat, drink and sickness. Fear rose in her throat. She tasted bile as she fought for self-control. In the shadows beyond the foot of the bed she could see the savage in a half crouch, ready to spring at the first sign of weakness, and she knew that for his sake she could not let her terror show.

"Don't listen to the big bag of wind!" she muttered defiantly. "He was going to kill me anyway— that's what he said. And when he does, he'll have nothing left to protect him from you!"

"Silence, you bitch!" Bosley pressed the knife harder against her jugular vein. She could feel the blade's sharp edge pushing into her tender flesh. He had only to let it glide forward or back and the slight motion would be enough to cut through her skin.

"I think you know what I'm capable of," Bosley said, glancing at Black Otter. "At my own whim, I can choose to let her live or die. More than that—I can choose to kill her swiftly, without pain, or perhaps allow her to live, say, without her nose or her eyes—

though it would be a shame to spoil what little beauty she has. I am my own man, Master Savage, and if you do not obey my orders, I shall do exactly as I please with this woman.''

Black Otter shifted slightly on the balls of his feet. He was still poised for attack but Rowena could sense his hesitation, and she knew that his fear for her would hold him in check. She forced herself to remain motionless as a desperate idea took shape in her mind.

''To the window, Savage,'' Bosley growled. ''You're to leave as you came. And if you survive the way down, without breaking your neck, there'll be a constable's party coming to hang whatever's left of you!''

Black Otter hesitated, then moved toward the shattered window, his eyes avoiding Rowena's. Would he risk her life by attacking, or would he guarantee her death by leaving? Rowena held her breath.

''Go on!'' Bosley snapped. ''Or would you rather watch me take out her left eye? It won't be pretty. Even if I don't kill her, she'll likely bleed to death. Just a simple matter of—''

''Don't believe him!'' Rowena blurted, flinging everything into one desperate gamble. ''The knife isn't real! It's nothing but a stage prop! A toy!''

Bosley started in surprise, dropping his guard just long enough for Rowena to twist her head and sink her teeth into the flesh at the base of his thumb. In a flash Black Otter was on him, seizing the arm that held the knife, wrenching it upward.

Roaring with fury, Bosley swung toward him and they began to grapple. The momentum of their struggle carried them to the window. Still gripping the knife, which was *not* a stage piece, Bosley used his

superior weight to force the savage backward, arching
his body over the stone sill. He pressed forward and
outward as his fist brought the blade closer and closer
toward Black Otter's face.

What happened next came about so quickly that,
afterward, Rowena could scarcely believe what she
had seen. Black Otter shifted backward over the sill,
carrying Bosley with him. Then, with the knife a finger breadth from his face, he brought his knee up like
a hammer between Bosley's legs. Bosley bellowed in
agony, lost his balance and pitched forward, his
weight carrying him over the top of the savage's body
and out the window. His long scream ended abruptly
as he crashed onto the flagstones two stories below.

Recovering his own balance, Black Otter glanced
out the window, looking down at the spot where Bosley had fallen. Then, still grim-visaged and breathing
hard, he turned back to Rowena.

In a moment she was free and in his arms. They
held each other tightly, both of them trembling as they
touched each other's faces, hands and bodies, as if
needing reassurance that this moment was real.

"We have to go," Rowena whispered. "Dickon
could be here with the constable any minute—and
without Bosley we have no proof of your innocence."

She felt him nod. Then, gently, he clasped her
shoulders, moving her a little away from him. "You
have no need to go," he said, looking into her eyes.
"Your home is free now, Rowena. *You* are free."

Rowena lowered her gaze, glancing around the ransacked room where she had spent almost every night
of her life. Her eyes took in the grim stone walls, the
valueless possessions, the lonely bed. She imagined
the years ahead, living here alone, or, perhaps with

her child, struggling to fill the empty days with some semblance of meaning.

She looked up once more at the man who had awakened her to life and love, and she felt a whole new world opening up before her.

Did she have the courage to embrace that world? Could she cast off the weight of this great, burdensome house, this life of grim tradition and plodding duty, to break free and soar like a bird in the open sky?

Aye, it could be done, she reflected, her thoughts flying. There would be danger at every turn, but wasn't danger the natural companion of freedom? Wasn't risk the very breath of life?

He was watching her, the depths of his ebony eyes shimmering with questions. He had never asked her to come with him—never so much as mentioned the possibility. But she knew that in his own quiet way, Black Otter was asking her now, and she knew what her answer would be.

Bending, she picked up the pouch of jewels Bosley had tossed to the floor. Then she slipped her free hand into his, as a lady would take the hand of her lord.

"Wendaxa," she said softly. "Come, let us go home."

Epilogue

A full harvest moon rose over the velvety darkness of the forest. Its golden light brushed the trees and glimmered on the waters where the great Mochijirickhicken flowed to meet the sea. Deep in the thicket, a herd of deer had bedded for the night, their bodies warm against the earth. From the sheltering branches above them, an owl took silent wing, floating like a phantom into the depths of night.

In the bark lodges of the Lenape village, the people, too, had settled into sleep. Only their *sakima*, Black Otter, lay awake, pondering as he lay on his bed of furs beside the smoldering coals of the fire.

On the far side of the lodge, Swift Arrow and Singing Bird lay wrapped in their robes, the firelight glowing on their sleeping faces. Black Otter had spent many nighttime hours watching them like this. Even now, after more than a moon, he found it hard to believe his son and daughter had been waiting for him, safe and well, cared for by the people of his village. He caressed them with his eyes, still half fearful that their beloved images would fade and he would awaken to find himself alone and in chains once more.

As sleep stole over him, Black Otter's arm tightened around his slumbering wife, pressing the roundness of her growing belly against his side. What a wonder she was, his Rowena. What limitless patience, understanding and love she possessed.

That love had embraced his children and his people, and had won their love in return. It had carried her through the trying days of adjustment to a new life, tempered by the joyous discovery that the great spirit had granted their petition. Their child would be born in the winter season, to be welcomed and loved by all the village.

Black Otter's thoughts drifted to the times ahead, the difficult, dangerous times, when the white men would surely come to their land. With Rowena's help he would prepare and protect his people, so that even without him they would be ready to deal with the English invaders. For now he could only pray for a few more years of peace, a few more years of this blessed contentment.

Rowena stirred beside him. Her golden eyes opened and she smiled, her hand reaching up to brush his cheek.

He bent and kissed her softly. Warm. Content. Home.

* * * * *

Historical Note

By the early 1600s, a number of Native Americans had been taken to England to be exhibited as "wonders." In 1584, two braves named Manteo and Wanchese attracted huge crowds wherever they were shown. In 1605, five Penobscots, including a woman, were kidnapped from the coast of Maine, taken to England and taught English habits. Perhaps the most famous "captive" of all was Pocahontas, who came to England in 1616 as the wife of John Rolfe and died, probably of tuberculosis, the following year.

Source: Emerson, Kathy Lynn, *The Writer's Guide to Everyday Life in Renaissance England,* Writer's Digest Books, Cincinnati, Ohio, 1996.

Be sure to look for Elizabeth Lane's
next Harlequin Historical,

NAVAJO SUNRISE,

available in early 2002.

Set in New Mexico in 1868, this is
the gripping tale of a headstrong beauty
who leaves Boston society behind—and a
wealthy fiancé—when a fearless
Navajo leader captures her heart
and nourishes her soul!

Please turn the page to read
the emotional prologue....

Prologue

New Mexico
March, 1864

Ahkeah stood in the cold moonlight staring down at the grave the *bilagaana* soldiers had forbidden him to dig. His hands were raw and bleeding, the nails worn to stubs from scraping away the half-frozen earth. His eyes and throat stung as if he had just walked through a forest fire.

Even now that the grave was finished, the top piled high with stones, he feared it might not be deep enough to protect his wife's body from the marauding foxes and coyotes that would close in after he was gone. She had died that afternoon, on the fifth day of the long walk from Dinetah to the place called Fort Sumner—died in unspeakable agony, her body swollen with a child that would not have lived even if she'd had the strength to give it birth. The passing soldier who'd fired a bullet into her temple had probably done her a kindness. Even so, it had taken three of Ahkeah's friends, gripping him from behind, to keep him from leaping on the blue coat and tearing him apart with his bare hands.

At the time he had wanted the solider to shoot him as well. He had wanted nothing more than to lie on the icy ground beside the body of his sweet young wife, free from the burdens of grief and shame and from the hunger that gnawed at his vitals. But even then reason had whispered that it was his duty to live. There were people who needed him—his small daughter Nizhoni, his mother's eldest sister who had watched her entire family die on the cliffs at Canyon de Chelly and had not spoken since. And there were others, so many others who needed his strength and his voice.

The crescent moon that hung above the mesa cast ghostly shadows across the desolation of the high New Mexico desert. Through the darkness, the lonely wail of a coyote drifted to Ahkeah's ears. The yelping cry was echoed by another, then another. Once Ahkeah would have welcomed the calls of his wild brothers. Now they only chilled his blood because he knew that the sharp-nosed creatures would be gathering around the bodies of the *Diné* who had fallen along the trail.

He had begun scraping out the grave as soon as he knew his wife was dead, but the soldiers, jabbing him with the points of their bayonets, had forced him to leave her and move on with the rest of his people. Only after the dismal procession had made camp for the night and settled into sleep was he able to slip past the sentries and race back along the trail to where she lay.

Now the grave was finished. The remains of his beloved were as secure as he could make them. But how many others lay unburied along this trail of tears and misery? How many bones would lie scattered on the sand because there was no one to dig the graves?

Turning in the darkness he faced the direction of the four sacred mountains that marked the boundaries of Dinetah, the homeland of his people. There the great headman Manuelito and the last of his followers were still holding out against the overwhelming forces of Kit Carson and his regulars. How Ahkeah longed to be with them in the mountains, to fight and die as a free man.

But Manuelito himself, his handsome face creased with weariness, had asked him to join the trek to the new reservation at Bosque Redondo. "Our people will need you, Ahkeah," he had said. "You grew up as a slave among the *bilagaana,* and you speak as they do. Go now, and be the voice of the *Diné* in this evil time. Go and speak for us all."

Speak for us all.

Swallowing his bitterness, Ahkeah turned his back on the sacred mountains and started back the way he had come. What words could he speak that were not hateful and angry? Once the *Diné* had been the Lords of the Earth, their herds, fields and orchards the envy of all the land. He himself had owned more sheep, cattle and horses than a man could count in half a day, and his beautiful wife had worn robes of soft wool and necklaces of the finest silver. Then the *bilagaana* had come, wanting their land, and everything had changed.

Be the voice of our people, Manuelito had told him. But the *Diné* needed more than a voice. They needed food in their bellies and clothes on their backs. They needed dignity, hope and pride—things the *bilagaana* had taken away and flung far beyond their reach, perhaps forever....

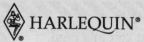

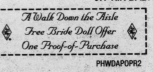